Murder

On The

Isle

Murder On The Isle

ANNA A ARMSTRONG

For Richard,
Thanks for all the fun.

No one is born hating another person because of the colour of his skin, or his background, or his religion. People must learn to hate, and if they can learn to hate, they can be taught to love, for love comes more naturally to the human heart than the opposite.

Nelson Mandela

Chapter 1

It was one of those heavenly summer mornings that make you thrilled to be alive – especially if you are lucky enough to be on the Isle of Blom – surrounded by sparkling blue seas and under a vast clear sky.

For one resident the day had not been auspicious; in fact, it had begun badly, and they now lay dead on a stunning coastal path with their blood seeping out and seagulls soaring overhead.

The killer observed their work with a curled lip and a dispassionate eye.

Murder is sometimes a messy but necessary part of business – a piece of the creative process.

'What could be better than to start the day with excellent coffee, toast browned to perfection, poached eggs and crispy bacon? And what a glorious view! Just look at the way the sun is catching the waves,' said Chief Inspector Nicholas Corman.

Neither his mother nor his father replied. Myrtle was toying with her fruit salad and George was looking out of the window.

Nicholas's enthusiasm was undaunted by their lacklustre response. Even at this early hour, he was clean-shaven and well-groomed. His dark hair was greying at the temples which gave him an air of distinction, as did his chiselled features. When people compare him to Cary Grant, he feigned embarrassment.

He glanced around the room. 'This B&B certainly lives up to the photos on its website. I like the classic look; I've always been partial to Archibald Knox fabrics, and those Nicholson prints are appealing.'

Myrtle looked away from her pineapple chunks and at the impressionist seaside paintings. She sniffed. 'Bit too old-fashioned for me. Now eat up your poached eggs before they spoil, love.'

His mother used the same indulgent tone he remembered from his childhood.

She hasn't changed much over the decades; still the same immaculate painted nails and lavish makeup plus a penchant for purple. With more than a touch of embarrassment, he wondered, *Where on earth did she find that mauve walking kit? And more to the point why did she buy a matching outfit for poor Dad?*

As if on cue, his father cleared his throat and put down the local paper he'd been reading. His father, George, rarely spoke – probably because Myrtle never gave him the opportunity – but this morning, inspired by the sea air, he commented, 'That's a headline to gladden a policeman's heart.'

Nicholas cast an eye at the paper. The first thing he noticed was a very small advert for a ballroom dancing competition at the villa.

Let's hope Mum doesn't notice that or she will have us all in sequins.

Fortunately, what his father was indicating was not the advert but a photo of a magnificent Loaghtan ram, its impressive four horns framed its proud face as it stared defiantly at the camera. Nicholas had an idea that Loaghtans were one of the many areas of contention between the Isle of Blom and the Isle of Man, with both realms claiming the sheep as native to their domain. The headline read, 'Rare Ram Rescued. Tony Pringle's Odin saved.'

Nicholas chortled. 'The Isle of Blom is certainly the place for a quiet life. A bit different from the spate of clown killings back in Little Warthing. The Cotswolds may be picturesque but it does have more than its fair share of murders.'

Myrtle patted his hand. 'That's why we suggested you joined us here for a little holiday. We thought you could do with recuperating.'

The mention of Little Warthing and murder brought to mind Zara FitzMorris.

'Are you alright, love? You've gone rather pink,' enquired Myrtle, solicitously.

'Er ... of course ... it's just rather warm in here,' he stammered and then swiftly changed the subject. 'I was thinking what a lucky chap Bob is to be in charge of policing a place where a ram rates a headline. No murders here!'

Myrtle smiled and took another dainty bite of toast before saying, 'I'm looking forward to our lunch with him. I haven't seen him since you were at police college together. But don't say things like that, love. It's tempting fate.'

'Like what?'

'About there being no murders here – it's asking for trouble.'

Nicholas laughed. 'Don't be ridiculous, Mum. Our plans are far too wholesome for any unfortunate corpses to turn up. We're going to spend the day taking the horse-drawn tram to the station, then a steam train to Port Saint Columba.' His eyes lit up at the mention of the steam train. If there was one thing that gave him more pleasure than his model train set, it was a real-life steam train. He folded the paper over and totally missed the article on an illegal gambling ring and next to it the contact number for the local branch of Gamblers Anonymous.

'Well, your father is looking forward to the walk back along Chough Drive. He hopes to get some photos of those rare birds. He's been talking of nothing else! Although what he finds so exciting about birds is beyond me.'

George was happily oblivious as he watched some oystercatchers paddling in the waves.

Meanwhile, in a guesthouse further along the promenade, Zara FitzMorris put down her guidebook. Elegant, even in her sensible green walking clothes, she had swept back her brilliant red hair into a loose ponytail.

'This coffee is excellent. If I had to make a guess, I'd say it's Colombian. I do like this guesthouse; they've put thought into every detail.'

Her mother, Dee nodded. 'The décor with all these blues and neutrals rather reminds me of that holiday we had on Nantucket.'

Zara glanced with affection at her mother. Petite and slim,

Dee might be in her seventies but she exuded vibrancy, from the top of her chic silver and saffron bobbed hair to the tip of her immaculately pedicured toe.

'I'm looking forward to us spending some quality time together and I'm so glad we're here. I've always wanted to visit the Isle of Blom. I suppose it was the result of growing up hearing you talk about your teenage holiday here. It's a shame Amelia didn't want to join us.'

Dee smiled. 'It's only natural at her age to want to be independent. Second-year psychology students don't tend to want to hang around with their mother and granny.'

Zara picked up the guidebook again. 'Did you know, Mother, the Isle of Blom is self-governing? Who'd have thought there'd be such a gem sitting in the Irish Sea? I can't wait to explore the rugged coastline, not to mention the medieval castles. I must say, it's wonderful to be out of the office. Much as I love selling properties, it's great to have a break. Now, if only you can manage to go for a week without finding any dead bodies, we should have a wonderful time.'

'I do wish you'd stop harping on about that. It's not as if I deliberately find corpses. I just seem to come across them,' replied Dee, as she happily helped herself to another kipper. 'These kippers are as delicious as I remember, especially with a bit of lime marmalade. Are you sure you don't want one, dear?'

'No, I'll pass, thanks; the smell is more than enough for me. I must say for someone as elfin-looking as you, you certainly do have a healthy appetite.'

'It's my morning Taekwondo drill. There's nothing like an hour of stretching and kicking to make lots of room for kippers,' Dee explained contentedly.

'Well, leave some room for these rolls – they're still warm from the oven.' Zara took a bite and shut her eyes as she savoured the perfect combination of crust on the outside and warm dough within. After she had swallowed, she grinned at Dee. 'I hate to say it, Mum, but their homemade blackberry and apple jam is nearly as good as yours.' After a few moments more of enjoyment, she pointed at the slim paperback book resting by her mother's plate. 'What's that you're reading?'

'Lavinia Loveday's latest,' enthused Dee. 'From her classical romance series. It's rather good – set in the art galleries in Florence.'

Zara smiled. 'Lavinia Loveday is clever in the way she has a series to cover everyone's tastes – you love the romance classics set in places like Paris and Rome; I go for her racier 'exotics'. Her descriptions of locations like Thailand and Vietnam are wonderful.'

Dee nodded. 'Then Amelia is totally enthralled by her Goth books where a heroine named Willow or Moon finds romance with young men called Thor or Hawk.'

Zara smiled. 'I just hope you keep your sense of adventure in your reading and not in the reality of the here and now.'

Dee laughed. 'The only adventure I'm looking forward to is seeing the choughs along Chough Drive. They're very rare and you know how much I love birdwatching.'

Zara did know and she tried not to think of the last time she had gone birdwatching with her mother and found that grotesque corpse, tied to a tree.

Her mother appeared untroubled by such worries as she chatted happily on. 'And the steam train to Port St Columba was always great fun when I was young. It's a shame your nice police inspector, Nicholas Corman isn't here. With his passion for model railways, he would love the steam train. Do you know he always reminds me of Cary Grant?' she added wistfully.

'He's not my anything!' said Zara crisply. 'Now hurry up; we don't want to miss our train.'

'I have plenty of water but have you got the sunblock in your bag?' asked Zara half an hour later as they hurried down the steps of their B&B. It was one of many along the seafront which were all built during the Isle of Blom's Victorian heyday.

'Yes, dear and—' Dee got no further as she was nearly sent flying by a dishevelled skinhead. He bumped into her with force.

Winded and surprised Dee looked at him – it was not a pleasant sight. He had a prominent forehead enhanced by a thick monobrow and a nose that had obviously been broken more than once.

He swore.

With a hand out to help her mother, Zara retorted, 'An apology would be more appropriate.'

He glared at them both but didn't say anything. As he stormed off, Dee gave her daughter a reassuring pat on her arm. 'Don't worry dear, we'll never see him again.'

Dee was wrong.

They caught the steam train with minutes to spare.

'It's just as I remember it – all red and shining brass – and these wooden carriages haven't changed a bit!' exclaimed Dee with delight as they found their seats.

The whistle blew and with a hiss they were off, rocking and clanging down the line with a puff of steam and a whiff of burning coal.

They disembarked at Port St Columba and had a glorious twenty minutes of walking by the coast, with the turquoise sea far below and the gulls soaring in an azure sky above. Zara had regained her sense of equilibrium but unfortunately, it was not to last long.

She was just turning her face to the sun and inhaling the sea air when all sense of peace was obliterated by the roar of an exhaust-blown engine. She glanced around and spotted the source of the noise; it was from a battered white van being driven erratically and – more to the point – it was heading straight towards them.

Dee froze, staring in disbelief at the van hurtling towards them, seemingly intent on sending them all over the edge of the cliff.

Zara screamed and grabbed her mother, dragging her to one side. The van missed them and continued on its unpredictable path.

Zara could feel her heart pounding. She was perspiring and angry – very angry. 'Are you alright, Mum?' she asked as soon as she had regained her breath.

'Quite, dear, no harm done,' Dee replied, calmly brushing some twigs and debris off her sleeve.

'It was the same man!' exclaimed Zara, staring down the now empty lane.

'What same man, dear?'

'The one from outside the B&B – the skinhead who bumped into you.'

Dee looked at her daughter with concern and very quietly said, 'I think you are probably letting your imagination run away with you. It's not surprising that your nerves are all on edge after the upset we've just had back at home with those clown corpses turning up all over the place. Thank goodness we're on this holiday. You'll feel much more yourself after two weeks of Blom tranquillity.'

Once again, Dee was wrong.

Chapter 2

For Nicholas and his parents, their journey to Chough Drive was less eventful. The gentle clip-clop of the horse-drawn tram along the prom gave Nicholas plenty of time to enjoy the sunshine, the sea with its picturesque folly of a Gothic castle and the Victorian frontage. It was a bit of a squash with all three of them on the hard wooden bench, still, the sea breeze was refreshing and the salty air made a change.

Myrtle was in full flow. 'That was the summer your father and I took the island by storm. Our Viennese Waltz was talked about for years. Shame the Palace has gone now. It was the biggest ballroom in Europe. I wore an elegant gown in lilac. It had sequins ...'

Nicholas let her words wash over him. He was ridiculously excited by the prospect of going on the steam train but he concealed it well beneath a demure façade.

His mother kept up a constant happy stream of reminiscences while his father was still, silently enjoying watching the oystercatchers paddling at the water's edge.

The relative peace was shattered by an ecstatic shriek from Myrtle, who had spotted a poster by the villa. 'Oooh, I say, Nicholas! There's a ballroom dancing competition at the villa. Good thing I packed some costumes.'

She elbowed him in the ribs. He winced, not only from the physical pain but also from the realisation that this holiday was to include shiny shoes and sequins.

So she's bought costumes – well that explains all those trunks she insisted on putting in the car.

He thought back to that evening at The Cuban Club, where, as part of their investigation, he and Zara had performed a sultry samba.

I wonder what it would be like to compete with Zara – perhaps we could tango.

'Are you alright, love? You've gone ever so red again. I do hope you're not going down with something. Summer colds can be the very devil.'

Nicholas cleared his throat. 'No, I'm absolutely fine.'

They arrived at the station a little later than planned. The ticket hall was filled with young families. Happy chatter echoed around the lobby. Every child was enthusiastically holding a bucket and spade, while each parent appeared to be weighed down by enough picnic boxes and windbreakers for them to survive an expedition to Everest rather than a day at Port Erin's beach.

The toot of the train sent a thrill through Nicholas's core but also a surge of frustration.

There won't be time for me to admire the engine and take photos before we leave.

He let go of his vision of enjoying the engine in all its gleaming polished glory, with billowing steam cushioning it. Putting a brave face on the situation, he said, 'I'm sure there'll be other occasions for me to look at the engines. If we're quick when we get out at Port St Columba I might get a chance to get a photo.'

No one was listening. Myrtle was totally absorbed in looking at the postcards of scenic landscapes, Loaghtan sheep and cliffs while George had found a book on local birds, with a red-legged chough on the cover.

His parents were so focused on their own interests that he only just managed to hustle them onto the platform as the conductor was waving his flag. He pushed them into the nearest carriage. The old-fashioned varnished door, with its thick leather strap, slammed shut as the shrill whistle blew and they were off.

With gentle, rhythmic, clanks and rocks the train pulled away from the station. The distinctive smell of oil and burning coal wafted into the carriage. As they steadily gained speed, the motion and noise increased. Nicholas gazed out of the window at streams, cows and cottages.

His mother was speaking. 'So I said to your father – didn't I,

George? I said …'

But Nicholas wasn't listening; he was totally lost in the heaven of being at one with a steam train.

He spotted a cluster of brown wiry Loaghtans and briefly wondered what the ram had been rescued from and then there was a flash of vivid endless blue ocean and all other thoughts were driven away.

They were slowing.

'We're coming into the station. We need to be quick disembarking,' he declared as he stood up and went to the door.

'Just a moment, love. My lipstick has rolled under the seat. Give me a hand, George!'

With a whoosh, the train drew to a halt. Nicholas threw the door open and, camera in hand, was ready to leap down onto the platform, sprint past the tiny passenger shelter with its flower display, and get a photo of the engine before it pulled out.

'Help me!' wailed his mother. 'I can see it but I can't reach it!'

Nicholas spun around. There were both his parents on their knees on the historic carriage floor, their purple behinds much in evidence as they groped under the seat for the missing lipstick.

Nicholas sighed and stepped forward, only vaguely aware of a couple of hikers disembarking.

Ten minutes later, with the lipstick rescued, they were walking downhill, with the sun filtering through the rich canopy of leaves. Periodically, his father held his binoculars up to get a better glimpse of some bird or other.

'I really don't know what you're making such a fuss about,' his mother grumbled. 'The conductor said it was no problem at all us holding the train up. They'll easily make the time up on the straight.'

Nicholas quietly sighed once more. 'We walk down this hill, along the road. St Columba Glen is on the right. Then we take a left turn,' he explained, repeating the walking guide word for word.

Once they had obediently turned left, Nicholas's frustration was swept away by the view. A majestic bay lay before them. The sea was a glorious shimmering blue, broken only by a fishing boat in the distance. Seagulls soared overhead. The verges were a mass of wildflowers and grasses. Butterflies fluttered around the yellow, white and pink blooms. The heady scents of coconut-smelling gorse and sweet honeysuckle filled the air. Nicholas inhaled deeply.

His mother sneezed loudly, then sniffed. 'George! Have you got my antihistamines? Ruddy pollen!'

There was a short delay while she rummaged in George's backpack. Amid tissues, sunscreen and water bottles the pills were found and they strode on toward Chough Drive.

Here the cliff plunged dramatically to the sea far below. Enormous rocks dotted the coastline lapped by white foaming waves. Towering up their other side was a steep rock face. The stone was striated with stacked layers squeezed out in different colours and folded together.

Myrtle was saying, 'Of course, as I said to your father—' when George exhaled a single rapturous word, 'There!'

Nicholas stood entranced as above him the famous black choughs flew. They were embroiled in an aerial battle. Angry squawks echoed around the cliffs as two parent choughs fought off a marauding crow. They wheeled and turned in a way that reminded Nicholas of footage of the Battle of Britain.

George had his camera out and was clicking away. Nicholas was enraptured until a distant whistle called his attention.

'Steam Train Weekly recommended standing on the headland to get a view of the five past ten from Port Erin. If I hurry, I should just make it,' declared Nicholas.

He hurried off to his mother's happy monologue, 'So then I said …' satisfied that he was going to get an iconic view of the train, embellished by puffs of steam winding its way around the rolling hills. A fairy tale image, complete with a turreted house that nestled near the line, the whole scene looked as if it was taken straight out of a storybook.

The train whistled and chugged into view.

It's even more beautiful than I imagined!

He sighed, and this sigh was one of pure happiness.

'Oh, dear! I haven't missed it, have I?' panted one of the hikers who had got off at the station.

Nicholas was about to smugly commiserate when he glanced over at her. Flaming red hair, neatly tied back, slim figure in a neat walking outfit, it could only be—

'*Zara FitzMorris!*'

His voice came out high-pitched. He coughed, swallowed and hoped he wasn't blushing.

'Hello, Nicholas.' Her voice was calm and she seemed quite unperturbed at the sight of him.

'I, er, you, er—'

'Yes.'

Is that the hint of a smile playing around her lips?

Suavely, she continued, 'It appears that we both had the same idea. After all that murderous unpleasantness, what could be better than a peaceful holiday on the Isle of Blom?'

'Er, yes, well, rather, well, er, spiffing ...'

Why is my voice so squeaky? And surely I didn't actually say, 'Spiffing'?

He coughed again. 'No chance of finding a dead body here!' he chortled and then a thought struck him. 'Where's Dee?'

'Oh, Mother is just around the corner. I left her watching a family of choughs. You know what an avid ornithologist she is. I simply couldn't tear her away and I did so much want to catch a glimpse of the five past ten from Port Erin. Steam Train Weekly said this was the spot to see it.'

'Does that mean that you—' He seemed mesmerised by those green eyes and never had her voice sounded sweeter. It took him a moment to collect himself and finish his sentence, '—like steam?'

'Crazy about it,' she purred and suddenly Nicholas felt dizzy. His heart was pounding but she appeared to be unaware of it.

'Mother will be thrilled to see you.'

She took him by the hand and he could but follow. He realised he was happy to go wherever Zara wanted to take him.

They rounded the corner and there was Dee, but she was not alone. At her feet lay the crumpled body of a man in a pool of blood, and in her hand was something pointed that dripped crimson drops of gore.

For a second both Nicholas and Zara just stared in silence then Zara exploded, '*Mother*! How could you! And after we specifically came here to have a break from dead bodies!'

'Sorry, darling! But honestly, it was just an accident.'

'Sorry? You think that's going to get you off the hook!' scoffed Zara, not even trying to hide her annoyance. 'And *what* is that in your hands?'

Dee blinked at the object she was holding. 'Well, unless I'm very much mistaken, they're a pair of Victorian sheep clippers. Those poor old shepherds must have got awful blisters when shearing a flock – they are very stiff.' She paused for thought, before adding, 'Perhaps they just need oiling.'

'I'll ring 999!' Nicholas was in professional mode.

At that moment, Myrtle bustled around the corner. She paused, took in the corpse and realised it was accompanied by two chic ladies with notable red hair.

She beamed and loudly declared, 'You must be Dee and Zara FitzMorris! Nicholas has told me *so* much about you both. He said that if there was a corpse, the FitzMorris ladies could not be far away.'

She strode towards Dee with her right hand outstretched. She glanced at all the blood. Dee shrugged apologetically, while Myrtle commented, 'Probably best not to shake under the circumstances. Nicholas will know what we should do. *Nicholas*!' she bellowed, although he was only a few feet away, still fiddling with his phone.

'Not now, Mother!' snapped Nicholas.

Dee crinkled up her nose and enquired, 'Does anyone else smell roses?'

Zara, observing her mother covered in gore, soothingly replied, 'It's probably the shock; it does strange things to your imagination.'

'I still can't get anything,' said Nicholas, holding up his phone.

His forehead was creased and there was an edge of desperation in his voice as he added, 'We need to get help as soon as possible.'

'Well, there was a jogger, but he seems to have run away,' said Dee, none too helpfully.

Nicholas, still battling with his phone, demanded, 'Why can't I get this thing to work? I don't seem to be able to get a signal.'

'There isn't any reception here!' came an authoritative male voice.

They all looked over to where the newcomer was standing. They had been so absorbed in Dee and the corpse that none of them had noticed his approach. He was tall and stood very erect. His eyes were pale blue and his hair the soft silver of someone who had been blond many years ago. He wore a lightweight navy sweater and had a red knotted handkerchief around his neck.

'If you're happy to stay here, I'll run to the end of Chough Drive; the phone reception is better there. You'll be wanting the police. The chap is beyond the help of a paramedic.'

'You'd better ask for an ambulance – for the body,' said Myrtle helpfully.

The man calmly regarded the cadaver, squatting down to get a closer look. It was difficult to tell how tall the corpse had been as he lay semi-curled on his side. He was thin; almost stick-like. He had scruffy jeans and a black T-shirt with a Manx TT motif on the front. Only half his face was visible, the other half rested on the tarmac. He looked to be in his late twenties or early thirties. His hair was mousey and collar length and his chin was covered in stubble.

'Who is he?' the man asked.

'We don't know. We're not from round here,' said Zara. She tilted her head to one side and regarded this commanding stranger.

'Well, I am from here and I've never seen him before.'

As he was speaking, he glanced up at Dee. As he looked at her, his eyes widened. Shock was written all over his handsome features, but it wasn't the sight of all the blood that was disturbing him.

'Dee! Is it really you?' he stammered. 'Fancy seeing you after all these years – and here, of all places.'

'Daniel!' was all Dee was able to say but Zara noted that her mother's face was as scarlet as the fabled chough's legs.

'Dee Drummond, you look as lovely as you did at sixteen.'

'It's Dee FitzMorris, Daniel dear.'

'Oh, so you did go back and marry him.'

Dee nodded. 'Yes.'

'I'm sorry to break this happy reunion up but we do have quite a serious situation here! Perhaps you could save the catch-up for later?' Nicholas fumed, his eyes narrowed and his arms folded across his chest.

'Of course! I'll be as quick as I can!' said Daniel as he set off at a jog.

Chapter 3

The rest of the day went by in a blur of statements and fingerprinting. Both Dee and Zara slept fitfully that night, their dreams haunted by echoing police corridors and stark interview rooms. The tang of institutional floor cleaners and uncertainty pervaded their slumbers. It was a relief when dawn came and they could get up and distract their minds.

For Dee, the night was troubled by more than just memories of finding a body. She had the added disturbance of meeting Daniel again.

Daniel! After all this time. She felt her heart flutter. *He's still the same as the first time I met him.*

Her mind wandered back to that summer when she'd been sixteen and heartbroken.

We were on the ferry to the Isle of Blom, I must have left my parents in the lounge or were they having lunch? Either way, I wanted to be alone to cry so I went up on deck.

She smiled as she recalled that back then her hair had been as long and lustrous as her granddaughter's was now. She'd had the same cascades of red curls which billowed around her face in the sea breeze as she'd sobbed her heart out.

Broken-hearted! My first major row with Zara's father and at sixteen I'd thought my life was over.

She chuckled silently at the devastation of youth.

I didn't notice him until he passed a pressed white hanky into my hand.

I seem to remember being impressed by how tall and slim he was in his denim jeans – bell bottoms were all the rage and he had on a jean jacket too – very trendy.

Although I seem to recall that I was quite on point, too, in my green-flowered flared trousers and crocheted sun-top.

He didn't say anything. He didn't bother me with questions. He just sat down beside me on the bench, took a sketch pad and pencil out of his bag and began drawing the seagulls.

After a while, I must have stopped crying enough to make furtive glances at him through my curls.

Once again, she felt a jolt of electricity as she recollected his aquiline nose, his blond, almost white hair and those eyes. His eyes were as blue as the summer sky and had an intensity about them as he focused on his sketching.

I must have shivered and I caught a glint in those dazzling blue eyes. I blushed, hot and crimson – he'd noticed me eyeing him up.

He didn't speak, he didn't embarrass me more by smiling; he simply took off his denim jacket and placed it around my shoulders. It was warm from his body.

And that was the start!

The next morning, after a light breakfast, they got into their hire car and headed out of St Aiden's.

'So where did you arrange for us to meet Daniel?' asked Zara. She was casually dressed in a pair of navy chinos and a polo shirt, adding some glamour with a stylish pair of sunglasses.

'Down south, at a café at the very tip of the island,' Dee replied.

'Is that where the guidebook says there are lots of seals and you can see a smaller island just off the coast?'

Dee nodded. 'The smaller island is called The Calf of Blom.'

Zara smiled. 'So, another similarity to the Isle of Man – they have the Calf of Man.'

'That's because they both were inhabited by Vikings so there are lots of similar names – like Balla for farm and Crink for streams.' Dee wasn't sure if she'd read that nugget of information in a guidebook or if Daniel had told her, decades ago. Thinking of him she said, 'Did I mention Daniel is bringing his grandson? I think they live together.'

'That will be nice,' commented Zara in a noncommittal tone. Not surprisingly, at the forefront of both their minds, were thoughts of what had occurred the previous day.

As Zara explained to her mother a few minutes later, 'I'm not sure which I'm more shocked at. You finding yet another corpse or discovering that all those tales, that you only ever had eyes for my father, until his early death, were a lie. I feel like a child who has just discovered that their parent has lied about the tooth fairy.'

'Really, dear, I think you're making a bit of a fuss.' Dee looked out of the window, admiring the rolling hills. 'Anybody could have come across that poor dead man. It just happened to be me.'

'But why is it always you? And what about this secret romance with Daniel?'

'Well, it was that summer that your father and I had had a bit of a tiff. Do you know I can't even remember what the fight was about? Anyway, I left for my holiday on the Isle of Blom, having told him that I never wanted to see him again.'

'So, one short ferry ride and you forgot all about my father and fell into Daniel's arms?'

'Honestly, darling, you make it sound so sordid. Actually, it was very sweet and innocent. I was only sixteen and I think he was eighteen. Why are you sniffing like that? Do you think it's hay fever or are you coming down with a cold?'

Zara sniffed again. 'Are you wearing scent?'

Hastily Dee demurred, 'I often wear scent.'

After a quick glance at her mother in the passenger seat, Zara raised an eyebrow. 'Is that your new silk scarf?'

'What if it is?'

'It's a little elaborate for a hike through the hills followed by a casual lunch with someone who is just an old acquaintance.' Zara was silent for a moment as she slowed to pass a girl riding a grey pony. With the obstacle safely behind them, she sped up and resumed interrogating her mother. 'And what exactly did Daniel mean by, "and here of all places"? What exactly did you and Daniel get up to on Chough Drive all those summers ago?'

Zara had had to slow down to a snail's pace once again; this time it was for a tractor with a trailer rattling behind.

'I think we turn left here, dear. Good thing we're behind this tractor – if we'd been going at any speed, we might have missed it. And for your information you've got it all wrong,' Dee replied calmly.

'So, what is the truth?'

'We're not having a hike followed by lunch, we're having brunch then a walk.'

'That's not what I wanted to know about, Mother,' laughed Zara.

They drove on for a bit, through a couple of sprawling villages with occasional glimpses of the sea on the near horizon.

Dee yawned and Zara was instantly concerned. 'Tired? You must be exhausted after yesterday. You were an age having all those forensic tests. I didn't think we'd ever get away from the police station.'

Dee shuddered. 'Silly of me to pick up those shears.'

Zara agreed. 'You should really have known better. After all, it's not as if it's the first body you've found.'

'But all that blood was a bit of a novelty. My top and slacks are ruined. And I thought the head policeman was a bit prickly – very unnecessarily brusque. So unlike that sweet constable. Do you know he even found some honey for my camomile tea – he said he'd made it just how his granny likes it.'

Glossing over the obliging nature of the constable, Zara honed in on the iniquities of the man in charge. 'Yes, that Deputy Chief Constable chap, Hadrian Macintosh, was not the most charming of men. But then in fairness, he had been called in on his day off. I doubt that I would have been at my most charming if I'd been anticipating a relaxing time at the golf course and then my day had been hijacked by having to hotfoot it back to the police station to deal with an unidentified corpse and an OAP covered in blood.' She concentrated on a tight turn before adding, 'Macintosh is very striking to look at. I must say I rather liked the contrast between his dark skin and red whiskers.'

'Yes, his appearance is distinctive,' said Dee. There was a long pause, and then she absently added, 'His moustache must take a lot of upkeep.' She exhaled some of her annoyance about Macintosh's behaviour. 'I suppose you're right, dear; I probably should be more charitable.' She wrinkled her nose with distaste. 'My discovery of that bloody body must have inconvenienced him. But I just can't help thinking it's a shame that Nicholas's old chum, the Chief Constable, wasn't around.'

Zara nodded. 'Someone said he'd been called away unexpectedly to a meeting in Liverpool.'

'Yes, most unfortunate as I'm sure if he'd been in charge things would have been a lot less unpleasant. After all, if he's a chum of Nicholas's I'm certain he's delightful.'

'Probably,' agreed Zara. 'Let's forget about all that unpleasant business for now and enjoy our day. I'll concentrate on driving and you can just all enjoy the view.'

Dee gazed out of the car window as they drove alongside a shallow shingle bay with the sparkling sea gently lapping against the shoreline. The scenery pricked at Dee's memory.

There's the little lane, just as secluded and with all those pretty pink thrift flowers as it was. We had such a lovely picnic.

With a slight smile, she recalled that what passed as 'a lovely picnic' to a sixteen-year-old was a greasy sausage roll in a paper bag and a bottle of bright orange fizzy pop.

That beaten-up old Land Rover of Daniel's gave us the freedom to roam all over the island.

She blinked at a stray thought. *I wonder what my parents made of it? After all, it was meant to be a family holiday, but as far as I can remember I spent the whole summer alone with Daniel. Were they hurt or relieved that I was busy and no longer broken-hearted?*

On the right of the road, set back from the sea, was a stone pub. It was isolated from any other houses and yet another reminder of former times.

But Daniel and I weren't alone all the time. That's the pub where we had a lock-in with his cousins, Tony and John Pringle.

She closed her eyes and could see the scene as vividly as if it had been yesterday rather than nearly half a century ago. She could smell the whiskey and beer, and hear the vibrant Celtic beat of the pipe and drum as she, along with the band and the other customers were locked into the cosy bar with its low ceiling and rough stone walls. The shutters were bolted, darkening the rooms and stopping any preying eyes who might report the publican for serving alcohol after hours. To a youthful Dee, it had been so new and dangerous. She almost chuckled out loud. *Although actually, it was rather innocent and wholesome – Daniel always did have an air of reliability about him.* She grew pink recalling the frisson of electricity that had passed between them as his bare arm had brushed against her skin when he'd passed the drinks out around their table.

Tony had spilt his and sworn but then he'd been in a bad mood anyway.

'It's no good taking it out on the drink!' jeered John. 'It's your fault for betting all that dough on your cockerel winning the Fur and Feather.'

John leaned back in his chair satisfied and Dee had taken the opportunity to take a good look at him. He had the same fair colouring and dazzling blue eyes as Daniel and Tony. *How were those three boys related? Was it a shared great-grandfather? That would account for what resemblances there were.* There were differences in their looks as well; John was heftier and his eyes were smaller. Of the three cousins, Daniel was easily the tallest, then John, with Tony being both the skinniest and the smallest. They had all been attractive in their own ways. *But then,* mused the older Dee, *youth by its nature is appealing.*

Tony's thin face, tight with rage, paled. 'It should have won, too!' he hissed, slamming his glass down on the rough-beamed table and spilling some more of his drink.

Dee had shifted on the uncomfortable bench and looked nervously down at her feet. She couldn't help noticing that Tony was angrily kicking his feet against the sawdust-covered floor. His sneakers were very old and worn. She'd glanced at Daniel for reassurance but he didn't seem bothered by the outburst – his face was as calm as ever.

John, on the other hand, was definitely gloating over Tony's discomfort. His piggy eyes twinkled as he nudged his neighbour, Elsie. She was a buxom girl, a few years older than Dee. She wore lashings of thick mascara and had scarlet lips. With delight he explained to Elsie, 'He's only gone and lost this month's milk money and his dad is going to beat the living daylights out of him when he catches on. After all, Tony, your family's virtually bankrupt at the best of times.'

Dee had noticed Tony's hands flexing into fists beneath his frayed cuffs. *I thought there was going to be a fight for sure but I'd reckoned without Elsie's charms.*

Elsie had pouted her full lips and wriggled towards Tony, exposing a liberal amount of her generous cleavage. 'Oh Tony, you never!' she purred, and Tony was so distracted by her body, if not her words, he stopped scowling.

John stared at Elsie and then at Tony and his relish had morphed into a sulky pout.

'We're here and just look at that view!' declared Zara.

And what a view it was. The churning sea ran between the end of the Isle of Blom and a smaller island. On the rocks, above the buffeting waves, basking in the sunshine were the seals. Sleek and content, they lay there, like voluptuous sea sirens. Beyond them and the Calf was rolling sea to a distant horizon. The whole vista was set off by dramatic heather-clad hills on either side. The purple of the flowers was so vivid that it seemed other-worldly.

Dee spotted Daniel and exclaimed, 'There's Daniel – on that bench! And he's sketching – he hasn't changed, he always had a pencil in his hand. I bet he's drawing those seagulls.'

Getting out of the car she called over to him. He stood up, smiling broadly.

Zara regarded him with interest; ramrod straight, he was undoubtedly striking to look at. In well-ironed chinos and a pale linen shirt, it was easy to see how he had made a sixteen-year-old

Dee's heart flutter. She glanced over at her mother.

And judging by her expression it's still fluttering! And Mother was spot on, now we're closer I can clearly see the seagulls – and rather good ones, too!

Depicted in confident pencil lines, were three gulls, caught spiralling effortlessly in a thermal.

Lurking behind Daniel was a youth, presumably his grandson. He had the same long limbs as the older man but he hadn't grown into them yet. The boy looked gangly and awkward. He was clad in faded black – actually, noir seemed to be his colour of preference from his made-up mouth to the expertly applied line around his Mediterranean blue eyes. He had a lip piercing which was large enough to make those of a weak disposition wince. The only thing that was remotely wholesome about him was his shiny blond hair, which was only slightly longer than conventional.

Dee gave him one of her warmest smiles. She enveloped him in an affectionate embrace and totally ignored his horrified rigid response and panicked wide-eyed stare. Instead, she enthusiastically declared, 'You must be Benedict. You'll have to meet my granddaughter, Amelia; she's a Goth, too. Well, some of the time, when she's not being a fairy. Anyway, that's another story. Now do tell me, what music are you into? Amelia loves the HU. They're Mongolian; do you know them?'

The boy stammered, 'Actually, I like Frank Sinatra.'

Daniel intervened. 'Shall we get some coffee? And for now, I vote we avoid talking about yesterday and focus on catching up.'

He ushered them into the spacious modern café. It had been built to be in sympathy with its magnificent setting. They found a seat by the window which gave them panoramic views of the coastline. Seagulls swooped around the outside tables, hoping to steal any morsel of food that visitors were careless with.

They decided what they wanted and briefly chatted about the scenery and the weather. Everyone carefully avoided mentioning the whole corpse and bloody shears incident.

'I thought that after this we could take a hike below the hills – that way you can see Tony and John Pringle as the path runs by their farms,' Daniel said, pouring Dee some more camomile tea out of a pot.

'Oh, that would be lovely. Have they changed much?' asked Dee.

Daniel laughed. 'Not a lot, only Tony is even more wiry and John is considerably fatter.'

'And who managed to win Elsie's heart?'

Daniel flushed pink and looked down at the table, all trace of a smile gone. 'Actually – I don't know about winning her heart but it was me who she decided to marry.'

Dee felt the room spinning around her. His words were like a stab to her heart and she was overwhelmed by a sense of betrayal.

'Oh!' was all she could say. She too stared at the table.

'It didn't last long. The Isle of Blom and the salary of an artist and part-time teacher couldn't give her a fraction of what she wanted, so she left me. Left us.'

'Us?'

'We had a son – Benedict's father.'

'Oh!' repeated Dee, frantically attempting to process all this new information. She kept her eyes on the table, unable to look at him.

Daniel cleared his throat. 'She went to America and made a fortune in cosmetics.'

'She always did wear rather a lot of make-up.' Dee's tone was neutral.

Zara intervened. 'Tony? John? Elsie?'

'Oh! Sorry dear, you don't know who we're talking about. Tony and John Pringle are distant relatives of Daniel's.'

'They're brothers?' asked Zara.

'No, cousins,' said Dee.

'We all shared a great-grandfather,' put in Daniel.

'When I knew them, they had a tremendous rivalry bordering on dislike as they were both madly in love with …' Elsie hovered over the table like the ghost of Christmas past.

'Elsie,' Daniel said; his voice conveyed bravery but his face was a little flushed.

'Yes … presumably, as er …' Dee stammered to a halt once more, the name seemed to get stuck in her throat and her mouth went dry at the mere thought of that buxom girl of yesteryear.

'Elsie,' supplied Daniel once more.

'Yes, as, er, she departed to distant lands, they were able to restore their relationship.'

Daniel looked towards heaven while Benedict snorted.

'If only! I do believe they are more at odds now than they ever were. They have transferred their rivalry to other areas: sheep breeding, ploughing competitions, and village vegetable-growing contests. I swear if either of them could cook, they would be at the forefront of any jam-making or cake-baking competition on the island.'

A flicker of concern crossed Dee's face. 'I hope Tony doesn't still bet on every race and competition.'

Daniel glanced around, making sure he could not be overheard and confided, 'Things are better now, but for a while, Tony's love of a flutter was a cause for concern.'

'At least if they're only distant relatives they don't need to see much of each other,' suggested Zara.

Benedict snorted again, which seemed to be his main mode of communication.

Daniel explained, 'Unfortunately, each of them inherited a family farm. There's only a lane dividing them and worse still the farmhouses actually face each other. It's the children I feel sorry for.'

Dee interjected, 'Oh good! So they both were able to get over … er …'

'Elsie.' This time both Zara and Benedict joined Daniel, as a sort of Greek tragedy chorus.

'Yes, so they were both able to get over her and find other loves!'

Daniel shook his head, while still avoiding making eye contact with Dee. 'They both still think of Elsie as the pinnacle of perfection and their wives – while they lived – were always second-best. Still, their kids are great, John's got a daughter called

Juliet while Tony's boy is called Christian. It's a shame; their fathers have never let them see each other.'

This was enough to elicit another snort from Benedict. Daniel didn't seem to notice. He cleared his throat, sat up straighter, shivered as if trying to shake off any lingering hint of Elsie and said, 'But that's enough about them. Tell me about you. So, you went back and married your childhood sweetheart. I'm glad it worked out for you but he's not with you at the moment.'

'He passed away.'

'Oh, I'm sorry.'

'Thank you, but I consider myself lucky to have loved two good men.' She looked coyly up at Daniel. Zara spluttered and tipped her remaining coffee over the table.

'Oh dear, must have gone down the wrong way. Never mind, I'll get some paper napkins. Give me a hand, Benedict,' Daniel said, getting to his feet.

When they were both safely out of earshot, Zara leant over to her mother and hissed, 'You've been lucky to have loved *two good men*? What about all your husbands? Did none of them make the grade as good men? As I recall one of them was even a vicar?'

With great dignity, Dee replied, 'I didn't say *only* two. Where is your sense of romance?'

'Firmly rooted in reality. Look, they are coming back. I think we should get going on our walk.'

Meanwhile, Nicholas was still in St Aiden's, ensconced with Betty Hobbs. She was the mother of his old friend from his police college days. They were in a café on the main shopping street and the smell of fresh coffee hung in the air. It was served hot and strong as Nicholas's burnt tongue testified. The place was busy with retired folk leafing through newspapers and young mums spooning gooey purée from pouches into squirming toddlers. Betty had opted for a cream bun and was set on reliving the police college days of Nicholas and her son, Ron.

'Such a shame you're not wearing that lovely tank top I knitted for you. Those sleeveless sweaters were all the rage.'

Betty Hobbs was just as he remembered her. Small and round, her pink lipstick was still in place; her style of floral dress was the same but now her blonde curls must be artfully enhanced by her hairdresser. She still smelt strongly of a rose perfume subtly underplayed with roll-your-own tobacco.

Nicholas winced at the memory of that sweater but politely replied, 'Well, Mrs Hobbs, it was lovely, but after twenty years it can't be expected to still look its best.'

She smiled sadly and there was more than a hint of accusation in her next comment. 'But it was so droll, you and Ron both at police college with matching navy tank tops. I remember they were the talk of the place.'

'Indeed they were.'

'And to think neither of you would have worn them if I hadn't insisted. I must say, I think, the old-fashioned police whistle I embroidered, coming out of the top pocket was an inspiration. It took me hours.'

Nicholas took another sip of his coffee; the memory of the humiliation and mocking still haunted him.

'And the brass buttons I sewed onto the shoulders gave them a touch of class. You and my Ron looked grand in them, like two little peas in a pod.'

She smiled happily at the recollection, then, without warning, she started tapping vigorously, on the café window. Glancing out, Nicholas, just caught a glimpse of a fit-looking young man jogging past. Redheaded and fleet of foot he was soon gone.

'Oh, dear! He didn't see me.' She was deflated. 'That was Joe – Joe Smith-Jones.'

She said the name in awed terms, as if, Nicholas, should know who he was. He stared blankly at her.

'My Ron must have mentioned him to you!'

Nicholas shook his head.

'He's a marvel. Only thirty and yet what he does for the youngsters he teaches is wonderful. He may be a maths teacher but his real gift is with troubled pupils. Take young Reggie for instance.'

'Reggie?' asked Nicholas.

Betty nodded. 'He's a boy with a troubled past. Joe is fantastic with him. He spends a lot of time sort of mentoring him. I do what I can too; I thought having a hobby would help, but the boy doesn't seem that interested in knitting.'

She bit into her bun and cream oozed out of the side. 'I knew his father.'

'Reggie's?'

'No! Joe's.' She blushed. 'We were just kids but he was quite the gent. Joe often says his dad, God bless his soul, is the inspiration for his life. Joe is tireless in helping those who get muddled up with drugs.'

'Is that much of a problem here?' asked Nicholas, thinking of the comforting newspaper heading of the great ram rescue.

'A bit. In fact, that's why Ron got called away off the island.'

The mention of Ron being away reminded Nicholas of the uncomfortable interaction he'd had the day before with Ron's deputy, Hadrian Macintosh. It hadn't gone well and Nicholas briefly thought of how much easier the whole Dee business would be if only Ron was present and in charge, rather than that ginger-moustached, dark-skinned and defensive Hadrian Macintosh.

Betty looked around the café theatrically, to make sure she couldn't be overheard, then she continued, 'He's having a meeting with the police in Liverpool. Of course, he wasn't to know that you'd step off the boat and immediately apprehend a killer.'

'I think you misunderstood the situation. I just happened to be on the scene as were Dee and Zara FitzMorris.'

'Friends of yours from somewhere, are they? Dee and Zara Fitz-whatever?'

'Well, sort of. I met them in connection with a recent case.'

She slammed her coffee cup into its saucer. 'You don't mean all those clown murders that were all over the papers? Goodness, I'm surprised the authorities let them onto the island! And now they're at it again but with sheep shears rather than clown makeup! I must say, Nicholas, you do have the oddest friends!'

Back down in the south of the island, brunch finished, Daniel led Dee, Zara and Benedict on a pleasant walk through lanes rich with wildflowers. Both Zara and Dee tried to engage Benedict in conversation but to no avail. The boy might look as beautiful and otherworldly as any anime hero, but talkative he was not.

Dee regarded his striking profile and mused. *He makes for an incongruous figure – all in black amid stone walls and sheep, one would imagine his natural habitat to be urban and nocturnal. Still, he does have magnificent looks. I bet Josh would love to draw him. He has quite a talent for drawing and he seems to find inspiration in unusual personalities like my granddaughter, Amelia in her Goth-meets-pixie guise.*

With the help of Daniel, Dee climbed over a style and then resumed her pondering of Josh. *That poor boy does have an uneasy time being Nicholas's professional police sidekick. If only Nicholas didn't get so frustrated by him when he crunches crisps into his immaculate car. Still, Josh might cause Nicholas stress, but he gives the rest of humanity a great deal of pleasure with his ready smile and good looks.*

They paused to admire a flock of small brown Loaghtan sheep with dark faces and legs.

'Gosh, the ram with his four curled horns is quite magnificent,' exclaimed Zara, pointing in her excitement.

'They are very striking,' agreed Dee, but most of her mind was still on Josh.

I know that Josh attributes both his looks and eating habits to his Korean heritage. How he manages to maintain his lithe figure with his addiction to junk food is a mystery, but I do think it's a little harsh the way he blames his parents and grandparents for cooking him endless delicious dishes for his junk food habit. He maintains their focus on fresh veg forced him into a rebellious attraction to pre-packaged food. She sighed. *I suppose the younger generation always has to find something to critique their elders for, still, I find the world is a delightful place full of aesthetically pleasing young men like Josh and Benedict.*

Their path took a turn and opened up a vista of heather-clad

hills. The view prompted Dee's thoughts to turn to old memories.
We must be getting close. I'm sure John and Tony's farms are somewhere around here. I seem to remember them being nestled in these very hills. I thought their homes were so picturesque – just like one of Beatrix Potter's illustrations – all stone walls and neat windows. I only visited the farms once and I didn't enjoy it. While the setting was beautiful there was an awful tension in the atmosphere.

If I recall rightly, Daniel and I had come in the old Land Rover to pick the boys up for a picnic, or was it a country show? Either way, we walked into one heck of a row – a fat man who turned out to be Tony's dad was yelling at Tony loud enough to send the yard hens scurrying and make the sheepdogs cower. I can see the boy now, standing forlornly, wringing his hands and staring down at his threadbare sneakers.

'You useless bit of filth!' spat the man, 'That's more money down the drain – if only you were more like your cousin John! He doesn't go around wasting his dad's cash!'

I remember grabbing Daniel's arm. I'd never seen anything like it – my parents were always so polite to me, even when I was being an impossible teen.

Daniel had looked at me, patted my hand, smiled and whispered, 'It's a family joke that Tony's dad doesn't like Tony much but then it all works out as John's dad would like Tony to be his son. The biggest joke of all is that the two boys, Tony and John, look as if they were swapped at birth – that large chap who is the image of what John will look like in thirty years is actually Tony's dad, while John's father is skinny like Tony.' Daniel had chuckled before adding, 'What's more, both the dads make it quite clear that they prefer the other's boy to their own child.'

I remember I wanted to scream, 'But it's not a joke!'

John had stood in his farmyard, which was directly opposite. He was enjoying the spectacle and looked smug. There was a thin older man nearby vigorously sweeping up –from Daniel's description I knew he must be John's dad.

And my sentiment that the family's turmoil was nothing to

laugh about was only reinforced when later on, I had, unwisely, asked John's dad if he minded taking a photo of us all – me, Daniel, John and Tony. I wanted to remember everything about that summer.

With a quick movement, he'd taken my camera in his thin hand and smiled warmly at me with the dazzling blue eyes that are a family trait.

'Delighted!' he said. 'Where do want it? In front of the house? Or by the gate? I think the light might be better by the house.'

So, we had all lined up by the pots of red geraniums near the front door. Tony mustered a weak smile, still subdued from the tongue-lashing he'd endured. John was beaming right up until the moment that his dad had snarled, 'Oi! John! Stand behind Tony, then you won't look so fat!'

Dee shuddered at the memory before putting her shoulders back and firmly telling herself, *Still it will be nice to see Tony and John again, I just hope they don't mention sheep shears.*

Sheep shears came up almost immediately when Dee was reintroduced to the Pringle cousins. For Zara, both men made a striking first impression. The cousins had been waiting for Dee and co while leaning on their gates and glowering at each other.

Goodness, thought Zara, *all Daniel's relatives seem to be blessed with deep blue eyes. Now from what Daniel and Dee said over brunch, the corpulent chap must be John – he's almost a perfect sphere! I wonder where he gets his trousers and checked shirt from? They are doing a manly job covering his ample form – which is no small feat. Is that binder twine holding up his trousers instead of a belt?*

She briefly switched her attention to the surrounding area. *This setting is picture-perfect.* The farms lay in the shelter of the hills with yards brimming over with poultry, and old farm machinery ranging from an ancient plough to a pair of equally ancient milk urns. The smell of diesel and a classic tractor were a nod to modernity. Zara chose to gloss over the less romantic elements of the buzzing blue bottle flies and the scent of manure.

'So, Dee, not back on the island for more than five minutes and you're already causing mayhem with some sheep shears of all things!' declared John in a jovial fashion. His cheeks were rosy and his smile warm.

Zara assumed she would be introduced but from the other gate, there was a roar.

'Sheep shears! You have the gall to bring up sheep shears when we both know it was you who sneaked into my house the night before last and stole great-great-grandfather's sheep shears!'

Zara presumed this was Tony, as he fit the description of being wiry. He was wearing blue overalls tucked into black boots. There was no excess flesh on him but you could tell that what there was of him was pure muscle.

'You know by rights them sheep shears should be mine, Tony Pringle. Grandfather always intended them to come to me!' John's many jowls quivered in rage.

'Poppycock! John Pringle, if it's thieving you are talking about let's talk about my prize ram, Odin. We both know it was you behind that attempt to rustle him.' Tony's sinewy frame was taut, his hands clenched into fists.

'Bit like watching a tennis match, isn't it?' whispered Dee to Zara. 'I suggest you just relax and enjoy the scenery; this is likely to take a while.'

'Were they always like this?'

Dee nodded. 'Only back then it all revolved around Elsie.'

Zara did as her mother suggested. The walk they'd had to get to this point had been highly enjoyable. The sky seemed to go on forever, then dip down to a distant blue sea. Sheep-grazed heather hills gave way to tiny pasture fields with intricate stone walls, a jigsaw of grey rocks painstakingly placed together and now embellished with moss and flowers.

The cousins' farmhouses were too high up to sustain more than a handful of trees. The few trees brave enough to attempt living at this altitude were bowed over by the wind. Both the cousins lived in traditional stone farmhouses with two small windows on either side of a front door and three neat windows upstairs.

Dee had mentioned that the windows were small and the walls thick to keep the winter storms out. Now, with the sun shining and swallows swooping in and out of the barns, it was hard to imagine that gales could ever rage in this idyllic spot.

'You call that a ram? He's not a patch on my Mannin.' John's bulbous arms were folded across his excessive stomach. His shirt buttons were struggling and failing to hold in his girth and bits of his string vest peaked through the gaps.

'Oh, is that the case? Then why did Odin win a prize at the Southern Agricultural Show? We both know that you were behind that attempt to steal Odin. You know he was odds-on favourite to win.' Tony's anger spilled out into agitated movement; his bony body swayed back and forth towards the gate.

John deliberately raised his eyebrows and tilted his head to one side. 'Trust you to know the betting odds! But who got Best in Show at the Royal, I'd like to know?'

Dee tapped on Daniel's sleeve. When he smiled down at her, she whispered, 'Surely they don't run bets on an agricultural show?'

He murmured back, 'They do but it's illegal.'

Dee persisted, 'I thought it was all online these days.'

Daniel nodded. 'But some people still like the thrill of actually being there.'

During this interchange, Tony and John continued their verbal combat but Zara began to lose interest in the repetitive nature of their squabble. As this was obviously going to go on for the foreseeable future, she continued to take in her surroundings.

There seemed to be an inordinate number of hens and cockerels busily scratching and clucking in both farm yards and spilling over to the dividing lane. A cat with no tail was languidly sunning itself on John's barn steps. *I wonder how Mother's rather pampered Persian is getting on back at home in the Cotswold – she must be suffering without Dee to wait on her hand and food.*

Zara's gaze moved on from the feline. She noted that the fashion for barns around here was for sturdy two-storey affairs, built of the local grey stone, with stables below and slit windows storage above. Substantial stone steps clung to the side of the building on the upper floor. She was just admiring the red geraniums planted in terracotta pots going up the steps when she recalled that John had a daughter called Juliet. *I wonder if those pretty pots are her work?*

As Zara was thinking of the romantically-named girl with a geranium in one hand and the trowel in the other, a pretty slim girl with long blonde hair slipped out of the barn door. She looked furtively around. The girl's eyes locked on the two men squabbling over their respective gates. Realising that her father and his cousin only had eyes for each other she turned back to make a beckoning gesture. From the same door emerged an exceptionally good-looking young man. Their hands touched lightly for a second and as he slipped past her, their bodies brushed effortlessly against each other. The folds of her light cotton frock billowed in a passing breeze and caressed his trouser leg. With a last, lingering look at her face, he turned and crept down the steps and out of sight with a smile still playing on his lips. The girl watched him go, and then quietly stepped back into the barn and closed the door.

Romeo, I presume, aka Christian. So that explains Benedict's snort at his grandfather's suggestion that the two were unable to meet!

Zara brought her attention back to her immediate companions to find that the Pringle cousins had stormed off.

'So that's that!' laughed Dee.

'Looks like it,' agreed Daniel with a grin. 'So much for a warm reunion.'

This left Daniel, Benedict, Dee and Zara to enjoy a peaceful walk back to their cars. It was agreed that Dee's old beau, Daniel and his grandson, Benedict, would meet Zara and Dee that evening and go for an early supper at a little fish restaurant that Daniel recommended along the quay.

'It's small and the fish is fresh.'

Duly at six-thirty, Zara and Dee were ready and standing outside their guesthouse. A couple of seagulls floated overhead and waves gently lapped the bay. Zara had opted for a navy and green wrap dress while Dee …

'Mother, laid-back chic?'

'Sorry, darling?' asked Dee while checking in her bag for her lipstick.

'Laid-back chic? Is that the look you're going for?' asked Zara, indicating her mother's outfit.

Dee blushed. 'What, this? Oh, I just threw on what was nearest to hand.' She hoped she sounded nonchalant.

'So, what was to hand was cream trousers, a silk blouse, those trendy canvas shoes and an array of layered necklaces?'

'Yes!' said Dee with conviction, while looking her daughter defiantly in the eye.

Zara grinned and regarded her mother. 'Well, you look lovely and Amelia would be proud of you.'

'How do you think she's managing without us?' Dee sounded concerned.

Zara laughed. 'I should think very well. What uni student wants their mother and grandmother constantly on hand?'

'You're probably right, but I think I'll give her a ring later, just to say hello.'

Daniel and Benedict strolled up to them.

'Ah! Dee, Zara there you are. Sorry we're a little late, we had trouble finding somewhere to park.' Daniel looked debonair and relaxed. He wore a linen jacket and Dee noted that Benedict had added some extra-thick eyeliner and a few more studded belts in honour of that evening's outing.

Daniel was smiling at them when he said, 'May I say how delightful you both look.'

Dee blushed a deeper rose colour.

'It's a beautiful evening. We'll walk to the restaurant; it's just around the corner.'

Daniel tucked Dee's arm comfortably into his, and then led the way down the steps and onto the prom. This left Zara to Benedict.

'Wonderful evening,' she tried and was rewarded with a grunt. 'I love the way it stays light here so late at night.' This time she thought she saw a nod but it might just have been her imagination. She wanted to ask him about the young cousins, Christian and Juliet; Benedict was bound to know exactly what the level of their friendship was. She felt that here was a tale of star-crossed lovers that was worthy of Lavinia Lovelace's pen. She was phrasing an opening comment in her mind when a whoop from in front of them interrupted. The cry was loud enough to make a boy peddling past on a bicycle stare, and a horse pulling the tram swish his tail and twitch his ears.

'Mummy! Granny!' came Amelia's familiar voice. And there she was all five-foot-one of her. Her black corset was laced tight, showing off her waspish figure. Her tutu was largely black but as a nod to summer, there were ribbons of green in it. Vibrant red curls cascaded around her face. What passed for Amelia's idea of minimal makeup adorned her face: black lipstick and lashings of thick mascara.

'Darling!' exclaimed Dee and Zara in unison as they rushed to embrace her.

Amelia, laughing, said, 'You didn't think we'd leave you both unsupervised when there's sleuthing to be done? The moment we heard that Granny was up to her old corpse-finding tricks we jumped straight into the car and caught the next ferry over.' Her green eyes were alight with life and her fair skin glowed with health and vitality.

'We?' queried Dee.

'Why, me and Josh, of course.'

Josh stepped forward from behind a parked van, smiling warmly. Dee liked him although she never knew what the correct term was to describe his looks. Gorgeous, was a safe and accurate adjective. He was lithe, reminding her rather of a panther, if it was possible to have a panther whose diet consisted of fizzy drinks and crisps.

It was his complexion that caused Dee concern. *Is it offensive to make reference to his delightfully rich skin tone and beautiful eyes, or is that raising his mixed Korean-European heritage in an unacceptable way? And is the very way I'm referring to his looks unacceptable? I mean, after all, if a man in his seventies mentioned a girl in her twenties was cat-like and gorgeous there would be no end of complaints.*

Shelving these social dilemmas, Dee settled for the safer ground of making introductions.

'Daniel you must meet my granddaughter, Amelia! Daniel is an old friend. And this is Josh, he works with Nicholas Corman.'

Daniel shook them both by the hand saying, 'Another policeman. Delighted to meet you, Josh. And Amelia, you look so like your grandmother did when we knew each other.'

Dee was flustered by this. *How can he say she reminds him of me? He never saw me in a black tightly-laced corset. Was it a dream of his?*

Dee moved swiftly on. 'And this is Benedict—'

She was about to explain that Benedict was Daniel's grandson when the lad strode forward. Positioning himself between Amelia and Josh, he took hold of her hand.

Their Goth eyes met.

When he spoke, his voice was as smooth as Frank Sinatra himself, 'Think of me as your personal guide while you are on the island. We can start by going to a fish restaurant nearby and then perhaps I could show you St Aiden's Head by starlight. Your grandmother says you have an interest in Mongolian music; I'd love to hear more about it.' All the time he was grasping Amelia's hand and gazing intently into her eyes.

Now he tucked her arm in his with as much aplomb as his grandfather had demonstrated with Dee and strolled passed Josh without giving him so much as a backward look. Josh watched them go, his mouth slightly open and his hands hanging slack by his sides.

Daniel raised his eyebrows and in a low voice he informed Dee, 'I haven't heard him use that many sentences since he was at primary school.'

How Dee would have responded Daniel never found out as a police car with its blue light pulled up and out of it stepped a tall WPC and a male officer.

The male officer approached Dee and formally asked her, 'Are you Ms Dee FitzMorris?'

Dee blinked, confused. 'Of course, I am. Don't you remember we met at the police station yesterday? You were so kind as to make me some camomile tea just like your Granny likes it.'

The police officer gave an embarrassed glance at the WPC and then proceeded. 'We're arresting you in connection with the murder that occurred on Chough Drive. You do not have to say anything but—'

Her hands on her hips and her eyes blazing, Zara's voice cut across the policeman's speech. 'Don't worry, Mother, we'll have you out of custody in a jiffy – we've done it before and I have no doubt we'll have to do it again in the future.'

It was only a matter of minutes before Dee was bundled into the police car and separated from her loved ones. She was touched by the send-off they gave her. Crammed in the back seat of the police car she craned her neck for a final view of them.

It rather reminds me of those old movies where the families line up on the train platform and tearfully wave their loved ones off to war. Although, in those movies, they always seemed to have white handkerchiefs to wave. We don't use hankies now. I suppose tissues are more hygienic but somehow waving a bit of crumpled Kleenex doesn't have the same poignancy. Goths too! That's another difference – you don't see a lot of tearful Goths bidding a fond farewell on screen, but other than that it was just like the movies.

Dee settled down more comfortably in her seat and hoped that the nice young policeman would make her another cup of camomile when they arrived at the station.

Chapter 4

A little earlier in the day, the actual murderer was pondering events while regarding the ever-changing ocean and breathing in the sea air.

Unfortunate! Yes, very unfortunate, but it's not the end of the world. Well, I suppose it is for the man I killed.

But the most important thing is that it won't interfere with my operation, I will still make a lot of money from the bets on the dance competition and then there are the drugs. The most important thing is that no one would ever suspect that it was me but just to be on the safe side I need to put myself right in the centre of the investigation. I hear on the grapevine that Dee FitzMorris is a suspect. It should be easy enough to get to know her or better still her daughter, Zara. That way I will probably be able to implicate the two of them for any further crimes I might commit.

They laughed out loud at their own cleverness.

After Dee had departed, the others stood, for a moment, dejected and forlorn.

Zara was the first to collect her wits. She grabbed her phone out of her handbag and declared, 'The first thing we need to do is get hold of Nicholas and get Mummy out of jail.'

'I think it might be an idea to get an advocate,' said Daniel, who also reached for his phone.

'An advocate?' queried Amelia, looking concerned beneath her black eyeliner.

Benedict, his white wing-collared shirt show-casing his fine features, spoke. 'We have a different legal system here. I'll explain it to you later.'

He was looking attentively at Amelia and using his height to dominate her line of sight, which wasn't hard as she was at least a foot shorter than him. He was suitably imposing; his slim black trousers and suit jacket elongated his height, his striking blue eyes were set off by black makeup, and then on top of it all was his shock of blond hair.

Zara suspected that Benedict was keen to keep Amelia's attention away from Josh. Poor Josh was hovering to one side; he was used to being the most remarkable-looking young man in any group but he didn't need his police training to tell him that this tall, stringy Goth was going to be a problem.

Zara focussed on her phone, as the ring-tone was answered. 'Nicholas, it's me. Where are you? Mother has been arrested.' She paused. 'What has you being out for supper with your parents and an old friend's mother got to do with anything?' Her voice rose to a pitch that caused a young couple walking past to stare. 'What do you mean you'll deal with it? We need to come up with a strategy.' She listened to his reply. 'No! I won't wait until the morning! Either you tell me where you are right now or I'll search every restaurant on the island until I find you! Oh? Really? How strange – that's where we were going to have supper. I hear their queenies are excellent.'

She cut him off and started to walk down the road.

'Queenies?' asked Josh.

Benedict just gave a derisive snort, so it was left to his grandfather, Daniel to say, 'It's a delicious local shellfish. We'd better hurry to catch up with Zara. I'm not sure she actually knows where the restaurant is.'

'That's all I need,' sighed Nicholas as he put his phone back in his pocket.

He'd been sitting at an outside table with his parents, Myrtle and George, and the mother of his old police colleague, Betty Hobbs. When his phone had rung, he had stood up and walked a little distance away to take the call.

He took a moment to compose himself. He inhaled a long slow breath. Gazing at the boats gently popping up and down in the harbour, he mindfully listened to the placid tapping of the rigging and the cries of the seagulls, but the joys of nature and mindfulness could not rid Nicholas of a sense of foreboding.

Damn! That's all I need!

The evening had not been going well. His father was not the problem. He never was, he just sat silently contemplating his own concerns and tracking the flight of the passing gulls. The source of his stress lay elsewhere …

I knew I was in trouble when I introduced Mum to Betty. He sighed. *The moment they clapped their eyes on each other, there was tension. Betty shouldn't have opened with that, 'My, aren't we purple?' comment. But then Mum's, 'My, aren't we floral? Presumably, you've just come from a 1940s re-enactment? I gather they are all the rage,' was a little harsh. It was quite a relief having to take a phone call and leave. I wasn't sure what to say with Mum bragging about my outstanding finishing time at the London Marathon – she knows I've never run a marathon in my life. I suppose Betty had been going on rather about Ron's sporting prowess. Strange he's never mentioned that he'd climbed Mount Everest for charity.*

Steeling himself he headed back to the table, his mind playing out the upcoming interview with Zara.

She'll be all revved up – keen to repeat the fun we had clearing Dee of those clown murders.

Despite his current anxiety, he smiled at the memory then, recalling his unfortunate interaction the previous day with the Blom constabulary, he grimaced and ran his hand through his hair.

If only I hadn't got off to such a bad start with the Acting Chief! There'll be no chance of me being involved in the investigation now.

His mind focused on his unfortunate meeting with Hadrian Macintosh.

I was on edge – not at my best, what with the surprise of seeing Zara and then Dee with that dead body. But still, I should have been more professional. That police waiting room didn't help. I'd been cooped up for hours, with that table covered in coffee cup circles and the constant chatter of that woman waiting for her son to be released. On top of all that, it was so hot and then there was that smell of cleaning chemicals – but still, I should have been more thoughtful.

I probably let my annoyance at being kept waiting show too much. I must have come across to Hadrian as a bit imperious, high-handed even. Naturally, Hadrian Macintosh, with his boss away, would be keen to assert his authority; I could have been more sensitive.

With a shudder, he recalled his ex-wife saying that he lacked the ability to be diplomatic. She put it down to him being an only child and not having grown up having to accommodate others. Pushing all thoughts of her to one side, he returned to Hadrian.

Odd looking chap; small and round. Unusual to have dark skin and red hair. I wonder if he grew that ridiculous moustache to hide his insecurity. Or was it to make himself look older? It looks like it's straight out of a Biggles' book – he must wax it, but perhaps it grows like that naturally, after all, his eyebrows do have a flyaway vigour to them. But regardless of his looks, he certainly won't want me anywhere near the case. And, more to the point Zara won't be pleased.

With that final thought, he found himself back at the restaurant. His mother and Betty both looked up as he returned.

'Zara is joining us!' he announced.

'Not Zara FitzMorris, the clown murderer?' gasped Betty.

'She was never accused of any such thing,' clarified Nicholas hastily.

'But her mother, Dee FitzMorris, was implicated!' persisted Betty. 'Why is she coming here?'

'Um! Er! It appears that Dee has been taken into custody.'

Betty triumphantly declared, 'I knew it! I think you'll find that Ron has got the Blom police force in tip-top condition. Even with him away in Liverpool, there will be no shillyshallying around with grannies who can't be trusted with sheep shears!'

Myrtle, in a heather-coloured dress and cardigan, had been visibly swelling with outrage. 'I think you'll find that my Nicholas is an excellent judge of people. If he says Dee is innocent, she is innocent. I can see it's a very good thing that he's here, otherwise, poor Dee would be the victim of a gross miscarriage of justice! Isn't that right, George?'

Without taking his eyes off a distant shag, George murmured, 'Yes, dear!'

Nicholas said nothing but feared that his worst nightmares were about to come true.

When Zara arrived, with Daniel, Josh, Benedict and Amelia in tow, he politely rose to his feet.

He did hope Zara didn't hear Betty saying, 'I knew that FitzMorris woman liked clowns but I didn't know she travelled with a circus.'

Betty did have a point; while Zara and Daniel looked respectable enough, pixie-sized Goth Amelia and the tall black-clad boy with her did lend the group a theatrical feel. He was both surprised and relieved to see his work subordinate, Josh, was with them.

Introductions were made and tables rearranged. It was fortunate they were outside as the quaint space inside, with its faux fishing nets and trendy paintings, could not have accommodated them all.

Pausing, only to order a plate of queenies, Zara launched into her agenda. 'So, Nicholas, what do you propose doing about Mother?'

'Miss FitzMorris – Zara – we really shouldn't interfere. Daniel has just told me that he has organised an advocate to deal with Dee's case. Other than that, we should let the Blom police get on with their investigation. I am sure they will establish Dee's innocence in next to no time.'

'Poppycock!' retorted Zara. Her green eyes flashed and, not for the first time, Nicholas thought, *She looks magnificent when she is angry. Scary? Yes! But there is a touch of Boadicea about the way she throws back her head with dignity and defiance. She would definitely inspire ancient Britons into battle. Or in this case, two Goths, an errant junior inspector and a local OAP.*

Zara was in full flow. 'That Hadrian Macintosh definitely had an attitude. He took against Mother the second he rather pompously asked her if she had anything to say and she said, "Do you have any camomile tea?"'

Betty, pink lipstick quivering and piggy face outraged, launched in to defend her son's deputy. 'I'll not hear a word against Hadrian Macintosh, he's one of the finest officers the police force has ever had. My Ron recruited him himself. He has an outstanding record. And what's more, he has a wonderful mother.' She cast a glance at Myrtle. 'I always think you can tell a lot about the calibre of a man by his mother, and Hadrian's mother is exceptional. So cosmopolitan – she was born in Mumbai, studied in New York and then met Hadrian's father when she was studying for her postgraduate qualifications at Edinburgh University.'

Nicholas could see that his mother had taken a sharp breath in order to make a retort and he was almost relieved when Zara spoke. 'Well if you won't help, Nicholas, I will just find someone who will!'

At that moment the waitress arrived with food. The smell of queenies, garlic and bacon carried on the sea air was intoxicating. Zara inhaled and gave the plate of food before her an admiring look before glowering at Nicholas. 'And just so you know, Nicholas, if I didn't believe it was a crime to waste food I would leave now.'

During all this interchange Daniel had been observing with a calm, detached interest. George was absorbed in observing some swans in the harbour.

Benedict and Josh were more animated. They were engrossed in trying to monopolise Amelia's attention. Sitting on each side of her, first one and then the other pointed out something of interest – a boat, a motorbike, a puppy; the actual object was not of importance as the aim of each boy was to cut his rival out. An observer would have noted that poor Josh was losing out to the novelty factor of Benedict.

Betty might not have taken on board all the subtleties of Josh's interactions with Amelia but she had seen enough to feel able to comment.

'My Ron always says it's a mistake for officers to get too friendly with suspects. Of course, you can't blame the younger officers, it's only natural that they should take their lead by the example set by their superiors.' Here, she pointedly looked at Nicholas. He was gazing forlornly at Zara. She had deliberately turned away from him and was concentrating on her supper.

This was too much for Myrtle who in a clarion voice announced, 'At least my Nicholas isn't some namby-pamby mother's boy. My Nicholas is full of manly passion! You should see his tango.'

Nicholas sighed and looked towards the heavens. *Could this evening get any worse?*

It was probably just as well, for Nicholas's state of wellbeing, that he was unaware that while the evening would not get any worse, he would think of it as a positively happy interlude before things got seriously tricky.

Chapter 5

The next day there was a fine early morning mist which boded well for a blazing hot day. Nicholas was down to breakfast first, which gave him a chance to read the local paper in peace. On the front page was the headline: *Today is the day we've all been waiting for*! Fascinated to find out what the population had been so highly anticipating he read on:

At St Bridget's Village Fair, we will finally find out who really has grown this year's prize carrots – will it be Tony Pringle? Or will John Pringle pip him to the post?

Other hotly contested topics are the jams. Mrs Roberts is thought to be the top runner.

The children of St Bridget's Primary School will be performing Blom dances – an annual treat.

The fair is sponsored by and will be opened by Sean Murphy. As many of you know, Mr Murphy is a newcomer to our island. In the short time he has been here, he has made quite an impact through his building firm and his philanthropic works.

It was opening at noon and the address was towards the south of the island.

Nicholas smiled. *Excellent! That is just the sort of activity which will get us away from St Aiden's and the FitzMorris ladies, not to mention Betty Hobbs. It will also keep Mother distracted!*

He read on and found the murder, which hadn't made the front page, but was mentioned on page three, with just a line or two about how the police had 'a person of interest in custody' and also that the owner of the sheep shears had been identified but the police had not released their name.

Evidently, for citizens of Blom, a village fair carries far more importance than a murder, he thought. *Poor Dee, I'm afraid she's in trouble. If Ron hadn't been called away to Liverpool, I would probably be able to put in a good word on her behalf.*

Daniel had rung earlier to say the advocate was hopeful that he would be able to get Dee out on bail. He'd also reported that she was in remarkably high spirits but that he would expect nothing less of such an admirable lady.

Yet again Nicholas had a futile qualm of regret. *I wish I hadn't rubbed Hadrian Macintosh up the wrong way. Maybe I could speak to him copper-to-copper.* Zara's disapproving countenance swum before him and he gave an inward sigh. Myrtle shimmied in, a vision in lilac slacks and a blouse. George followed in her wake. Myrtle was ecstatic when Nicholas suggested going to the fair and even more overjoyed by the reality when they arrived at St Bridget's a couple of hours later.

'Why, George, isn't this just like village fairs when we were children!' she exclaimed as she had her first glimpse of the fair. The three of them stood and admired the merry scene. Canvas tents dotted the field, adorned with bright bunting. There was a coconut shy and – judging by the number of children running around clasping toffee apple or candy floss – there must also be food stalls. The sky was a clear vivid blue such as you only get on a small island. The air was filled with the sound of laughter and a lusty brass band.

Myrtle had changed into a fit-and-flair summer frock in lilac. Her tiny waist was defined by a wide belt. To fend off the intense sun and to add glamour she had added a straw hat and a rather dashing pair of winged sunglasses.

'Come on, George! There's the flower tent.' With that, Myrtle disappeared into the throng, firmly holding George by the hand, just in case he made a bid for freedom.

Nicholas permitted himself a smile of satisfaction.

I think I can safely congratulate myself on successfully removing us all from stress – at least for one day!

Then through the hubbub came the piercing shriek that destroyed his hope of serenity.

'Nicholas Corman, how adorable of you to come and support me! How sweet of you to realise that with my Ron away I could do with a bit of company. I imagine you're simply longing to look at my knitting!'

There was Betty Hobbs, in fuchsia from the top of her head to the tip of her toes. Nicholas could not help but gawp. She gave him a girlish smile and twirled around. 'Quite something, isn't it?'

Nicholas stared, his eyebrows raised to his hairline, but he managed to say, 'Er, yes! I've never seen anything so … How did you get your hat and shoes decorated like that?'

'It took some doing – I had to attach every flower by hand.'

'But there are so many of them!' gasped Nicholas.

'Well, I like to make the effort. But Nicholas, how did you ever find out about my little surprise?'

'Surprise?' Nicholas swallowed nervously; he knew from experience that Betty's surprises were never good.

'Yes! My entry for the knitting competition.'

Nicholas was perplexed. Betty gave him a none-too-gentle jocular nudge in the ribs with her elbow.

'It's no use playing coy with me! I suppose it's your police training! Still, how did you know that I've knitted you a pair of swimming trunks and that's what I've entered for the knitting competition?'

'Swimming trunks made of wool?' queried Nicholas, his heart beating faster.

Betty beamed. 'I knew you'd be pleased! They used to be all the rage – I've no idea why they went out of vogue. All these modern trunks are so unattractive.'

'You've knitted me some swimming trunks?' he stammered.

'Well in all honesty they were going to be for Ron but with him being away I made them a lot smaller so they'll fit you nicely for the photoshoot.'

'Photoshoot?' Nicholas's anxiety was rising to panic.

'Yes! On Port Erin Beach. I've got photographers from the Blom Independent and the Courier. I shouldn't be surprised if it didn't make the front page.'

'Photographers?'

'Yes! You really don't seem to be at your sharpest this morning, dear. Perhaps it's the heat. We need all the publicity we can get. How else will we bring about a fashion revival?'

'Fashion revival?' Nicholas was baffled but scared.

She nodded enthusiastically. 'There's a huge gap in the market. I've researched it thoroughly and no one else is manufacturing knitted trunks!'

Nicholas was lost for words which didn't matter in the slightest as Betty had enough words for both of them.

She grasped his arm, so tightly, her pink lacquered nails bit into his flesh.

'Oooh, look who it is! There's Joe. And bless him! He has Reggie with him – he's so good to that boy!'

Her voice was full of girlish enthusiasm. He could imagine her as a teenager, with a blonde beehive hair-do and a pink flowered mini skirt, shrieking at the Beatles in a similar fashion. He scanned the sea of people. There were old folk indulgently watching cute toddlers, teenagers trying to look cool while eating toffee apples, and there was even a lady with seven dachshunds but he couldn't discern anyone who merited that degree of excitement.

'Coo-ee, Joe! I'm over here!'

At the summons, the lanky redheaded man stood still and looked over towards them. Nicholas remembered seeing him running past the coffee shop when he'd been with Betty in St Aiden's. Now he was stationary Nicholas was able to get a proper look at him; he was tall, about six-foot-two but his extreme leanness made him appear taller. His hair was strawberry blond, and even at this distance, Nicholas was struck by his pale eyes; they reminded Nicholas of pictures he'd seen of the Arctic ice. His complexion matched his eyes; he was pale to the point of being almost translucent.

Nicholas noted the second that Joe had registered that it was Betty hailing him.

Was that a flicker of disdain on his sharp features? If it was it, was quickly replaced by a genial smile!

Joe exchanged a word with the youth, Reggie, who was standing beside him. The boy was as tall as Joe but built on a burlier scale. He had dark hair, milk-white skin and spots – a red, angry rash of them. He was dressed in a way that Nicholas knew his subordinate, Josh, would term 'flash'.

Joe strode towards Betty and Nicholas, with Reggie trailing behind. Before there was a chance for Nicholas to introduce himself, Betty had clasped both Nicholas and Joe about the waist.

'How blessed am I! There was I thinking I was going to have to do today alone and unsupported, what with my Ron away in Liverpool, but both of you came here to be my boys. We are all going to have a wonderful day. Now Joe, Nicholas is very excited about my swimming trunks and is just longing for me to show him the craft tent.'

'Betty, my love, much as I am longing to see your creative talent, duty calls.' Joe nodded over to the side of a tent where Daniel's grandson, Benedict was standing; a black stick of Gothdom against the white canvas. He delivered this excuse smoothly, as his pale silver eyes smiled into Betty's and his masculine hand affectionately patted her pudgy paw while at the same time, he skilfully removed himself from her clasp. He made his escape with an ease that Nicholas could only envy.

Far from being hurt or affronted by the gesture, it only seemed to confirm Betty's admiration for him.

'Isn't that just like him?' She sighed. 'Never thinks of himself and his own enjoyment. His father would be so proud of him, he's such a fine young man. Look, there he is, talking to that boy you had at supper.'

She indicated to where Joe had cornered a very reluctant Benedict. The youth, in his habitual black and studs, was scowling and looking at his feet. Reggie hovered to one side.

'I must say, Nicholas, you do have some very peculiar friends. That boy – just look at him! Must be on drugs! That's probably what Joe's gone to talk to him about. He's tireless in his efforts to get his pupils onto the straight and narrow. You know I knew his father?'

A wistful note entered her voice.

'What, Benedict's father? How? I mean I thought you only came to the island when Ron got his job,' asked Nicholas in surprise.

Impatiently Betty answered. 'Not the Goth's father! Joe's! He lived on our street – of course, he was a bit older than me. He had a way with him – all the girls liked him. And Joe is the spitting image of him.'

She was looking longingly at Joe in much the same way Nicholas could have imagined her looking at Joe's father many decades earlier and Nicholas realised she was repeating the conversation they had had at the teashop.

There was a crackle over the loudspeakers then a cough, followed by the announcement: 'Ladies and gentlemen, I'd like to welcome you all to today's fair. If you will kindly make your way to the stand, the band will lead us in the National Anthem, then the children of St Bridget's School will demonstrate some Blom dancing before our generous sponsor for today, Mr Sean Murphy, will say a few words to officially open today's proceedings.'

Betty sighed. 'Oh, dear! Looks like you've missed your chance to see the trunks. But not to worry there'll be plenty of time later. Oh, look! Joe seems to be free now. I'll just go and have a word.'

She buzzed off, rather like a large pink bumble bee, leaving Nicholas to make his way, along with everyone else, to the stand.

The stand consisted of a few wooden pallets comprising a makeshift stage. On it were a handful of dignitaries. The band struck up the opening of the Blom National Anthem. With one accord the whole seething mass of people stood to attention. Heartily they sang a stirring song, foreign to Nicholas, but obviously as familiar to the locals as God Save Our Gracious King is to folk in the UK.

As the last notes finished, a variety of children in homemade costumes, shuffled in front of the podium. One or two of the reluctant older boys had to be forcibly shoved into the limelight. Once the jolly folk music of fiddle and drum started, they all danced credibly. The audience applauded with enthusiasm. Nicholas never ceased to marvel at the blind admiration that parents and grandparents have for their offspring.

The dancers took their final bow and walked away from the podium and into their loved ones' embraces. A gentleman walked confidently to the centre of the stage. He was small but what he lacked in stature he made up for by what Nicholas's mother called 'presence'. He just stood there and within seconds the hubbub had died down and every eye was upon him. Nicholas regarded him with a professional eye: dark hair, dark eyes – which held an unmistakable roguish twinkle – in his fifties and vibrant with good health. His watch of note and expensive suit denoted money and attention to detail.

When he spoke, he had the softest of southern Irish burrs, like a gentle seductive mist. His voice carried effortlessly to the furthest corners of the field. Nicholas found himself disliking the man and feared it might, just might, be due to jealousy.

'Ladies and gentlemen, as some of you know, my name is Sean Murphy. I am honoured to be here today. I've had the privilege to have a preview of the competitors and I must say the standards are exceptionally high. I was impressed by a pair of knitted swimming trunks – I haven't seen those since I was a boy.' A faint snigger ran through the crowd and Nicholas felt his stomach clench at the thought of Port Erin Beach and a photographer. Sean Murphy scanned the crowd with the easy assurance of a born orator.

Is it my imagination or is there one figure he seems especially interested in?

Nicholas glanced around, trying to see who Sean found so fascinating but his view was obscured by a middle-aged couple of generous proportions.

'The WI have baked a fine array of cakes which you can sample in the tea tent. They are also putting on a display of axe throwing and jujitsu, so make sure you don't miss that. And without more ado, I declare this year's St Bridget's Fair open.'

There was a cheer and the band struck up with 'For he's a jolly good fellow' which Nicholas thought was quite unnecessary and a bit excessive.

Sean Murphy left the stage with the certainty of a guided missile. Nicholas had been right; during his speech, Sean Murphy had been drawn to one person in particular. As the large couple waddled towards the tea tent, Nicholas could finally see who he had been so entranced by. Hawk-like, Sean was focused on his prey: red-haired, petite and vibrant, it was Zara FitzMorris.

'May I introduce myself?' said Sean smoothly, never taking his black eyes away from Zara's green ones. He took her hand firmly in his. 'Sean Murphy, at your service.'

Nicholas watched and thought, *I knew I didn't like the chap from the moment he stepped onto the stage. And what is Zara up to? Is that look demure? More like a thin coating of demure and a heavy overcoat of 'Come hither'!*

Without even realising what he was doing, Nicholas stumbled towards the couple, stopping abruptly at Zara's side, just as she was replying, 'Zara FitzMorris.'

Without letting go of Zara's hand, Sean regarded Nicholas coolly. 'Is he with you?'

'Only a vague acquaintance,' said Zara with chilling finality.

'In that case, let me show you a prize marrow,' said Sean, tucking her arm in his and leading her to the vegetable produce tent, leaving Nicholas alone amid a milling crowd of people.

They had only got a few steps when John Pringle, very smart in his Sunday best, lumbered up. He was perspiring heavily, evidently feeling the heat.

'Did you hear the news?' he demanded of Zara.

'Sean Murphy, this is John Pringle, a childhood friend of my mother's.'

'How do?' nodded John, not really looking at Sean. 'So, have you heard? It was *my* antique sheep shears, that your mother was caught red-handed with, so to speak, over the corpse.'

'What do you mean *your* shears? You know, by rights they're mine,' bellowed his cousin who had, silent as a ferret and just as slim, sidled up to them.

'And this is his cousin, Tony Pringle,' continued Zara, calm despite the commotion.

Nicholas, who could hardly be blamed for having heard the interchange, joined them.

Sean stopped walking and, obviously surprised, said, 'Let me get this right. Between the two of you gentlemen there lies the ownership of the Victorian sheep shears that were the unlikely murder weapon of a man on Chough Drive.' The two cousins nodded at him. He now turned his attention to Zara. 'And your mother is the lady who was found with both the body and the weapon?'

'Yes,' replied Zara. 'But what's your interest?'

'The dead man worked for me. Patrick O'Connor.'

'Did you say Patrick was murdered?' started Tony, his thin face contorted.

'You knew him?' enquired Sean, one eyebrow raised.

'I think I met him once,' said Tony. His voice was light, but his eyes darted from side to side while he spoke.

Sean smiled a full-wattage beam at Zara and purred, 'Perhaps, Zara, you wouldn't mind foregoing the pleasures of the produce tent? I think we should all put our heads together and see if we can work out what's going on. The police don't seem to be getting on very fast and their constant enquiries are playing havoc with my work schedule. The sooner this is all sorted out, the better.'

'My sentiments precisely,' agreed Zara, throwing Nicholas a smug glance.

'Grand idea! But after that, Zara, you must come and see the veg.' John's ample chest swelled with pride. 'My carrots won Best in Show.'

'That's only because you've been giving that Judge Mr Bee extra eggs all summer. Whose potatoes came first? Tell me that! And what's more, I did it fair and square,' declared Tony as they walked away.

Once again, Nicholas was left alone.

In a different part of the field, Josh was doing his best not to suffer the same lonely fate as his superior officer.

He had been quite enjoying himself. It was a glorious day and he did like a traditional country fair. Visiting them in the summer was one of the highlights for him of living in the Cotswolds. The news that Dee was expected out on bail soon had put Amelia in buoyant spirits. Josh had found Amelia's exuberant happiness infectious. The drive down to St Bridget's had been fun; they had exchanged a teasing banter over inconsequential things. Yes, all in all, he thought the day was going to be good – then they ran into Benedict.

Josh did not like the exuberance with which Benedict and Amelia greeted each other. It was a bit like watching two ravens courting, Benedict in his tight black trousers, with rips and studs and Amelia in her trademark black corset and tutu. He hated that they looked good together, right down to the way his blond hair and her red hair were set off to perfection by the contrast of their black outfits. Josh in his clean-cut trainers, chinos and button-down shirt felt distinctly out of place.

Amelia enthused, 'Hey Benedict, I'm so pleased your granddad suggested us coming here. It's wicked. And otherwise, we'd have just been hanging around waiting for Granny to get out of jail.'

Amelia was hanging on to Benedict's arm and giving him the full benefit of her sparkling eyes and dazzling smile.

Benedict surveyed the bunting, the band and the coconut shy and shrugged. 'It's OK, I guess. Hey, Amelia, do you fancy grabbing a ciggy behind the veg tent?'

Josh, aware he'd not been included in the invitation, chimed up. 'I'm a bit old to be sneaking off behind the bike shed for a smoke. I left school a long time ago. Besides neither of us smoke – filthy habit.'

To his horror, he realised he didn't sound like the mature man-about-town he was aiming at, but rather like the nit-picking, middle-aged Nicholas Corman.

'Suit yourself, old man,' said Benedict, taking Amelia firmly by the hand and leading her off. To Josh's annoyance, Amelia didn't mind. Obviously, her last term's lectures on female equality had been wasted.

Josh glanced around the bustling field, taking in the people, the coconut shy and the toffee apple stand. He couldn't help thinking how much fun he and Amelia would have been having if only Benedict had not appeared. Reluctantly, he followed Benedict and Amelia as they wove a path through the milling crowd and behind the produce tent.

It was a secluded spot, protected on one side by the cream canvas of the produce tent and on the other by a thick green hedge. In between, on some straw bales, lounged a stunning couple. The young woman was long-limbed, slim, with golden hair that cascaded down her back. She looked as if she would be better placed in a lifestyle advert for Swedish yoghurt, rather than puffing on a fag behind the veg tent. The man matched her perfectly – they could be a pair of classical statues.

The girl observed them and then, ignoring Amelia and Josh, addressed Benedict. 'We'd just about given up on you.'

'Hi Juliet, Christian, I got collared by Smith-Jones.' Benedict scowled.

The young woman, Juliet, pointedly still did not acknowledge Amelia and Josh's existence, let alone ask for an introduction, instead, she replied sharply, 'You shouldn't let him bully you. I need to tell you a thing or two about that prat, Smith-Jones. Stuff that will give you major leverage. Of course, your problem is you look wicked so everyone assumes you are up to no good. You look like a villain, whereas in reality you are just a softy with a vinyl collection of Frank Sinatra hits. You want to take a leaf out of my book – if you look like an angel, you can get away with murder.'

Josh had been watching her and privately agreed she did look like a heavenly being. The cigarette in the corner of her mouth and her condescending manner did detract a bit from the image but still, she was gorgeous.

The equally beautiful young man, Christian, then spoke in a softer sympathetic tone, 'Was he doing the whole, "teacher takes an interest in the troubled boy with an absent father" act?'

Benedict sat down beside Juliet, took her cigarette and after a long drag, said, 'Nah, I could handle that.'

'Tell us,' said Juliet, taking back her cigarette.

'We'll talk when we're alone,' said Benedict. He gave Josh a filthy look and added with a sneer, 'He's a copper.'

Josh, who had been standing awkwardly next to Amelia, gave a weak smile. 'Hi, I'm Josh.'

Amelia, irritated at Benedict leaving her out, added, 'I'm Amelia – my grandmother and Benedict's grandfather knew each other years ago.'

Unsurprisingly Juliet gave her a dismissive nod but the young man stood up and shook her and then Josh by the hand.

'Great to meet you. I'm Christian and that's Juliet – along with Benedict, we're all distant cousins. So, Josh, you're in the police, that must be interesting.'

'It has its moments,' said Josh with a modest half-smile.

'And what about you, Amelia?'

'Second-year psychology student.'

'Wow! Love to hear about that – Juliet and I both graduated this summer.'

Juliet finished her cigarette. 'Oh, for goodness sake, you're not interviewing her for a job.'

Christian enquired, his beautiful blue eyes alight with interest, 'Presumably your gran is the OAP who found the bloke stabbed with our shears?'

'Your shears?' queried Josh, in a tone that implied his inner bobby was longing to get out. He leant forward, his face alert.

'Yeah! They were our shears, but how they got out of the house, let alone into the bloke is beyond me,' nodded Christian, shrugging his shoulders.

'I have a confession to make,' laughed Benedict.

They all stared at him. Josh automatically reached for his absent handcuffs.

'Oh, Benedict! You plonker! You didn't?' hissed Juliet.

'Didn't what?' Benedict looked confused.

'Kill that man,' stated Juliet.

Horrified he spluttered, 'No! But I did take the shears out of Christian's place as a lark.'

'Some lark. You idiot! You know our dads hate each other as it is and you've just given them something else to fight over,' sighed Juliet.

Christian gave her a commiserating look and squeezed her hand before saying, 'So if you took the shears, how did they end up being involved in a murder on Marine Drive?'

'That's what I was wondering,' said Josh, his exquisite almond eyes narrowing with curiosity.

Chapter 6

Naturally, there was only one way for the FitzMorris ladies to celebrate Dee's release: tea.

It didn't take Dee long to shower and change and then they headed out and found a tearoom situated in a bookshop. It had attractive books arranged enticingly around the tables and a large enough variety of herbal tea to impress even Dee. Not surprisingly she went for a pot of camomile flowers, while Zara and Amelia chose mint.

'Doesn't it smell wonderfully refreshing?' commented Zara as she carried the tray over to a free table.

'Heavenly,' agreed Amelia, as she paused to admire a Cavapoo puppy. Inevitably, Amelia exchanged with the pup's owner and got permission to tickle the fluffy mutt's tummy.

Dee and Zara left her to it and settled down at a nearby table.

'I can't wait for you to meet Sean,' smiled Zara, flicking back a stray saffron curl.

Dee regarded her daughter and dryly replied, 'I feel as if I've known him for years, with the number of times you've mentioned him in the last twenty minutes.'

'Well, he is very charismatic.'

Amelia sat down beside them. She rolled her eyes and said, 'Don't say Mum is still banging on about that Sean bloke?'

Amelia was embracing the rural vibe of the island and so was wearing a tawny colour corset and tutu. She had swapped her heavy black makeup for brown and had even found some mahogany boots. Zara was wearing tan ballet flats, a chino skirt and a cream blouse. Dee thought it was fortunate she was in navy or they would look as if they were all off on safari.

'You're a fine one to talk,' retorted Zara. 'Isn't Benedict a bit young for you? He's still at school.'

'Oh, Mum! That's such an oldies thing to say! Besides, he finished this summer and he's only a year younger – he retook his upper sixth – I'm a bit vague about why.'

With a slight sigh and a faraway look in her eye, Dee poured herself some more tea, and commented, 'He takes after his grandfather, he has the same tall athletic figure and those blue eyes …' Her voice trailed away as she smiled into her steaming teacup.

Zara and Amelia regarded her, Amelia with amusement, Zara with more caution.

'While your grandmother recovers from thinking about her old paramour, you can clarify for me what exactly is going on with you and Josh versus Benedict? After all, I presume it was you who dragged Josh up to the Isle of Blom and now he's following you around like a lost puppy, while you hang out with Benedict.'

Amelia gave her mother a withering look and calmly stated, 'You are obsessed with putting everything and everybody in boxes! Relationships can't be confined like that!'

There was an edge in Zara's voice when she replied, 'I'm sure you've got some clever psychological term to define my beliefs but I like things neat and tidy and poor Josh looks miserable.'

Dee had rallied enough to pick up on the rising tension. She glanced at Zara, bristling with annoyance and Amelia who looked as if she was getting ready to flounce off in a swirl of tawny tutu.

It must be this hot weather – the two of them aren't usually this touchy! she thought.

By way of distraction, she asked, 'So what did you find out about the case while I was stuck in a police cell?'

Amelia beamed. 'Well, it turns out Benedict took the shears from Tony's and Christian's home. Christian is Tony's son and I must say he's a lot nicer than Juliet – she's very snippy,' Amelia explained all this before taking a sip of her tea.

'Why?' asked Zara.

Amelia looked thoughtfully up at the ceiling. 'Perhaps being that beautiful has gone to her head.'

Zara shook her head. 'Not "Why is Juliet a pill?" but "Why

did Benedict take the sheep shears?"'

'To quote him: "For a laugh".'

'Bit immature wouldn't you say?' Zara raised one eyebrow and regarded her daughter with her head slightly tilted to one side.

Hastily Dee intervened, 'But how did it get from Benedict and into the deceased?'

'Can't help you there – Benedict shoved it in his backpack and didn't realise it was missing until a day or so later.'

'Where had he been?' enquired Zara.

'As far as I can gather, he'd been everywhere – on the bus, home, school, town – you name any spot on the island and he'd been there. Hey, Gran, while we're on the subject of Benedict, how come his granddad has so much money?'

'Daniel? I don't think he has – as far as I know, Daniel worked as an artist with a bit of teaching on the side – you don't make much money out of that. In fact, when we were walking to the Pringles' house together he mentioned that he thought lack of funds was one of the reasons his son was so driven to make money. Do you know Benedict's father more or less abandoned him, following one lucrative project after another?'

'Really?'

Dee nodded, regarding her camomile tea with a hint of melancholy around her eyes. 'Actually, it seems that lack of money has caused a lot of problems in his life. First, Elsie deserts him for the lure of big bucks in the States then his own son, feeling he'd been hard done by growing up in modest circumstances, turned his back on the Isle of Blom and Benedict in order to earn lots of money in the Far East, none of which he seems to have sent home to help raise his son.'

'Goodness, Mother,' commented Zara, stirring her tea. 'You did have a good old heart-to-heart – presumably in the thirty seconds Benedict and I were exchanging grunts.'

'Well, it was quite a long walk,' smiled Dee.

'Where's Benedict's mother?' enquired Zara.

Dee shrugged. 'She never came up in the conversation – presumably, she's not in the picture.'

Amelia looked impatiently from her grandmother to her mother. 'No, that can't be right,' she insisted, shaking her head in such a way that her long vibrant red curls quivered. 'You should hear Benedict talk about all the exotic holidays he's had with his grandfather. When we visited the tea tent at St Bridget's fair he talked about nothing else – much to Josh's annoyance. I thought I'd seen most of the world backpacking with you two but he's been everywhere and with luxury all the way. And when Benedict needed to redo a year at school, Daniel wanted him to go to one of those posh boarding schools and you know they cost a fortune. The only reason Benedict didn't go was because he refused.'

Zara's jade eyes regarded Dee. 'So, Mother, it seems that your beau is a man of mystery – perhaps he is behind all the illicit gambling on the island and that's where he gets his money from.'

'I think that's highly unlikely, dear. Let's get back to the point.'

'This is to do with the matter in hand. According to Sean, Patrick O'Connor had a major gambling problem, which was one of the reasons he was working on the island. He needed to get away from some nasty types he owed money to in Liverpool. I would say illegal gambling is a pretty good bet why Patrick O'Connor ended up dead.'

Dee sounded a note of caution. 'Isn't that a bit … well, a bit simplistic? I mean it's a bit of a jump from – here's a chap with some sheep shears in his chest – oh and by the way he had a bit of a gambling problem – to bingo he was killed because of his involvement with gambling. It's a bit like person A shops at M and S, person A has a heart attack, therefore shopping at said retailer caused the heart attack.'

Amelia leant forward her pretty face animated by excitement. 'Not quite. I think Mum is onto something. I was talking to Benedict and it seems Tony Pringle – apparently, he's the skinny one, father of Christian' – Zara and Dee were polite enough to nod while Amelia clarified Pringle parentage although they were both well aware of this fact – 'used to have quite an issue with an illegal gambling ring on the island and they were a vicious mob – real villains – and they placed bets on everything, from village fete jam competitions to Best in Show and the big agricultural events.'

Dee settled back in her chair, looked from her daughter to her granddaughter and with a contented smile said, 'In that case, all we need to do is infiltrate the gambling ring and we can find the killer, clear my name and have an enjoyable holiday.'

'I say cheers to that!' agreed Zara and the three of them clinked teacups.

'So, what's the next big event on the island where there could be gambling?' asked Dee.

'Quick! Hide!' hissed Zara, holding a nearby newspaper up to her face. Dee saw Amelia glance around, then saw shock register on her face before she grabbed a glossy magazine and buried herself in it. Totally bewildered, Dee looked about her. All she could see was a rather plump, late middle-aged woman, in flamboyant pink with matching high heels. The woman was talking, or rather verbally assaulting, the girl behind the counter.

'Of course, you can put this up!' she declared emphatically. She was brandishing a poster advertising the dance contest at the villa.

Meekly, the girl took it and the woman stomped off in triumph.

When she had safely departed, Zara and Amelia lowered their paper and magazine.

'Phew! That was close! Thank heavens she didn't see us,' said Zara, taking a recuperative sip of mint tea.

'She was too busy harassing that poor girl about advertising a dance contest to notice us,' commented Amelia.

'Who is she?' asked Dee.

'Ghastly woman. Name of Betty Hobbs, a friend of Nicholas's,' explained Zara with a shudder.

'To be exact, she is the mother of some police bigwig that Nicholas knows,' elucidated Amelia.

'The police bigwig must be the chap who has been called away to Liverpool leaving Hadrian Macintosh in charge,' mused Dee.

Amelia wasn't listening. She stood up and went over to the

counter to look at the poster. When she returned to the table, she beamed at her mother and Dee. 'I think we have the answer as to where the next contest will be. And where there is a competition, there is bound to be gambling. Mother, we need to find you a dance partner.'

'Nicholas can dance, can't he?' said Dee hopefully.

'I was thinking of someone a bit more ...'

'Dangerous?'

'No, *interesting*. I'll give Sean a call.'

A couple of hours later, it was Josh and Nicholas who were discussing the situation. Rather than chatting over a pot of tea, Josh had a half of Okell's and Nicholas a Fynoderee gin and tonic. Seated in a sleek wine bar by the station; they were both staring morosely at their drinks.

'I don't know what she sees in him,' sighed Nicholas.

Josh nodded in agreement.

Simultaneously they both spoke, totally oblivious to what the other was saying:

Josh: 'It must be the eyeliner.'

Nicholas: 'It must be the money.'

Josh: 'All that bad boy vibe.'

Nicholas: 'All that dangerous charm.'

Josh and Nicholas: 'The only solution is for us to dive right in and solve the murder.'

Chapter 7

Not far away the murderer was musing on events while preparing to go out. *I may have killed Patrick but he did have it coming to him. This evening should push things along.* They glanced at themselves in the mirror. *Looking good!* They smirked at their reflection. *I reckon the villa contest will bring in quite a bit of cash and then there's the big drug drop-off to come.* Contented with both their looks and their plans they headed out the door.

Totally ignorant of the motives and grooming habits of the Blom killer, Nicholas was still with Josh. The longer they sat in this wine bar, the more Nicholas liked it. It had a relaxed atmosphere; the spacious, light-wood and steel interior was both contemporary and restful. The gin and tonic he was sipping was exceptional – citrussy, woody and with just the right degree of sharpness.

'My gran loves a spot of gin,' commented Josh as he watched Nicholas savouring his drink.

'Is that your granny who cooks up the delicious Korean feasts? The traditional banquets you tend to go dreamy-eyed about when you are tucking into a vindaloo on the high street?' asked Nicholas.

'Nah, that's Granny Park. I'm talking about Granny Kim – she lives in Croydon.'

'Oh,' said Nicholas. He had a brief mental picture of an older oriental lady, as beautiful as Josh, sipping gin in Croydon when the door swung open.

'Great! That's all I need!' sighed Nicholas as with a swirl of bonhomie, Sean walked in. He was looking swish – or to Nicholas's mind 'flash' – in a jacket with a shirt whose top two buttons were undone, and rather a lot of bling on his watch and signet ring.

'Why does he go around as if he owns the place?' muttered Nicholas.

Josh smirked. 'From what I've heard he's so rich there's not much that he doesn't actually own.'

Nicholas scowled at Josh but his approbation was lost on him, as he was chortling at his own joke.

Sean's eyes alighted on Nicholas and he walked over to their table.

'You're that vague acquaintance of Zara's,' stated Sean with charm but little interest.

'Nicholas Corman,' said Nicholas, standing up and introducing himself with an overly firm handshake. He looked Sean in the eye with the steely regard he normally reserved for hardened villains and added, '*Inspector* Nicholas Corman.'

Sean was unruffled and just smiled. Nicholas's dislike of him went up a notch.

Much to Nicholas's surprise, Zara chose this moment to come in. She looked fresh and vibrant in a long-sleeved green wrap dress with a multi-layered pearl necklace and ballet flats.

'Ah! Sean, I do hope I haven't kept you waiting.' She gave him a winning smile and bestowed a light kiss on his cheek. Nicholas received a waft of delicate scent and a cursory nod.

With regal benevolence, she directed her attention to Josh. She noticed that the sea air had fanned his dark good looks to sleek perfection.

'Amelia will be here in a moment.'

Josh sat up straighter and smiled, his panther-like charisma back in evidence.

'She's meeting Benedict and his cousins.'

Josh slumped back to his gloomy contemplation of his Okell's; whatever feline spirit had inhabited him now oozed out, leaving him more like a moggy caught in a rainstorm.

Zara took a step closer to Sean. Nicholas watched in helpless horror. Huskily she enquired, 'Do you tango?'

Sean, his eyes firmly locked on Zara's, murmured, 'For you

Ms FitzMorris, I'd dance to the end of the world.'

He reached over and plucked a white carnation from the vase on the table. Clamping it firmly between his teeth, he pulled Zara to him, holding her so tightly that there wasn't so much as a shaft of sunlight between them. When he dipped her, their faces were only millimetres apart.

Nicholas rolled his eyes. *For goodness sake! Is this really necessary? A simple 'Yes' is all that's required.*

When Zara was released, she was a little breathless, her fair skin flushed and her abundant burnished hair attractively tousled.

'Well, that answers that question,' she purred.

Sean gave her a rueful apologetic smile. 'Not exactly, love. I'm afraid I've got two left feet.'

'Oh!' said Zara, and Nicholas found himself smiling.

Perhaps, this evening isn't going to be all bad.

Amelia and Benedict arrived, both dressed in black leather and studded chic. Following them were those rather beautiful blonde and willowy, distant cousins, Christian and Juliet. They had entered in time to witness the interchange.

Amelia, with her arm still linked through Benedict's, asked, 'You don't dance by any chance, do you?'

Only mildly surprised by the question he shook his head. 'No! But Juliet and Christian are the next best thing since Fred Astaire and Ginger Rogers.'

Amelia's raised eyebrow and intrigued, 'Really?' was cut off mid-flow.

'Will you stop yabbering and shift! You're blocking the bloody door!' growled a tattooed skinhead as he barged passed the group, deliberately knocking against Benedict. Amelia felt his body tighten and, keen to avoid a fight, she hastily nodded towards a far alcove.

'Let's grab that long table at the back. It's got a window and there're loads of seats if the oldies can manage to get onto those tall chairs. It's a great spot and best of all we won't be overheard by anyone.'

'It's that man again! No manners! He's a positive menace!'

announced Zara as she walked towards the alcove. She glowered at the man as she passed him. He appeared out of place leaning against the bar with his crewcut hair, his vest top and his grungy trousers against the backdrop of jewel-coloured gin bottles and tubs of sliced lemons. He didn't look around. 'I've come across him before. First, he nearly knocked Mother over on the pavement outside our B&B, then he almost killed us by driving his white van recklessly by Chough Drive.'

Sean took her elbow and guided her to a seat. His voice took on an extra soft burr, as comforting as an Irish whiskey on a stormy night. 'Don't let him get to you, love. People like that aren't worth bothering with. Now, what can I get everyone to drink?'

Josh and Nicholas exchanged a brief glance then, uninvited, they picked up their glasses and moved to the new table.

With such a lot of them, the introductions took a bit of time but they were not nearly as complicated as the seating arrangements. It was a long, rectangular table.

Amelia, with a rustle of black tutu, sat in the middle of one side and her mother, Zara, alighted gracefully, on the opposite side.

Josh, sleek, clean cut and agile, managed to get a prime position to Amelia's right, while Benedict, younger, taller and distinctly more Goth-culturally appropriate, sat on her left.

Sean was easily able to secure the chair next to Zara as he still had her elbow.

But Nicholas's innate good manners meant that somehow he was pushed out by the fair and long-limbed cousins, Juliet and Christian. Consequently, he found himself perched uncomfortably at the end on a stool, marooned from the central hub of conversation and from Zara.

When everyone was settled with a drink in hand, Benedict glanced at his blond and statuesque relatives and repeated his question. 'So Juliet, Christian, are you going to enter this dance competition at the villa? There are posters up all over the place.'

He gestured to one of the eye-catching adverts which was displayed on a nearby wall.

Before answering, Juliet, with her long golden hair framing her exquisite face, took a sip of her iced gin and tonic and grimaced. 'Is it just me or does this taste funny?' She looked around the table. There were general murmurs of, 'Mine's fine, delicious' so she carried on, 'Yeah! Christian and I could do with the money – the first prize is generous and what's more, it's cash.'

The more observant at the table noticed that at the mention of the 'generous cash prize' Sean looked conspicuously modest.

Odious man! thought Nicholas.

Benedict drew his eyebrows together, a gesture of concern that emphasised his black eyeliner and blue eyes. 'Isn't it a bit dodgy? Your parents might get wind of it. It was one thing you guys competing in all those dance competitions when you were at uni but this is right under your dads' noses. If you win it will be in the paper. Tony and John will go ballistic.'

Avoiding eye contact with his girlfriend, Christian muttered, 'That's what I think but—'

Juliet gave a wicked smile. 'But I like to live dangerously. Who knows I might even have a flutter on the side. If we make enough dosh, Christian and I will be off to travel the world.'

'Why do your fathers hate each other so much?' asked Amelia. She was gazing at Juliet with her head tilted to one side.

This led Zara to wonder at what age Amelia would learn that the psychiatrist's couch questions should be left for the psychologist's office, not for the social setting of a wine bar.

'You're one nosy little psychologist, aren't you?' sneered Juliet, leaning back and crossing her arms in front of her, all the while giving Amelia a cool look.

Christian, who despite his good looks, obviously shared Amelia's inability to read a room, replied, 'From what I've heard through village gossip it started more or less from birth. There were genetic abnormalities.' At the blank looks around the table, he expanded, 'John took after Tony's dad and Tony after John's and the dads didn't try to hide the fact they preferred the other's child.'

How interesting, thought Zara in a rapid mental turnabout.

Perhaps it's not such a bad thing that young people can lack tact. Although to my mind the real quirk of genetics isn't that Tony and John didn't take after their respective father, but that the unprepossessing John and Tony should have had such beautiful offspring – the statuesque Christian and stunning Juliet. They had obviously tapped into the genetic strain that gave Daniel and Benedict their good looks.

Amelia nodded sympathetically. 'That must have been very hard on them growing up.'

Josh, his dark eyes alert, spoke up. 'What did you mean by "having a flutter on the side"?'

'Shit! I forgot you're the law,' complained Juliet.

Zara smiled. 'Actually, we know all about the illegal gambling ring currently operating on the island. That's why I'm looking for a dance partner.'

Nicholas, who was perched at the end of the table nearest the bar, leaned forward in an attempt to be heard over the low murmur of newly-arrived customers. 'Why the interest in illegal gambling?'

'The victim, Patrick O'Connor, had a problem in that direction.'

Christian's fair skin flushed and he shifted uneasily on his high seat. 'You don't know for certain he was gambling on the island. He might have turned his life around – lots of people do, especially if they join Gamblers Anonymous.'

Without even looking up, Sean shook his head and carelessly said, 'Unlikely.'

Christian looked down at his drink. His lips pressed into a tight line.

Nicholas continued. 'That's a bit of a narrow field of enquiry. Personally, I'd like to know more about the victim.'

'Like what?' asked Benedict with all the interest of a Goth Sherlock Holmes.

'Like, why was he on Chough Drive? He didn't look like your average birdwatcher or walker. I could be wrong, but he was wearing a conspicuously new pair of trainers. Anyone else have any thoughts? What do we know about the victim?'

Zara lifted her head which sent a tremor through her saffron locks and narrowed her jade eyes. 'He smelt of roses. That's what Mother said and she should know as she got rather too close to the corpse.'

Everyone stared at her.

It was Christian who politely enquired, 'Are you sure? I mean could Dee have been mistaken? There's lots of gorse along Chough Drive – that smells of coconut. Or could it have been honeysuckle? There are sometimes honeysuckle bushes growing on the cliff face. You can't see them but you catch wafts of the scent when you are walking.'

Zara shook her head.

Nicholas tilted his face towards her and Zara thought, *Dee is right! With his dimpled chin, generous mouth and aquiline nose, he does look like Cary Grant.*

He said, 'I didn't notice, but then my sense of smell isn't that great. It wasn't the smell of blood, was it? After all, there was rather a lot of it.'

'No, it was definitely roses.' Zara was emphatic.

Nicholas leant back and murmured, 'Smelling of roses is hardly a motive for murder.'

Amelia laughed. 'Well in Betty Hobbs' case, it should be. She reeks of the stuff. Even though we were outside at that fish restaurant, it was overpowering.'

Conversationally, Benedict added, 'Do you think it's to cover up the smell of her smoking? There's a faint undercurrent of tobacco – you know, the raw, roll-your-own stuff.'

He was very striking to look at, his black garb emphasising the length of his limbs and the sunshine brilliance of his hair. Amelia allowed herself a pleasurable moment observing him before saying, 'I wonder what else she is covering up about who she is? Secret smoker? Secret what else?'

Nicholas felt a prickling of loyalty to a fellow copper's mother. 'I think we're getting off track. Sean, do you know if he was into drugs?'

Sean paused. He fiddled with his cufflinks, giving Nicholas

yet another flash of bling, before he said, 'I don't think so.'

Nicholas pressed on. 'You don't sound very sure.'

Sean shook his head. 'I'm pretty certain he didn't take drugs but—'

Zara filled the pause. 'If he was desperate for money he might have been involved in selling.'

Nicholas leant even closer. 'Or smuggling. I would imagine that a building firm would provide lots of opportunities to bring substances in. You must import a lot of building materials. Illegal drugs can be very lucrative.' He allowed his eyes to linger on Sean's wristwatch, twinkling in the light from the window.

Sean's black eyes narrowed. He leant back in his chair and took his time before languidly enquiring, in an accent that had grown as thick and menacing as an Irish fog, 'Why, Inspector, are you accusing me of something?'

Calmly Nicholas replied, 'Just trying to establish the facts.'

Sean smiled. 'I think you need to speak to someone who knew Patrick better than I did.'

'Like who?' asked Zara. 'Was he close to anyone at work?'

Again, Sean paused to consider. 'He wasn't a chummy sort of bloke. Good at his work, mind. Excellent at getting his team to work to schedule. That's why I kept him on after he had that trouble with loan sharks in Liverpool. I suppose the person he spoke to most was Jill. She works in the office – she's an ace at admin but—'

Sean's words were cut off by a high-pitched scream and the sound of shattering glass coming from the bar area. They all looked up. The scene could have rivalled a particularly dramatic night at the Queen Vic on Albert Square.

The skinhead Zara had deemed an 'unpleasant chap' was on his feet. There was a wild look in his red-rimmed eyes, his arms were flexed and he was brandishing a broken beer bottle. His opponent was a good foot taller than him and dressed in smart casual wear like the rest of the clientele. What marked him out were the rippling muscles straining under his crisply-ironed white shirt. He had the stance of an athletic bodybuilder.

Wine tasting and canopies were obviously more the norm here for the general customer than bar room brawls and they gawped in amazement rather than ran to safety.

All eyes were focused on the violent scene unfolding before them so no one observed the cool, assessing look in Juliet's magnificent blue eyes.

Zara noted that the girl behind the bar was on her mobile, presumably calling the police.

Nicholas, Sean and Josh were all on their feet and ready to help.

Somehow, Zara was not surprised that Sean's contribution was to rescue the very pretty young woman who had screamed. Putting his arm around her waist; he swept her to the relative safety of their table.

Meanwhile, at the bar, Nicholas and Josh had separated; one going to each side of the two men. The skinhead was visibly sweating, his eyes were bulging, and his lips were pulled back, animal-like so he was baring his teeth. His bodybuilder opponent was confronting him with the firm wide-legged stance of a professional fighter. Although he was outwardly calm, Nicholas could see the vein on his thick neck pulsing and his chunky hands were clenched into tight fists.

Nicholas and Josh were now in close proximity to the two protagonists. Nicholas deliberately took a slow breath and relaxed his own body. When he spoke, his voice was commanding but unhurried. 'Now gentleman, I would like to inform you that we are both officers in His Majesty's Police Force. I'm sure we can sort this out without violence.'

The skinhead took a menacing step into Nicholas's body space, his head jerking from side to side. 'Get out of my face, you, posh, southern git! And mind your own bloody business.'

Nicholas blinked but did not move or change his demeanour. Zara realised she was holding her breath; she felt her heart beating uncontrollably.

Josh, with feline grace, approached the strapping bodybuilder. 'Sir, would you mind taking a step back?'

The bodybuilder continued staring down his opponent. 'No one messes with my girl,' he boomed.

The girl, who was trembling in Sean's arms, let out a plaintive wail. She was little more than a wisp, so fragile that she looked as if she would break in two if her muscle-bound boyfriend so much as hugged her. Her huge blue eyes were surrounded by rivulets of thick black mascara from her copious tears. 'Oh, Rickie don't! Just leave it! He ain't worth it!'

A fight looked inevitable. Zara hoped that Nicholas was as proficient in fist-fighting as he was in model-making.

Fortunately, the tension was broken by the cacophony of police sirens. Blue lights flashed through the roadside windows. For the first time, both the skinhead and the bodybuilder looked unsure. Josh and Nicholas took a step back and watched as the uniformed officers swarmed in and took the offenders away. The girl broke free of Sean's arms and with another wail of, 'Oh, Rickie!' followed them out of the door.

The whole room seemed to let out a collective sigh of relief. There were one or two nervous titters of laughter then spontaneous applause.

Amelia was on her feet, taking Josh by the hand and leading him back to his seat. Her lips were slightly parted and her tone soft as she said, 'Come and sit down. You deserve a drink. I didn't realise you could be so ... so commanding.'

Josh looked modest – or as modest as a triumphant panther can look.

Benedict pouted and started to sulk.

When calm had been resumed, Sean said, 'Well, before that bit of excitement I had been about to say that I know there was some sort of a rumpus with Jill's boyfriend and Patrick. And that girl I had in my arms, was Jill and the hefty bloke, we've just seen, was her boyfriend, Rickie.'

Zara filled the ensuing silence, 'OK! So it looks like we have another possible motive for murder and another suspect. That beefy chap definitely looked as if he was capable of murder.'

Before more could be said, their table was approached by the slim redheaded man that Nicholas recognised as the teacher Betty Hobbs was so keen on – his name escaped him for the moment. Behind him was the spotty youth whom Nicholas recalled was named 'Reggie' – as in the Kray twins.

Betty's friend smiled genially at the group. He had an aura of assurance and exuded confidence, unlike Reggie, who skulked behind, looking at his feet. Once more, had anyone been regarding Juliet instead of the main action, they would have seen her eyes narrowing in a cold assessing look. She was as shrewd and calculating as she was beautiful.

Reggie's companion focused on Sean. 'Mr Murphy, that was quite a show, wasn't it! Let me introduce myself. I'm Joe Smith-Jones and I just wanted to thank you for all you're doing to sponsor the dance competition. The money raised will be such a help in our fight against drugs.'

'It's an honour and a pleasure to be able to do a little something to help,' said Sean with practised humility.

'Is there much of a problem here with drugs?' asked Zara.

Joe looked over at her with his pale eyes. 'Not generally but just at the moment there seems to be a spike. There are all sorts of things from cannabis to heroin getting onto the island.'

Zara was intrigued. 'How?' she asked.

'That's the issue; normally the route has been using drug mules and the ferry but the police and port authorities have upped their security and the drugs are still getting in.'

'So the dealers have found another route,' said Zara.

Joe nodded, pressed his thin lips together then added, 'Someone is getting very rich and it's at the cost of our young people's lives. Actually, I'm here to talk to our police chief, Hadrian Macintosh, about this issue and the event – ah, there he is, just arriving now.'

He indicated the door where Hadrian, resplendent with his red whiskers and dark complexion was courteously holding the door open for a lady.

With a sinking heart, Nicholas recognised that lady as his mother. She scanned the room and spotted them all at the table.

With a gracious smile at Hadrian, she waved her hand and called over to them, 'Coo-ee!'

Nicholas swallowed and rose to his feet. She swept in, a swirl of purple and high heels. Without waiting to say hello she announced, 'I'm so glad to have found you.'

'Er, Mother – why are you here and where's Dad?' stammered Nicholas. He was painfully aware of Sean's keen and amused interest. She glanced back at Hadrian, then at Joe Smith-Jones, Zara and Amelia.

'Gosh, It's like a ginger convention!' She smiled and tittered at her own joke, before swiftly proceeding. 'Actually, George is the reason I've come and I'm not here to see you, Nicholas, I came to speak to Zara. I met your mother and that gorgeous-looking man of hers, on the prom and she said you were at this bar.' She paused to give Zara a wistful look. 'They were looking ever so chummy. Anyway, my George has twisted his ankle. It's not serious – would you believe he did it racing down those steep stone steps onto the beach? He'd spotted a white ibis.'

'Oh, I am sorry,' murmured Zara.

'Quite! But then he tends to be inconsiderate. So now we can't enter the dance competition at the villa.' She gave Zara a smile worthy of any stage. 'So you will simply have to enter it with Nicholas.'

Chapter 8

Myrtle had a habit of unsettling people. When she had accosted Dee on the prom and demanded to know where Zara was, she had left Dee quite unnerved.

After Myrtle had scurried away, Dee attempted to get back to that delightful sense of time not existing. Before her romantic walk with Daniel had been interrupted by Myrtle in purple and her restless energy, Dee had been totally content on his arm. The sea was gently lapping, and the breeze was obligingly warm and held just the right amount of saltiness. Daniel was the perfect romantic companion; attentive, amusing and good-looking.

But since the interruption, cold reality consumed Dee. Something was bothering her –it wasn't really Myrtle, it was something Amelia had said. She had been carefully pushing it out of her mind but now …

'Dee, penny for them?'

'Sorry, Daniel, what was that? I was miles away.'

'A penny for your thoughts?'

She tucked her arm more firmly into his. She liked the feel of his warmth and strength close by her side. 'Oh, I'm not sure they're worth a penny.'

'A ha'penny then.'

She smiled, 'I was just thinking of something Amelia mentioned.'

'Yes?'

'About all the travelling you and Benedict have done.'

'Yes, how about you?' He looked inquisitively into her eyes. 'Have you travelled much? I seem to remember you dreamed of seeing the world.'

'I've been very fortunate,' said Dee while wondering how

they had jumped from his travels to hers in a single heartbeat.

'So you travelled a lot with your husband?'

'No, not really, you know what it's like when you're young, just married, with a baby – we hardly had enough money for food let alone exotic trips. But Zara, Amelia and I have backpacked over much of the globe – all on a shoestring, but that's where the adventure comes in, you know, sleeping on floors, eating street food?'

She was tempted to add some little phrase along the lines of, 'Amelia says that from what she has heard from Benedict, all your travels were champagne-fuelled and five-star accommodation. Kindly explain how on earth you were able to afford that as a jobbing artist and teacher?' but her courage failed her.

Daniel smiled, 'They must be fun – very authentic.'

'And you?' she prompted.

'Well, it's all been with Benedict. I was determined to get it right with him. As I said before, I feel partly responsible for the lad's father going off and deserting him in his quest for wealth. As you can imagine, an artist and part-time teacher doesn't earn a lot. I can't help thinking that if my son hadn't grown up with so little money it wouldn't have become his all-consuming passion.'

'But you are still an artist and teacher?'

He nodded. 'You've been to Italy of course – have you been to Florence and Rome?'

'Yes, I can imagine how much you loved all the galleries.'

'And Paris.' He stopped mid-stride and pulled Dee around to face him. 'We should go together, see the Louvre, the Musée D'Orsay. What do you say?'

In a desperate attempt to get the conversation back onto the issue of 'pounds, shillings and pence', Dee said, 'It sounds lovely – but expensive.'

He laughed. 'Don't worry, I've got lots of money tucked away.'

'How come?'

'Oh, you know, I've done this and that. Some things have been surprisingly lucrative.'

No, Dee didn't know and as they continued their walk, she couldn't help wondering exactly how much she really knew about this man and why he'd been on Marine Drive at the same time that Patrick O'Connor had been murdered.

That evening, the prom seemed to be the place for uncomfortable discoveries …

The party at the bar broke up, goodbyes were said and the group dispersed.

Zara assumed that Amelia would walk back with her to the B&B. However, Amelia didn't feel sleepy, so after a brief discussion, Zara went back alone and Amelia decided to visit the impressive sunken gardens behind the prom to listen to the gentle sound of the waves.

Protected by a wall from sea winds these gardens flourished; beautifully cared for and planted up by the skilled government gardeners, they were a riot of colour, scent and texture. Benches were placed so that passers-by could sit and admire the flowers. These benches were hidden from the prom by the wall, but in the still of the night, sounds carry. Sitting on her scenic bench, Amelia actually ended up hearing more than the sea.

As she sat quietly admiring the view, she heard familiar voices.

'What's eating you, Christian? You haven't said a word since you popped into that late-opening shop and got me this stuff.' Amelia recognised Juliet's voice.

'Are the crackers and water helping? Or are you still feeling sick?' asked Christian.

'Not really! I still feel queasy. I must have eaten something. But what's wrong?'

Christian paused. 'When I was in the shop, I saw something.'

'What?'

'The latest edition of the local paper.'

'So what?'

'There's a photo of the dead bloke – Patrick O'Connor – on the front page,' Christian stated in a flat voice.

'So?'

'I recognised him.'

Amelia mentally gasped at this but Juliet was unfazed.

'So, it's a small island. You might have seen him in a pub, on the beach, at Tesco – anywhere.'

'No, I've seen him several times.'

'Where?'

'At home, chatting with my dad.'

'Oh!' said Juliet.

'Exactly!' replied Christian sombrely.

'But hasn't your dad, Tony, straightened out his life? Isn't he still going to Gamblers Anonymous? I thought he was doing so much better.'

'So did I.' His voice cracked with emotion.

Amelia heard the sound of movement and assumed that Juliet was giving Christian a hug. 'You know that whatever happens, you've always got me.'

'I know,' said Christian in a husky voice. 'I'm scared though – the old man is capable of anything when he's gripped by his demons. What if he's involved in that man's death? After all, there's the shears—'

'Don't even think it!' interrupted Juliet.

Their voices fell silent and for a moment there was just the reassuring rhythm of the waves.

When Christian spoke again, he was calmer. 'I wouldn't have got through all those really grim years if it hadn't been for you. All that time he was so erratic, the lies, the uncertainty.'

'You know it's an illness.' Juliet sounded gentle; it was a side of her that Amelia wouldn't have expected.

'You've always been so stable.'

'And I always will be. But now we need to get going. I'm dead tired. Perhaps I've got a bug; I've been exhausted for the last few days. Besides which, I need to be fit tomorrow for us to rehearse. We'll need to practice if we're going to get our hands on that prize money.'

Christian agreed, 'And we need the money if we're going to

be able to go away together.'

'I think I'll die if we have to stay here. When we were teenagers all the sneaking around and hiding from our dads was exciting, but now I just want us to be able to live together like any other couple.' An audible sigh escaped her.

'Me too and we'll get there.' He didn't sound convinced.

'Not without money. I've been thinking, if we don't win, I know another way to get money. I can have a word with someone. They'll pay big money for me to keep quiet about what I know.'

There was a crafty edge to her voice as she spoke and there was no mistaking the horror in Christian's voice when he swiftly retorted, 'No! It's too dangerous. I don't want you going anywhere near that world. Drugs are worse than gambling.'

Juliet laughed. 'You worry too much. Come on, let's go.'

Their voices grew softer as they walked away. Amelia didn't feel any sleepier than when she'd parted from her mother; if anything, the revelation had sent adrenaline coursing through her veins, leaving her wide awake.

When Christian got home, he found that sleep eluded him. His mind was whirling with thoughts of the present and memories of the past.

He lay silently in his bedroom, staring up at the ceiling until the early hours of the morning, just thinking about Juliet.

She'd always been there from his earliest memories. Her eyes were so large that they dominated her slender face. They were as blue as the sea on a sunny day and held an intensity in her gaze that a man could easily drown in.

Sometimes he didn't know where he stopped and she began; their lives and bodies were so intertwined.

His first distinct memory of her had been playing together in the reception class at the village primary school. They were in the Wendy house with its diminutive chair and table and inviting wooden stove, complete with saucepans.

He had known she was his forbidden cousin – the blonde-haired girl he was not allowed to talk to. She was a figure of intrigue. He had caught glimpses of her through the yard gate; she'd had skinny arms and legs and was always moving fast, whether she was feeding the chickens or playing with the dogs. She'd sung frequently – her voice, high and melodic, floated over from her home to his.

He smiled to himself in the darkness. *I think I was her slave from the moment she looked me in the eye and thrust a child-sized broom into my hand and commanded, 'You sweep and I'll get the tea on.' And, open-mouthed, I'd obeyed.*

Our reception teacher, Miss Jones, let us share a desk, so at school, we sat side by side – more like twins than cousins – then at home we obediently pretended not to know each other.

Then things began to change. He chuckled. *Was it the second or third year of high school that I noticed that her sparrow legs and scraped knees had become graceful and willowy? She was still all arms and legs but now it was in a good way. It didn't take me long to notice other signs of her metamorphosis from a little girl to a woman. Suddenly she had budding breasts and a slight curve suggesting a hint of a waist above her jutting hips. She was sylph-like with her long golden hair waving over her slender shoulders. Somehow, her button nose became refined and her lips full. When I told her that from that point on, I no longer hoped for sightings of her feeding the hens in the yard, but for illicit glimpses of her through the small red gingham-curtained bedroom window, she had roared with laughter.*

He clenched his jaw as he recalled the next phase of his life. He rolled over onto his side and pulled the duvet close around him.

It was at about that time that her mother left and my mother died.

He swallowed, trying to think clearly about his life's narrative.

Those tragedies might have made us cling together but they didn't, not then. I suppose I was so overwhelmed by my loss and the kitchen sink overflowing with dirty plates. I had to work out how to clean – in a haphazard way – my school uniform. I hadn't been able to focus on my schoolwork. He let out a bitter laugh. *I couldn't even sit still, let alone tackle a maths problem.*

He'd heard teachers comment on how he was losing weight. In a frighteningly detached way he'd thought, *Well, that's hardly surprising – I'm living off white sliced and if I'm lucky a tin of baked beans.*

At that time, Juliet had been suffering too. *She started nervously pulling and twisting her hair. Sometimes I saw bald patches.*

But he'd been too wrapped up in his own grief to give her much thought. They became irritable with each other and in the end, they hardly spoke. They took to cold-shouldering one another on the school bus as effectively as their fathers did at the cattle market.

That was until that night – that stormy night.

In his mind, he could see the scene again, with painful clarity. There was his father, crumpled on the sofa. He was a pitiful shell of a man far removed from the hero he had been to the infant Christian. The concept of his father as his idol was shattered forever.

That day Tony had bet on the Grand National – apparently it was a sure thing. A sure thing that had not only lost the race but every penny the household had. *That week there wasn't even enough money for a tin of baked beans.*

Tony had glanced up at his fifteen-year-old son with red tear-filled eyes. They were eyes that pleaded for sympathy and at the memory he felt again that tangled mixture of emotions: love, pity, disillusionment but overriding all was disgust.

I couldn't stay there – I'd had to get out. I'd turned and run.

He'd bolted out of the house and into a magnificent storm. It was raging in full force – powerful and unforgiving. Black heavy clouds blocked out any light the night stars and the moon might have given. Strong, gusty winds rattled the corrugated iron roof on the sheds that surrounded the yard. The rain pounded down on the metal roofs and the muddy yard proved a relentless procession.

He'd stood, forlorn and alone in the centre of the yard with the ferocious thunder echoing around the valley. He'd heard the frightened whimper of one of the dogs.

His shirt was soaked through.

Vindictive lightning split the sky.

He felt devastatingly alone, isolated and abandoned – that was until he felt Juliet's arm encircle him.

She'd approached him from behind. He hadn't been aware of her presence until the moment she'd enveloped him in a comforting hug, clasping her hands around his waist.

The warmth of her body pressed against his back.

He was no longer alone.

They might have each other but there had never been anything restful. Even their first kiss had been far from sweet and innocent. They'd been in their last year at school at the time.

I was angry – filled with a fury that only Juliet can ever evoke in me. I was sweating, my chest was pounding. We were at some seedy party – I hadn't wanted to go but Juliet had insisted and we'd already had one row over it. I'd caved like I always do and there we were in some rundown flat with all the lowlifes from school. The neighbours had already complained about the music being too loud and the air was thick with tobacco and cannabis smoke. But just being there wasn't enough for Juliet. She had to march up to the seedy middle-aged guy in the corner who was openly selling ecstasy. I watched her go, my fury mounting with each step she took.

When I grabbed her by her wrist she winced from the pain of my grip. I knew I was hurting her and I didn't care. No one commented as I dragged her out. She yelled and protested but I didn't let go until we were by the old bus shelter – no one ever goes there. I more or less flung her against the wall and she glowered at me with big enraged eyes. Her chest heaving, she rubbed her wrist. 'What the hell do you think you're playing at?'

I'd glared back at her, too angry to speak.

She turned to go. I grabbed her by the shoulders.

'Leave me alone!' she'd spat, so close to me I'd felt her hot breath on my face.

'I can't!' I'd yelled back.

*'What I do is none of your bloody business!' she'd screamed
and I'd kissed her then, angrily, passionately. She'd kissed me
back, holding onto me so tightly her nails dug into my back.*

The thought of kissing Juliet gave him tingles along his spine.
He smiled in the darkness – going off to university together had
given them lots of opportunities to kiss away from prying eyes and
the risk of their fathers finding out. Juliet might find the danger of
parental fury added a frisson of excitement to their embraces, but
he just found it worrying.

Uni had provided them with privacy and it was there they
had got into ballroom dancing and discovered they had a flare for
it. They both loved everything about it, the music, the closeness,
even the discipline of endless rehearsals.

The first time they'd made love had been after the euphoria
of winning their first competition. The actual lovemaking had
been clumsy and brief – he chuckled; they'd got a lot better at it
since. Afterwards, they'd giggled, and for days to come every time
they'd caught each other's eyes, they'd blushed and giggled. He'd
made her breakfast in bed, a small gesture of love.

*And now? How do I talk to her about our future? Doing the
dance competition at the villa is nuts! Our dads are bound to find
out and there'll be all hell to pay, but I'll go along with it as I
always do whatever Juliet wants. She's so focused on getting some
cash – as if a little bit of dosh is enough to settle our future. I need
to tell her that I've been looking at courses at Blom College. If we
both get some financial qualifications, we can then get our careers
on track and it's such an opportunity to get sorted without going
into debt – living rent-free.* He sighed. *But Juliet won't like it.*

He rolled over and reached for his phone. Bright in the
darkness, it stated two o'clock.

'Shit!'

*But it's not just Juliet keeping me awake – there's Dad too!
Juliet is right; he's got his life so much more on track now but so
many coincidences? The shears? Him knowing the man? Surely
he isn't capable of murder?*

Christian swallowed down his knowledge that his father was

capable of anything including gambling away his child's lunch money.

Unlike Christian, Zara fell asleep more or less the moment she got into bed. Before sleep engulfed her, she'd just had time to run through the arrangements she'd made for the following morning.

Sean had initiated it. 'Look, if you want to find out about Patrick, why'don't you talk to Jill, casual like, ask a few questions? She won't open up to me; I'm her boss. She'll be in work at nine.'

'OK, just give me your office address,' Nicholas had said, taking out his phone to jot down the details.

'I didn't mean you. I was suggesting that Zara has a word with her,' returned Sean with satisfaction. 'This requires a woman's touch. Besides, she'd think it odd if you suddenly turned up.'

'Won't she think it equally odd if I appear at your work?' asked Zara.

'Not really. She saw you with me tonight and my office is at home.' He honoured Zara with what was obviously a well-practised, suggestive smile. The twinkle in his eye was working overtime as he added, 'By my bedroom.'

Zara gave Sean a quelling glance and said, 'Give me your address and I'll be there at nine.'

'Eight-fifty would be better – we don't want her seeing you arrive, far better if she thinks you spent the night.'

'Fine, eight-fifty,' agreed Zara, then she turned her attention to Nicholas who was trying not to pout. 'In that case, Nicholas, we can meet at eleven to rehearse our tango. After all, even if we're primarily at the dance contest to look into the illegal gambling ring, we want to put on a creditable show.'

Nicholas nodded, 'But let's make it twelve. I want to see if I can mend some fences with the local police force and perhaps get Hadrian Macintosh to tell me a bit about that skinhead. He must be a good suspect, judging by his behaviour tonight and the fact you saw him near the locality of the crime.'

Zara looked pleased. 'Excellent idea. Do you think that chap is on drugs? I mean there's definitely something off about his erratic behaviour, and did you notice his cold sore?'

'Could be,' agreed Nicholas.

Sean, feeling he'd been left out of the conversation for quite long enough, interjected, 'So Zara, my love, I'll see you bright and early tomorrow.'

The next morning, at eight-fifty on the dot, Zara drove up to Sean's home and office. It was just like him, obvious and flashy. Set on full display near the road, rather than discreetly down a drive, it was a large, square mock-Georgian, but with embellishments. Sean was waiting for her. Despite it being first thing, he looked sleek and well put together. Even at fifty yards, Zara just knew that he would have started the day with a brisk thirty-minute swim in his basement pool, followed by a workout in his gym. She suspected that he would follow a programme devised for him by his personal trainer, who would inevitably be female and attractive.

He came out and held her door open for her, and then led her into the palatial entrance hall which was complete with a grand sweeping staircase.

The décor's a bit overdone but that's easily changed, thought Zara.

'Coffee?' asked Sean.

'Mint tea, please.'

The kitchen was open plan with a lot of marble, and large windows overlooking an expanse of landscaping – there was little evidence of anyone ever having cooked in it. When he showed her his office, it had a similar air of magnificence again with no hint of any work going on in its vicinity, apart from the perusal of a variety of horse-racing papers, which were scattered on several surfaces.

A little later Sean was proudly looking out of one of the four grand windows, saying, 'It's a great view of the lake. It took no end of organising, permits, diggers ...'

Zara wasn't listening; she was observing Jill.

The woman's office opened out from Sean's and she was so absorbed in what she was doing that she was quite unaware that

Sean and Zara were close by.

The first thing that struck Zara was a pot plant – green and leafy – it adorned Jill's desk, alongside pens, pencils, post-it notes and files. It was the only thing that Zara had seen in the place that was real. Admittedly, the whole house was filled with magnificent white orchids, but they were all silk – excellent and attractive in their way, but they weren't real.

The second thing that struck Zara was Jill herself. She was small and painfully thin. She was still blonde and she maintained her dress code of short skirt and even smaller top embellished with layers of cheap jewellery and lashings of makeup. What had totally changed was her demeanour. *Admittedly, perhaps I didn't see her at her best last night. Being caught in the midst of a brawl with skinheads and bodybuilders getting overexcited would test any lady's poise, but today she is like a different person – there's no hint of scattiness.*

Zara watched, fascinated by the focused way Jill was checking files, jotting down notes and consulting her computer.

That girl is one bright cookie! And it's not just her glasses that make me think that.

'Ah! I can hear Jill – let's get started,' announced Sean, taking Zara's arm while holding his phone in the other hand.

He marched through the door. At the sound of their approach, gone was the calm Miss Moneypenny and back was the dizzy airhead of last night. She fumbled with a file and dropped papers all over the floor with many high-pitched shrieks of apology.

Does her boss make her nervous? He's intimidating, perhaps, but not that intimidating. Or did we just catch her doing something she shouldn't have been doing? Perhaps looking at a file she shouldn't? Transferring funds to some secret offshore account?

Sean glanced at the file on the floor. 'Leave those plans for the new public convenience in Ramsey and be a dear.' He held up his phone. 'I've got to take this call. Could you please show my friend, Zara, around the grounds?'

Was that a flicker of shrewd assessment? wondered Zara as Jill glanced from Zara to Sean.

But Sean was already talking loudly, to an imaginary work colleague, about building regulations in Turks and Caicos as he walked back into his study and shut the door.

'So, Sara, just give me a minute to sort this out and shut down my computer,' Jill gushed, while hurrying around to pick up the papers.

'Zara.'

'Eh?' She looked up in confusion, her large blue eyes framed by improbable lashes.

'I think you misheard my name. It's Zara, not Sara.'

'Oh! Silly me! My granny always said I'd forget my head if it wasn't screwed on!' She snickered and Zara smiled. 'You will have seen around inside so let's head outside. Now where have I put my keys?' She rummaged in her bag and pulled out a tissue, several lipsticks and a bottle of nail polish before retrieving some keys on a teddy bear key fob.

'We'll start by walking around the lake. Sean is very proud of it.'

Zara was surprised by how fast Jill walked. *Obviously she is an extremely fit will-of-the-wisp.*

'Sean had all this landscaped,' said Jill as she whisked Zara through a landscape that reminded Zara of an unimaginative urban municipal garden.

The sun was already hot and Zara decided to use the weather to steer the conversation.

'Is it always this sunny here?'

'No. Sean got in loads of diggers to do this, then he had to get the topsoil and the turf.'

'So, have you always lived on the island?'

'No. Sean stocked the lake with koi carp.'

Sensing that she was about to find out more about fish than she wished to, Zara resolved to be more direct, 'It was rather ... uh ... disturbing, that fight last night.'

'Umm! Would you like to feed the fish?'

'Nasty-looking chap, that skinhead. What did he do to provoke your boyfriend?'

'We keep the pellets down here.'

'Sorry?'

'For the fish,' said Jill happily. 'It's great fun! You just throw them into the water and all the fish come running.' She giggled. 'Or rather, swimming.'

She handed Zara a scoop and Zara obligingly threw the pellets in. Frenzied feeding ensued. Splashing and jumping, they vied for their breakfast more like a school of half-starved piranhas than prized pets fit for an emperor.

'Actually, I'd seen him before,' persisted Zara.

Jill was watching the fish with all the rapt enthusiasm of a child.

Relentlessly Zara continued, 'It was on the day we found Patrick's body.'

Jill swung round to face Zara. She looked at her sharply; her eyes narrowed and there was the same alert expression on her face that Zara had seen when Jill had thought she was unobserved. She remained silently looking at Zara, who had the distinct impression she was being weighed up.

'Sean said you and Patrick were close. It must have been a terrible shock for you. I'm sorry for your loss.'

'What's your connection to Patrick?' There was a keen edge in Jill's voice.

'None, we just happened to be on Chough Drive and we just happened to come across his body.'

'And now you *just happen* to be getting very friendly with Patrick's boss and you *just happen* to be asking me all sorts of questions about Patrick.' It wasn't a question, it was a statement; then abruptly she ended the conversation. 'We should be getting back to the house. I have work to do.'

With that, she strode off, even faster than before.

In Douglas, Nicholas was having even less luck trying to get information about the skinhead. The receptionist at the police station had flatly refused to give Nicholas Hadrian's private number – it was not surprising but still annoying. So here he was, sitting in the same police waiting room that he'd been in the day the body was found. The side table had been cleaned so the coffee cup rings were in different places. There were the same sounds of people talking, doors shutting, the occasional wail of a siren or someone who was drunk. The leaflets on victim support and household security remained pristine and untouched. This time, mercifully, he had the place to himself. It was a relief not to be trapped with some chatty person, but on the other hand, when Hadrian Macintosh finally made time to see him, there was no need for them to go into Hadrian's office. Nicholas stood up and held out his hand as Hadrian walked in through the door. The other man did not take the proffered hand, nor did he show any sign that he was going to sit down.

His dark eyes were cold and his voice brisk. 'What is it you want?'

So much for a friendly cuppa and chat, one police officer to another. This man really doesn't allow for second chances!

Nicholas was now in a quandary. If he sat down would that look disrespectful? On the other hand, if he remained standing, they would both be sort of hovering, which would hardly be conducive to a free and frank exchange of information. He decided to compromise – he stayed on his feet but adopted a relaxed, 'I've got all day' body stance.

'I'm afraid we got off on the wrong foot.'

'We didn't. Now, can you make this quick? I'm extremely busy.'

'Of course. Sorry to hold you up, I know how pressured one is during a murder investigation.'

Hadrian did not even flicker one of his beetling red eyebrows at this allusion to Nicholas being an inspector.

'So? Why are you here?'

'I was just curious about that skinhead who was in that skirmish at the bar last night. Are you still holding him? I understand he was seen near the scene of the crime.'

'Mr Corman, I suggest you keep your curiosity to yourself and focus on enjoying your holiday. Now, if that's all, I'll say goodbye.' His tone implied that mentally he had added, 'And good riddance'.

Chapter 9

The big day arrived. Myrtle had had Zara and Nicholas rehearsing relentlessly. For Nicholas, it had been an unnerving experience to hear his mother shouting, 'More passion, Nicholas! You need to exude *sex*!' The command in itself would have been enough to evoke disquiet in the policeman but his discomfort had been magnified a hundredfold as he'd had Zara FitzMorris in his arms at the time. For her part, Zara had remained cool and professional.

Nicholas was at the villa in what he hoped was good time. He found that the venue was already a hive of activity.

The chosen theme of the evening was Old Hollywood Musicals and people had certainly dressed for the occasion. There were gentlemen in black tie and even a few in top hats and tails. The ladies were an array of beautiful fireworks in bright, flowing dresses that sparkled with sequins. There was the obligatory red carpet for grand entrances, framed by an archway of red balloons. The organisers had arranged circular tables around the perimeter of the dance floor. Each table had a tasteful candle and flower arrangement – shades of the 1990s.

Waiters and waitresses were bustling around with trays. The band was tuning up. A few early-arrival guests were getting drinks at the bar. It was easy to tell the audience from competitors; it was a matter of hairspray, makeup and nerves. The female contestants had thickly painted faces, hair-dos rendered immovable by pins and spray, and were nervously running through steps. The male competitors were fidgeting and asking their partners repeatedly, 'Are you OK?' while perspiration dripped from their faces onto their exceptionally shiny shoes.

In the centre of this hive was the Queen Bee herself, Betty Hobbs. She seemed more agitated than any of the competitors.

Her dress was a ballgown of pink, glittering sequins and lace. Her hair was stiffly curled and her lipstick was almost fluorescent with gloss. She had a clipboard and was hurrying in high heels from one corner to the next, ticking things off. As she went, she muttered to herself, 'The raffle is all in order, the steam packet tickets look excellent displayed in that box, the bar – yes that looks good, the band's music list is correct, now where are Sean and Hadrian? At least I don't have to worry about dear Joe – he is always on time and in the right place.'

She almost bumped into Amelia, Benedict and Josh as they were looking for their table. Amelia was looking splendid in a black tutu that shone under her corset. Benedict wore a Gothic version of tails and Josh could have passed for James Bond in his black tie.

Betty Hobbs regarded them in surprise. Looking pointedly at Benedict, she said in a piercing voice, 'I didn't expect to see *you* here! We are, after all, raising money to fight *against* drug use on the island.'

Benedict flushed and stammered, and Amelia bristled, but it was Josh who suavely took control. 'You must be proud, Mrs Hobbs, that the island boasts such fine, upstanding young men who are prepared to do their bit for the good of society as a whole.'

Betty Hobbs 'Hmmphed' and bustled off to check the microphone.

Under his breath, Josh said, 'Don't let her get to you. Remember we are here to get evidence of the illegal gambling ring and hopefully clear Dee's reputation.'

Nicholas was vaguely aware of his friends' arrival but he was more concerned with finding Zara. He decided to wait for her just by the entrance. It was a warm evening and nerves were already making him perspire, so he hoped there would be a cooling sea breeze outside.

When he stepped outside, he found the longed-for cooling sea breeze but also saw that people were flocking in. He hadn't expected the event to be so popular. He tugged at his collar and looked at his watch, wondering where Zara was.

Christian and Juliet arrived. Christian had his cousin by the arm and was pulling her towards the door, saying, 'Come on, we're late as it is.'

Juliet was looking beautiful in a fairy princess dress in blue. Her long blonde hair was artfully piled on top of her head with attractive curls framing her heart-shaped face.

'Hang on a moment. I need to catch my breath. This dress is so tight I feel like I'm suffocating.'

Christian stopped, ran his hand through his hair and checked his watch. 'We really haven't got time for this.'

'Lay off!' snapped Juliet, then suddenly she swallowed and exclaimed, 'I think I'm going to be sick.'

'It's just nerves. You'll be fine once you get on the dance floor,' snapped back Christian.

The pair may not have noticed Nicholas but he was observant and could see that Juliet was very pale and decidedly green.

Her equanimity was not about to be helped by the arrival of her father, John. He was big, round and irate; evidently, he had come in a hurry as he was still in his work clothes. He bellowed, 'So that Hobbs woman was right! When I bumped into her at the corner shop, she said you were in this dance contest with *him*.'

The venom with which he glared at Christian made Nicholas think he was going to have to intervene, but worse was to come. Now Tony, a skinny whirlwind of fury, arrived. Addressing his son, he declared, 'I can't believe it! That Betty Hobbs woman was right. Here you are trussed up like some Christmas turkey and about to display yourself as a namby-pamby for all the world to see!' He glowered at Juliet and pointed an accusing finger at her. 'I blame you for this!'

Christian protectively stepped between his father and his girlfriend. Nicholas also took a step towards them but Daniel was there before him. Daniel's height and unexcitable demeanour made him an effective barrier between the crossed lovers and their irate fathers.

In a calm voice, brimming over with authority he said, 'Tony, John, this is not the time or the place for a fight. Everyone is staring.'

Tony and John looked around them and indeed there was quite a circle of curious onlookers; a few had even taken out their phones and were filming.

Daniel took each of them firmly by the arm. 'We can discuss this later. Juliet and Christian, you head inside and get ready. Your dads can sit by me – don't worry, I'll take care of everything.'

As they departed, Nicholas looked at his watch yet again. *Where is she? Perhaps she's changed her mind and isn't coming.*

'Oh, Nicholas! I'm so glad I've found you! I have something extremely important I need to tell you,' exclaimed Dee as she breathlessly grabbed his arm.

'Isn't she coming?'

'What? Who?'

'Zara.'

'No! It's nothing to do with her. I've just seen something that—'

'So where is she?'

'I don't know. Look, Nicholas, this really is important, I've just seen—'

'She should be here by now.'

'I need to tell you—'

'Oh, thank goodness, there she is.'

'Nicholas—'

He wasn't listening; he had seen Zara. He stood and stared; a still point in the hurrying crowd, he was unaware of anyone but her.

'It'll have to wait. Tell me later.'

'It can't wait,' wailed Dee as Nicholas strode off to offer Zara his arm.

Zara looked demure in an elegant green dress. The colour perfectly complemented her porcelain skin and fiery hair. The dress was cut to give her freedom of movement while at the same time showing off her figure.

'You look delightful,' he said in a low throaty voice.

'Thank you,' she replied giving his arm a friendly squeeze.

'But …' faltered Dee only to find Myrtle at her side.

'Doesn't she look a picture? I had a friend courier the dress over – I knew Zara would look splendid in it. There were a few small alterations to make, but I've always been a dab hand with a needle.' She had taken Dee's arm and was propelling her inside. 'We need to find our table quickly. They'll be starting in a moment. Where's that handsome escort of yours? Oh, there he is. That must be our table.'

Myrtle propelled Dee towards a table by the dance floor. Dee momentarily wondered why both Tony and John were there and why they were both sulking. The cousins were hunched in their chairs with their backs to each other.

With relief she spotted Josh, sitting by Amelia. 'Oh, Josh! I'm so pleased to see you. I must tell you, as I was walking here, I've just seen—'

Josh rose to his feet but Daniel intervened. Yet again, his height and imposing manner formed an effective human barrier, stopping Dee from telling Josh her urgent news.

'Dee, my darling, I'm so glad you've come in time.'

He clasped her hand and looked intently into her eyes. Dee was trying to look over his shoulder to Josh but as Daniel towered above her it was a forlorn hope.

'Yes! Yes! Lovely to see you too, Daniel, but I must speak to Josh.'

'I wanted to give you this.' He pressed a small jewellery box into her hands.

'What?' stammered Dee, staring at the neat velvet box. She had been feeling flustered before but now she just felt sick. He was gazing at her with big adoring eyes that reminded her of an old, loyal, golden Labrador.

'I designed it myself and had a talented friend make it for me. It's Manx gold.'

Dee was touched, confused and more than a little frustrated.

Why do men always believe that what they have to say is more important than anything a woman might have on their mind?

'That's – uh – great but I really need to have a word with—'

The orchestra let out a commanding chord. The lights dimmed

and a spotlight fell on Betty Hobbs.

Betty smiled graciously then with a slight tightening of her lips glanced at where Dee and Daniel were standing.

'If I can kindly ask *everyone* to take their seats so we can begin.'

She paused while there was the normal shuffling of feet, scraping of chairs and clearing of throats. When calm had settled, she continued.

'I would like to thank you all for coming here tonight to support this wonderful cause. As you know, if we are to successfully fight against the drug issue, it has to be approached from several angles. We are fortunate here that we can offer a truly 'joined up' approach. I would like to thank Hadrian Macintosh who is here tonight representing the police force.'

Hadrian, stood beside her, looking uncomfortable. He was unsure how he should respond – smiling seemed inappropriate but then glowering was not likely to encourage donations. His discomfort was short-lived as Betty was speaking again.

'As you know the police work hand in hand with our medical services. The emotional side is admirably represented by Joe Smith-Jones, whom many of you know as a talented teacher, but he also tirelessly and generously organises counsellors for those in need.'

Joe seemed far more assured than Hadrian had been. He managed to look serious yet approachable with the spotlight on him.

Nicholas glanced from him to the shadows and was not surprised to see Reggie there. The boy hadn't dressed up for the occasion. *Or perhaps he has – who am I to say? That could be his best hoody, ripped jeans and trainers that only come out for special occasions.* Nicholas screwed up his eyes to get a better look and what struck him was the youth's expression of admiration as he watched Joe's competent handling of his moment in the limelight. *That's interesting – Reggie hero-worships Joe.*

Betty was speaking again.

'Finally, I come to Sean Murphy, whose generous patronage

has made this grand event possible.'

Sean, unlike the others, positively glowed when the spotlight reached him. He gave the audience an inclusive smile and looked as if he would have said a few words but Betty Hobbs had moved on.

'We, ladies and gentlemen, will be the judges of tonight's event so without more delay I call on our first contestants.' She glanced down at a card in her hand. 'Juliet and Christian Pringle, who will be dancing a Viennese Waltz.'

The panel hurried to their table as the orchestra played the opening bars to a familiar Strauss waltz. Dee could feel the tension on her table, emanating from the two fathers.

John muttered, 'That good-for-nothing son of yours, dragging my Juliet into making a spectacle of herself.'

Tony half-rose to his feet, his fist clenched. 'Why you—'

Daniel pulled him back to his seat and hissed, 'Shhh!'

The music played, and on a beat, the blackened room was illuminated by a golden globe of a spotlight. In its centre, poised and elegant, were Juliet and Christian. They looked like a painting from Napoleon's time.

Before the pair began to glide and swirl around the dance floor, there was just time for Tony to sigh, 'My boy!' and wipe a tear from his eye, and for John to gulp, 'She's a princess.'

Light as a cloud they floated. When they spun by Dee's table, she could see both fathers' faces rapt with awe and joy.

The music intensified to its climax and the audience held its breath in anticipation of the grand finish, but instead of a triumphant final pirouette, Juliet suddenly pulled away from Christian. With both hands covering her mouth she ran from the room, leaving her Prince Charming staring after her, without so much as a glass slipper for company.

The band ground to a halt and there was a weak spattering of applause, but Betty Hobbs was a match for any complication.

On her feet, with her microphone in hand, she briskly announced, 'So let's give Christian and Juliet Pringle a big hand for that graceful opening to our evening. Watching them I could easily imagine I was in Vienna.'

The room echoed with applause. When it had died down, she continued, 'So, we now travel from Europe to the Argentine with Zara FitzMorris and Nicholas Corman.'

Betty Hobbs scurried back to her seat next to her fellow judges. She was never one to allow silence when she had perfectly good words to fill the void. As she took her seat next to Sean, she regarded him; he appeared to be mesmerised by Zara, in her well-fitting dress and currently in the spotlight. She was standing, unmoving and magnetic, with her eyes fixed hypnotically on Nicholas. Sexual tension crackled in the air. The audience was hushed into awed silence. The band struck up its first passionate notes.

'Sean!' Betty dug Sean painfully in the ribs and in a stage whisper said, 'Stop gawping at Zara like that! This is supposed to be a dance contest, not a competition to see who can squeeze themselves into the tightest dress.'

To the beat of the music, Zara took several hip-swivelling, sensual steps towards Nicholas. Inches away from him, she thrust her arms into the air before provocatively trailing her fingertips over her body.

'Oh! Is that allowed? I mean there are children present?' enquired Betty of her panel. There was no response – all three men were leaning slightly forward in their chairs.

Zara enticingly beckoned Nicholas towards her. He was standing with all the majesty of a matador: feet together, shoulders thrust back and head erect. Carefully they circled each other, never quite touching but very much in each other's orbits. As the music took an emphatic note they each took a dramatic step back only to lunge towards each other, front knee bent and other leg taut behind.

'Looks a bit like fencing, doesn't it?' whispered Betty. 'You know when they lunge forward with the foil? Or yoga? Good job Zara's dress has that big split in it or there would have been a few ripped seams.'

Nicholas took Zara powerfully by the hand. The first touch

was electric and a ripple of appreciation run through the crowd. He spun her in three tight concentric circles, she pulled away a fraction and effortlessly kicked her high-heeled foot into the air before bringing it to rest on Nicholas's shoulder. As Zara did the splits, Nicholas held her to him. There was a gasp from the audience followed by applause.

'Yoga! It definitely must be yoga she does, rather than fencing. They do a lot of hip-opening exercises in yoga,' Betty explained conversationally.

Within the powerful, narrative of the dance, Nicholas rejected Zara, despite her impressive demonstration of flexibility. He cast her to one side after an elaborate display of spins. The final twirl left her seated on the floor and Nicholas striding manfully away.

Passionate chords continued to echo around the hall as every observer was willing Zara and Nicholas back together. Zara gazed longingly at his departing back. When all seemed lost, she lifted herself to her feet and ran after him. She leapt into the air as if she meant to throw herself onto his back, but as she launched herself at him, he turned and caught her in his arms. He held her there in mid-air, suspended in time and an arm's length away from him. No one in the audience dared take a breath. Then, with incredible strength Nicholas slowly lowered Zara to him. Her hands clasped his face. The intensity of their gaze electrified the room. Their foreheads met but still, their lips were tantalisingly separate.

Another beat, another bar and both moved in for a consummating kiss, only to have the unmistakable sound of a gunshot reverberate through the building.

In surprise, the band stopped playing, someone screamed and several people leapt to their feet, fearing a gunman was about to burst into the hall.

Hadrian Macintosh seized the microphone and calmly insisted, 'Can everyone please take their seats and can we have the lights turned on?'

The lights flashed back on, people blinked in the unaccustomed brightness and, sheep-like, they resumed their seats.

Nicholas looked at Zara and had been about to say, 'Stay

here!' but she was too quick for him.

'Come on! The shot came from behind the stage.' She grabbed him by the arm and started to run up some steps to one side of the stage and behind the curtain. Instinctively Zara turned to the green room. They reached it at the same time as Hadrian Macintosh.

Nicholas would have liked to tell Zara to be careful but she was already throwing open the door. Nothing could have prepared them for what they found inside.

There was Dee, standing apologetically in the middle of the room. In her hand was a pistol. At her feet lay the crumpled, inert body of Tony Pringle. In his limp hands there was an open black and gold metal cash box and strewn like confetti over the floor were old-fashioned betting slips, banknotes and coins.

Chapter 10

The malefactor or, as they preferred to think of themselves, 'The greatest criminal mastermind in Blom, if not the whole world,' surveyed the chaos at the villa. External confusion soothed their inner demons. They paused and inhaled, observing the crying, frightened crowd, the fast-moving police officers and the calm and confident paramedics.

So, things haven't gone quite as I hoped. Shame, I was looking forward to all that money. Still, it will work out to my advantage. That nosy Dee FitzMorris sticking her oar in could be the best thing that comes out of the evening; everyone will be focused on her, leaving me to get on with making money.

They glanced over at the ambulance, where Tony was on a trolley.

I'll need to visit the hospital – boring, but still, it's all good cover. And best of all, no one will suspect me.

'It must be a little trying,' commented Myrtle.

She was standing next to Zara on the pavement outside the villa and Zara was still in her magnificent dress with the lights reflecting off the sequins. They were watching Dee being escorted off to the police station.

'I mean my mother had her little foibles, especially towards the end – I think a lot of mothers do – but this habit of hers of being arrested must be a bit inconvenient.'

'Not arrested, just taken in for questioning,' corrected Zara flatly.

Further along the road, there was an ambulance, its blue light flashing but the siren off. It had been called for Tony. As Zara watched, the paramedics were skilfully loading him into the back.

Close by were Amelia – petite and anxiously watching, Daniel – who, as ever, was exuding calm – and Benedict – lean and unsure, standing slightly to one side.

Christian was distraught. Even at this distance, Zara could see that his handsome face was pale and his startling blue eyes were streaming with tears. Juliet, who didn't look much better than her boyfriend, had her arm around him and was trying to comfort him. She now looked like a very wilted and bedraggled Disney Princess in her blue, twinkling ball gown. Her father, John, was watching. His round face sagged towards his equally rotund body. It was difficult to tell what he was thinking as he observed his daughter's distress at his cousin and foe being taken to hospital.

'Yes, dear, not arrested, just taken in for questioning! And looking on the bright side, at least the body she found this time wasn't actually dead – just unconscious – so perhaps she's getting better.' Myrtle's voice was encouraging. She glanced at Zara and said, 'Now, we'd better get inside. I know it's a warm evening but we don't want you getting a chill. After all, you were mid-exertions when you got – er – interrupted.' She began to lead Zara inside. 'The pair of you were magnificent – Nicholas always did a good matador.'

Inside there was a hubbub of hushed whispers. The police were taking note of people's contact details.

Zara sat down at an empty table and within moments, Joe Smith-Jones walked up. She was surprised both by the speed with which he arrived and by the solicitous tilt of his head beneath his strawberry blond hair.

With his pale, narrow fingers he proffered a white enamel cup and saucer. 'I thought you might appreciate this. Camomile is wonderful for calming the nerves.'

A single tear trickled down Zara's cheek. 'Sorry,' she said, brushing it away. 'Camomile is my mother's favourite – she drinks it by the gallon.'

He sat down next to her; his light, almost transparent blue eyes looked steadily at her. They were comforting and concerned. He leant towards her and when he spoke his voice was soft. 'You must be very worried about your mother.'

'Well, yes and no.'

'Umm.' Joe's course on counselling and empathic listening obviously hadn't covered this.

'You see, it's not the first time. In fact, she makes a bit of a habit of it.'

Joe was doing a valiant job of maintaining a calm, non-judgemental listening ear. 'She makes a habit of what exactly?'

'Oh, you know, the usual – finding dead bodies, getting carted off. If she's not being abducted by murderers, she's being taken in for questioning by the police.'

'I see,' was all Joe could think of to say. Zara suspected his training had instructed him to make some validating statement such as, 'That makes sense' or 'I quite understand'. Zara glanced at him. *Presumably, even with many counselling courses under his belt, he can't bring himself to pretend he can follow the situation.*

After a pause, he enquired. 'Did she say anything? I mean when you found her.'

'Only something about her needing to tell us something in private, which was odd.'

'Odd? In what way odd?' Joe leant forward and appeared thrilled to have something concrete to talk about.

'Well, there was only Nicholas and Hadrian Macintosh there with me. Tony was unconscious, so he doesn't count. I can't imagine what she could possibly have to say that couldn't be said in front of her daughter and two high-ranking policemen.'

'What indeed?' said Joe thoughtfully.

There was a halt in the conversation. The crowds were thinning as members of the audience were given permission to leave. The cleaning staff had also been told that they were allowed to begin taking away glasses and balloons.

'How do you know, er, what's his name? The victim,' enquired Joe.

'Tony Pringle. My mother knew him when they were teenagers. Well, actually she was more friendly with Daniel.'

Joe nodded. His pale skin looked even transparent under the

lights and Zara felt his long limbs looked, somehow, disconnected to his bony fingers. *Are his fingers really super-elongated or do I just need more camomile and an early night?*

'I see,' he said, back in empathetic mode. 'I've come across Daniel Pringle in my work. I taught Benedict. He is lucky to have Daniel as his grandfather.'

At the mention of youthful, troubled Benedict, his eyebrows rose and his lips pursed in concern, then as he moved on to Benedict's dependable grandfather, Daniel, his features relaxed into an 'all is well with the world' serenity.

Zara was beginning to find Joe fascinating – but not in a good way. *The man has one of those mobile, almost plastic faces that are overly expressive; a bit like a pale, zombie Mr Bean.*

Amelia walked with dragging steps and stooped shoulders to the table. Her thick black eye makeup had run a little and Zara suspected the odd tear had been shed.

Joe sprang to his feet. 'Do have my chair. Can I get you something to drink? Water? Tea?'

'Water would be lovely, thank you,' replied Amelia, sitting down.

Joe went in search of the kitchen.

Zara watched his departure and commented, 'I hate to have to admit it but I rather agree with Betty Hobbs. Much as it goes against the grain to find that she's right about anything, Joe Smith-Jones is exceptionally kind.'

Amelia screwed up her face as if someone had left a particularly pungent cheese on her side plate. 'I think it's creepy the way she's got such a crush on him. Benedict doesn't like him much, nor does Juliet. But that doesn't mean a lot as Juliet doesn't like a lot of people.'

Zara thought of the ambulance and asked, 'Any change in Tony's condition?'

'Not really, he's stable but still not conscious.'

'How is Christian doing?'

'He's extremely upset.'

'That's understandable.'

Amelia toyed with a ringlet by her ear and bit her lip. 'I think it's more that – I suspect he's worried about that stuff I overheard him tell Juliet on the prom.'

'You mean about him having seen the corpse, Patrick O'Connor, with his dad?'

Amelia nodded. She had filled her mother in about what she'd overheard and Zara had meant to go into sleuthing mode and follow up on this clue but then she had started rehearsals. Nicholas's mother, Myrtle had set a demanding pace but Zara couldn't delude herself that that was why she'd failed to ask any questions. For the last forty-eight hours her every thought had been taken up with her dashing dance partner. Even now, the intensity of his gaze as he danced with her sent a thrill through her body.

Perhaps her thoughts about him conjured him into being, as she looked up to find Nicholas standing beside her. At the same time, Joe walked up with Amelia's water.

'Any news?' asked Zara, shaken out of her stupor by the sight of Nicholas's elegant figure. *No doubt about it, that matador costume does great things for him! Shame there's not much call for a policeman in the Cotswolds to wear tight-fitting breaches and a snappy bolero jacket. He is so capable I'm sure he will have chatted to that acting police chief, Hadrian, and miraculously, secured Dee's release.*

He shook his head. Zara looked at him with hope in her jade-green eyes – a look intensified by her stage makeup – and he hated having to disappoint her.

'No, but to be fair, I would have taken Dee in under the circumstances. It doesn't help matters that Hadrian Macintosh seems to have taken against me.'

Joe handed Amelia her water. 'I could have a word with him. Hadrian and I get on quite well together, but I don't think it would be of much use.' He drew his eyebrows together and compressed his lips. 'It doesn't look too good for Tony Pringle. He must be behind the illegal gambling ring and it looks like he's responsible for Patrick O'Connor's murder. The links are evident – the betting connection and then the sheep shears. Still, it was a bit dim of him to use a murder weapon that could be traced back to him so easily.'

Zara bristled but wasn't sure why – perhaps some strange loyalty to her mother's teenage beau's distant cousin?

Amelia was having a similar reaction to Joe's accusations; while she didn't like Juliet, she did like Christian, and she wasn't about to remain silent while Joe accused the boy's dad of murder.

She drew in her breath, ready for a stinging retort but Nicholas was speaking. In measured tones and looking Joe firmly in the eyes, he said, 'Those are a lot of suggestions but none of them are known facts. Probably better to let the police do their job before you go around repeating them.'

Joe held Nicholas's gaze for just a second longer than suggested contrition, before saying, 'I'm so sorry, I didn't mean to offend.'

There was an uncomfortable silence, and then Nicholas looked around. 'Where's Sean?'

'No idea – I haven't seen him all evening,' muttered Zara. She was unimpressed by Sean's absence; it suggested a lack of gallantry. If there was a rating system for maidens in distress and in need of a knight in shining armour, having one's mother taken away by the police had to be high in the ranking.

Amelia shrugged and Joe said, 'He was on the panel table right up until the gunshot but then he vanished.'

The crowd had thinned to a trickle of people. Now there were just a couple of police personnel and some villa staff with brooms.

Nicholas regarded both Zara and Amelia, they both looked tired; even their matching red curls seemed slightly less vibrant.

'We may as well go back to our rooms and get some sleep. We won't be able to find out much more until Tony regains consciousness and can tell us exactly what happened.'

Amelia sighed, her heavy Goth look at odds with the concern in her voice. 'I wonder how they are getting on. Poor Christian was in quite a state.'

Christian disliked hospitals, the vast pale walls with all their sockets, the even bigger windows with their inadequate blinds, the stiff adjustable beds, and the smell of cleaning fluid and latex gloves. He hated it all but most of all he abhorred seeing his father lying there helpless. He had an oxygen mask on, a drip and a monitor. He was wearing one of those hospital gowns and there was no sign of the vibrant energy that was the essence of his father.

Christian was biting his lip so hard it hurt, but somehow it was an anchor amid the chaos. He felt a warm strong hand on his shoulder and heard Daniel's calm voice, sounding like a distant echo. 'I need to make some phone calls, let people know what's happening. I won't be long. Juliet is here and John is just getting you some tea.'

John? Getting him tea? The world really had gone upside down. He had only ever treated him with disdain before. Had that really been genuine concern he'd seen on John's face, as his dad and his long-time enemy, was carried away on a stretcher?

Juliet was next to him, her small hand clutching his, her chair pulled up close and their knees touching. Was she speaking in a whisper so the uniformed policeman stationed at the door couldn't hear or was it so as not to wake up his unconscious dad?

'It's lucky that he wasn't shot, although that blow to the back of his head must have been vicious to lay him out like this.' She squeezed his hand, her voice was breathy. 'Don't worry about what the doctor said about there being a risk of permanent brain damage – your dad's got a thick skull – he'll be fine.' Her voice became stern and now she spoke rapidly, 'You mustn't tell the police about your dad knowing the bloke who was murdered – it will make things complicated.' Christian glanced over at her, confused. Both her face and her face were hard and emphatic. 'We need to keep things simple. We must use what we know, the info, the dirt, to get cash. Then we can get off the island and start a life together.'

Juliet was talking, saying things that were wrong, even dangerous, but Christian didn't care about that now. He just wanted his dad to open his eyes.

Meanwhile, in a police cell in Douglas, Dee wasn't happy.

She had an ability to be happy almost anywhere and under

any circumstances, but now she was more than just worried, she was scared.

Even here, in this small room, with the furniture fixed to the floor, the thin mattress, the sound of footsteps echoing along passageways and the unfamiliar smells of stale food and tobacco, she would, under normal circumstances have been able to find peace. Normally, she could have lost herself in a daydream about Lavinia Loveday's latest book.

Would the dashing Count propose to blushing Belinda by the Birth of Venus, while the sounds of Florence drifted into the Uffizi Gallery?

But even a dream of Tuscany could not distract her from what she had seen.

If only I'd been able to tell Nicholas what I saw on the way to the villa. I should feel that a police station is the safest place in the world, but if I'm right about Hadrian Macintosh then I need to get out of here. Oh! I do hope that the nice policeman brings me some camomile tea soon.

Chapter 11

After a night's rest, Dee was in a more positive mood.

As she explained to her daughter over the phone, 'No, Zara, dear, really, I'm fine. Daniel and the advocate are here. They say the earliest I'll be out is late afternoon, so there is no point in you coming down and hanging around the police station. I really need to speak to Nicholas, perhaps you could call him and ask him to meet us at our B&B at five?'

Zara was puzzled as to why Dee was so keen to meet Nicholas but now wasn't the time for questions as Dee obviously needed privacy to say what she wanted to say, so she just nodded, 'OK, love you and see you later.'

Dee put the phone down. The police seemed to have confiscated her mobile so she was using their desk phone. She was out of the habit of using a heavy landline and she glanced at it with nostalgia.

That went well; I don't think Zara picked up how worried I am. It will be a relief to speak to Nicholas. With all his experience in the police force, he will know what to do.

Zara clicked her phone off. Amelia looked at her, expectantly. They were having breakfast or, in Amelia's case, a smoothie. Zara thought that her daughter's appearance suggested she was both tired and remarkably young. Not surprisingly, neither she nor Amelia had slept well. Evidently, Amelia hadn't felt like putting on her layers of heavy makeup this morning. Fresh-faced, her daughter was youthful and pretty, but Zara knew better than to comment on it.

'Was that Granny? How is she?'

'Yes, it was and I think she's OK. You know what she's like; she was obviously very worried but was desperately pretending to be fine so that I wouldn't be concerned.'

Amelia nodded. 'I'll just finish my smoothie and we can go down to the police station.'

Zara shook her head. 'She said not to. Daniel and the advocate are there and she won't get out until much later. She wants me to contact Nicholas – oh, speak of the devil! Here he is!'

Nicholas, looking newly shaved and well-ironed, smiled.

Josh, who was crumpled and stubbly, glanced warily at Amelia, as if unsure of his welcome. He noted her more natural appearance and an involuntary gaze of appreciation suffused his face, accompanied by a gentle blush.

Zara smiled at them. Her eyes shone as she said, 'Hello you two. Have a seat. Coffee? Breakfast?'

They both accepted a seat but declined coffee.

When they were settled Zara stated, 'I've just been talking to Dee.'

Nicholas took the lead. 'That's why we're here. How is she? Is there anything we can do?'

'Not until she's let out.'

'When's that likely to be?'

'Late afternoon. She's very keen to speak to you, Nicholas.'

He nodded. 'We need to go through what happened last night. I know I quashed that Joe Smith-Jones chap's accusations about Tony Pringle, but honestly it doesn't look too good for him.'

Zara sadly shook her head in agreement. 'All those old-fashioned betting slips and the cash box might have been rather theatrical but they're still pretty incriminating.'

Amelia added, 'Actually, it's worse than that.' She swallowed and looked around the table. 'I overheard Christian saying that he'd seen the dead man, Patrick O'Connor, with his dad at their home.'

'Has he told the police?' asked Nicholas sternly.

Amelia shrugged. 'I doubt it. Let's hear what Granny has to say then if Christian hasn't already come clean, I'll make a statement. Benedict won't like me dobbing in his relatives, but it can't be helped.'

Nicholas drew in his breath and was about to say something about how he'd accompany Amelia straight down to the police station, but he was cut off.

'So that's all settled.' Zara's tone was firm and brisk, then she directed one of her most brilliant smiles to the table at large. Her eyes sparkled and her enthusiasm was infectious. 'What are we all going to do until Dee's release?'

Josh, a little hesitantly and eyeing Amelia hopefully, said, 'I was reading in a guidebook about how you can cycle to St Cuthbert's along the old railway line. St Cuthbert's sounds brilliant – there's a castle, a beach and loads of places to have lunch. There's a chap in a kiosk who does the best fish on the island.'

'Excellent. Amelia loves cycling and castles. You'd better hurry though and hire some bikes; it's going to be another scorcher of a day, so you need to leave soon before it's too hot. And for goodness sake take lots of water and sunblock.'

Nicholas was looking at Zara with speculation. He enquired, 'What about you?'

Zara turned her full attention on him; he had the sensation of being a recently caught butterfly being pinned on a board by an avid Victorian lepidopterist.

'I don't cycle,' she lied, 'so why don't you and I find some secluded beach and have a picnic?'

She smiled. Her green eyes sparkled as she looked at him. The sun's rays coming through the window caught her hair, making its vibrant saffron colour flicker with flaming highlights. Her glowing complexion gave no hint of the trials of the previous night.

'Oh, er, rather. I say, is it rather hot in here?' stammered Nicholas, wondering why in Zara's company he so often sounded like a character from PG Wodehouse.

He was not sure of the exact steps it took but half an hour later, he and Zara were in his car and winding along the dramatic coastal road heading towards St Ia. On the left were towering grey rock cliffs and to the right, there was an electrifying drop down to the churning sea far below.

Zara's landlady had provided direction to what she described as, 'A right romantic cove with a grand woodland walk'. She had even supplied a picnic in a wicker basket and a rug.

Despite everything, Nicholas was in jocular spirits. He broke off humming the theme of the tango to say, 'You must be concerned about your mother but you're not to worry – we're getting to the bottom of things. Last night was useful in uncovering the gambling ring.' He paused to concentrate on overtaking a couple of bicyclists. 'Of course, it's unfortunate that Dee put herself in the thick of things. It doesn't look good. Still, you say the advocate is confident she'll be out today?'

Zara replied in a relaxed tone. 'That's what Dee said on the phone this morning.'

Nicholas's brow creased with concern as he said, 'When I speak to Dee, I'd like to ask her about the gun. It seems odd. And she must have seen someone or rather several people, judging by the number of betting slips and cash on the floor. I wonder who the punters were. Did you notice people coming and going from the audience?'

Zara shook her head. 'No, but then I was rather focused on you.'

She spoke casually, as if her words were merely light conversation. He glanced over at her; she was gazing out the window at the cliffs and sea. She looked very poised; she reminded him of Grace Kelly in *To Catch a Thief*. He would have liked to have brought up Sean's sudden disappearance but somehow he didn't want Sean to intrude on their time together.

Instead, he said, 'You looked beautiful last night.'

'Thank you. We dance well together.' She was demure.

Nicholas cleared his throat and opened the window. 'It's hot, the weather, I mean the weather is hot. We must be in for a storm soon.'

They passed through St Ia which was a quaint, scattered village on a hillside. They nearly missed the turning to the cove but Zara spotted it at the last moment. The turning led to a narrow lane, sheltered by tall trees. Eventually, there was a flash of vivid blue sea and they arrived at a pretty bay with trees and greenery behind and low rocks framing the ever-present sea.

Leaving the picnic in the car, they got out. Zara lost no time in heading towards the rolling waves. It was a pebbled rather than a sandy beach and the smooth stones clanked underfoot. She threw her head back and closed her eyes, just enjoying the feel of the sun and salty breeze on her skin, and Nicholas wondered what it would be like to kiss those upturned lips. The happy thought was quickly overshadowed by the memory of the last woman he had kissed: his ex-wife. He shivered and looked out to sea.

'This is heaven,' Zara murmured as gulls circled overhead. She glanced over at him. 'Are you OK?'

He swallowed, blinked at her and thought fast. *Probably better not to mention my ex on our first date.* He swallowed again. *Not that this is a date – far from it. It's* – he looked at her beautiful open face and eager expression – *it's more like a business meeting. A chance for two fellow sleuths to exchange thoughts in a congenial setting. With a picnic.*

'Fine, just thinking about the case. It's all so nebulous. Unless Tony regains consciousness and confesses, we need more concrete evidence of the illegal gambling and Patrick's demise. We must find some facts and irrefutable links if we're to clear Dee.'

They stood, side by side on the shingle beach and watched the sun-dazzled waves roll in with a gentle rhythmic whoosh. There was a reassurance in the vastness of the ocean and the regularity of the waves.

Eventually, Zara sighed. 'I could stay here all day but I can feel that I need to get out of the sun for a bit. This weather must break soon. How about a walk before we have our picnic?' said Zara, turning to go.

Nicholas followed and with a chuckle, added, 'My mother insisted we brought endless waterproofs as she was adamant it always rained on the Isle of Blom.'

'That's just what my mother said too,' laughed Zara. 'Come on! That must be the path, by the stream and heading into the trees.'

It was delightfully cool once they reached the forest.

'I love the dappled light,' said Zara as she held out her hand for Nicholas to help her over a broken branch that blocked the path. Once over the obstacle, he let go of her hand and she felt slightly disappointed. The path led steeply uphill, flanked by towering trees. Close to a cool, cascading river, there was the faint scent of damp moss and tiny gnats flitted over the surface. As they reached the summit, the trees opened up to reveal a panoramic vista of distant purple hills and an undulating blue ocean.

'Magnificent!' declared Nicholas, turning around 360 degrees and looking to the far distance.

'Definitely worth the climb,' agreed Zara who, despite the heat and the ascent, still looked cool and collected with her stylish sunglasses and neat slacks, 'but I'm getting hungry.'

Nicholas laughed and once again thoughts of his ex-wife crept into his mind. She always insisted she wasn't hungry while starving herself and agonising over every calorie. He found Zara's attitude refreshing.

The walk downhill was rapid and they were soon back at the car. They found a spot on a little rise with a view of the sea but shaded by trees. With a certain degree of amusement, Zara watched Nicholas's pedantic efforts to lay out the rug perpendicular to the beach and without even the hint of a wrinkle. He then placed the Tupperware, all with the same ordered precision that she could imagine him lining up his model trains.

He looked up, aware of Zara watching him. 'What?'

'Nothing.' Zara settled herself on the rug and began opening the Tupperware boxes. 'This looks amazing: sandwiches, boiled eggs, cake, fruit – it's very Enid Blyton.'

'*Five go on a picnic.*'

'Exactly! Amelia's father, Freddie, loved picnics.' She smiled but Nicholas could see her sadness. 'He would insist that we put on our mittens and waterproofs and go out, picnic in hand, even in the middle of winter. Amelia used to love it too.'

'You've never bought him up before,' said Nicholas quietly. He didn't mention that he'd overheard Zara talking to Freddie back in a café in Little Warthing. She'd spoken with anguish of her loss and referred to her subsequent hesitancy to enter into any romantic relationships.

She shrugged and firmly kept her eyes away from Nicholas, focusing on the sea. 'Well, a husband dying in a car crash doesn't exactly make for light conversation.'

'I'm sorry – it must have been hard for you.' His hand lightly rested on hers. She gazed at it for a moment, strong and still, covering hers on the red plaid rug then she pulled away hastily.

'It was worse for Amelia; she was so young. We wouldn't have gotten through it if it hadn't been for Dee. Let's talk about something else. Have a sandwich. I wonder if Amelia and Josh have found something to eat in St Cuthbert's?'

Josh and Amelia's first desire upon reaching St Cuthbert's had been to find a cold drink and some shade followed by some ice cream.

'It was further to cycle than I thought. In hindsight it probably would have been better if I hadn't kept on challenging you to race,' confessed Amelia as Josh handed her a dreamy Davidsons ice cream. It was already melting and dripping down her hand. She quickly licked it.

Josh laughed. 'You look as if you're a kid, about six years old, when you do that.'

Amelia grimaced. 'It's because I haven't got my gear on.' Furtively, she gazed around, checking no one was observing her. 'I hate just appearing ordinary. Being so small, people always think I'm a kid.'

And a kid is powerless whereas a Goth is kind of scary, thought Josh and he suddenly liked Amelia a whole lot more.

They ate their ice cream and watched the sea and the hurly-burly of the sandy beach. The huge expanse of sand was alive with brightly coloured beach towels, sun umbrellas and people. There were teens with footballs and toddlers with oversized sun hats and diminutive buckets and spades. The smell of burgers cooking and coconut suntan oil hung in the air. Seagulls swooped and dived, keen to steal any unguarded morsel of food. Their cries merged with the sound of the waves and the children's shrieks of joy as they played in the cold sea.

'I feel so sorry for Christian,' said Amelia.

Josh would have preferred it if she'd said something like, 'Gosh Josh, I was so impressed with how fast you went on your bike.' If she'd accompanied the statement with a flutter of eyelashes, so much the better.

As it was, he nodded and said, 'He will have already been through a lot growing up with a dad addicted to gambling.'

'Poor chap, he was so certain his dad was in recovery.'

Josh could feel that this romantic date or outing was slipping away from him. He tried to lighten Amelia's mood. 'We don't know for certain what happened. We'll have more facts when your gran is out and can tell us exactly what happened. And when Tony regains consciousness, he's sure to be able to give us lots of details.' A smile lit up his dark handsome face. 'Let's look on the bright side. Apart from your gran, there are lots of other suspicious characters.'

'Like who?' asked Amelia as she crunched on her cone.

Josh had to think on his feet. He'd been so busy contemplating Amelia that he hadn't really considered possible culprits.

'Well, that Betty Hobbs is odd, then there's Benedict's grandfather, Daniel.'

Amelia looked at him with large green eyes, 'Daniel? I don't see why he's suspicious, unless it's because he has more cash than your average artist.'

Encouraged by her interest, he leant forward, nodding. 'Exactly. And top of my suspect list is Sean. Bit odd the way he disappeared so suddenly.'

Amelia smiled. 'It was rather. Mum wasn't impressed.'

Josh pressed on. 'And let's not forget that skinhead your mum saw near the scene of the crime. He looked like a nasty piece of work when we saw him in that bar.'

It worked – Josh had succeeded in cheering Amelia up. She became animated, 'You're right and talking of the bar, what about that bodybuilder boyfriend – Sean said he'd had a bit of a barney with Patrick over the secretary – what's her name?'

'Jill,' supplied Josh. 'Now, if you've finished your ice cream, do you see the ruined castle at the end of the bay?'

Amelia nodded.

'I'll race you to it.'

Amelia carefully put her napkin in the bin by their chained-up bikes. 'OK. I just wish Granny was getting out earlier – I'm longing to ask her loads of questions.'

She gave Josh a mischievous smile that made his stomach spasm and then, with no warning, she set off, sprinting towards the castle and calling over her shoulder, 'Come on, you slowcoach!'

She just caught the sound of Josh's deep laugh over the noise of the waves, the gulls and the people.

Unbeknown to Amelia, Dee had already been released from police custody, a lot earlier than expected. Elated to be free she was soon thrown back into despondency by being unable to contact her family or Nicholas.

'I really need to tell them as soon as possible,' she muttered.

'Tell them what?' asked Daniel.

'Oh, nothing.'

Chapter 12

Daniel was shaking hands with the advocate and saying his thanks and goodbyes; Dee gathered they had been at school together. She was glad of his distraction as it gave her a brief reprieve from his attention. The desk sergeant returned her personal belongings: her phone, her lipstick and the small square jewellery box Daniel had given her the previous evening. She still hadn't opened it. For some reason she couldn't quite put her finger on, she was reluctant to see what was inside. Hastily she thrust it back into her handbag.

'That's that then,' said Daniel happily, as he resumed his laser-like focus on Dee. He was rather like a giddy schoolboy and appeared not to notice that Dee was preoccupied.

'Well, I am rather pleased that you can't get hold of Zara or Amelia, as it means I have you all to myself,' he confessed as he walked, arm in arm with her, along the prom to her B&B. The sun was hot and they had to dodge young children on bicycles with stabilisers, mothers pushing prams and all sizes of dogs and their owners, from tiny chihuahuas to sturdy bulldogs. The horse-drawn tram clip-clopped past and Dee thought how idyllic it should feel.

Daniel was chatting away. 'I'll drop you at your place so you can freshen up and then I'll carry you off on an adventure.' A look of concern flickered over his face. 'Unless you're tired. Do you need to have a little lie-down?'

Dee smiled and shook her head, 'No, I'm OK, or I will be after a bath and a change of clothes.'

'Excellent and here we are,' he declared as they reached the door of her B&B.

Dee bathed, relishing in the liberal amount of scented oils she'd splashed into the water. She applied a face mask as she always found it was a wonderful way to subdue troubles. As she luxuriated in her bath, she tried not to think of anything but the soothing notes of Bach playing in the background.

When she judged it time to once more embrace life, her first concern was the jewellery box gift from Daniel. She deliberated over whether she should transfer the box into her day bag or leave it in her room. She decided to take it with her; Daniel was bound to ask her if she liked whatever 'it' was and he'd be hurt if she admitted that not only had she not bothered to open it but she had abandoned it in her B&B.

Her next problem was what to wear. Daniel hadn't specified the nature of their adventure and obviously, the dress code would vary according to the activity. If it was rock-climbing, sturdy boots would be required, whereas if he had hired a helicopter and was whisking her away to Paris for a gourmet lunch of oysters and champagne overlooking the Eiffel Tower, something a little more formal was required. After pondering her options, she decided to go down the safe route: slacks, a blouse with a small silk scarf and sensible shoes.

She squirted herself with a light scent, applied her lipstick and went downstairs to find Daniel waiting for her.

His eyes melted as he looked at her and Dee could not deny the delightful flutter of butterflies he provoked in her. He handed her an enormous bouquet of flowers, fragrant and tasteful.

'Lilies – my favourite,' said Dee, taking a deep appreciative breath of the heady perfume.

'I remembered,' beamed Daniel.

Dee laughed. 'You're just like the hero in one of my Lavinia Loveday books; so romantic.'

He flushed and stammered, 'Let's leave the flowers here and head out.'

They drove over heather and sheep-dotted hills, with the odd mine chimney to break the view. The sea and the hills of Ireland were blue against the horizon.

'This heat will break soon and we'll have a heck of a storm,' he said conversationally and she wondered if an approaching storm was a metaphor for their relationship; unexpected heat followed by a downpour. Mentally she shook herself and diagnosed either too much camomile tea at the police station or too little.

As Dee admired the majestic countryside, it occurred to her that it was slightly strange that Daniel hadn't bombarded her with questions about what had taken place at the villa. *Could it be that he doesn't need to ask because he was in some way involved?* She glanced at his handsome profile and stated, 'You haven't asked me what happened at the villa.'

'I guessed you could do with a break from answering questions,' he said lazily.

Is he amazingly, almost unbelievably thoughtful or doesn't he care? She looked at the azure sea far away, beyond mauve valleys and an alternative unwelcome thought popped into her mind. *Perhaps he has other, more self-centred, potentially criminal reasons for not asking.*

When she didn't respond he added, 'So?'

She shrugged. 'It's really all a bit of a storm in a teacup.'

What's of far more significance is what I saw on my way to the villa, but I don't think it's wise to tell him.

He laughed. 'Only you, my dearest, could be found with a gun in your hand, an unconscious man at your feet, not to mention cash and betting slips galore and describe it as a storm in a teacup. Tell me what happened step by step; starting with why you left the table when Zara was mid-tango?'

'I saw Tony get up, which seemed odd, so I followed him. Of course, he could have been just visiting the gents', but somehow he seemed to be being furtive. The next thing I knew I was in a dark corridor – it was literally pitch black – and someone brushed past me, or rather banged into me, thrusting what turned out to be a gun into my hand.'

'Who was it? Did you get a look at them?' There was an edge to his voice and she noticed he was giving her a sideways glance.

'Not really.'

Why do I not want to let Daniel know that I think it was that unpleasant skinhead?

'And then?' he asked.

She didn't feel comfortable with his tone. *Perhaps I'm just extra sensitive with all the upset.*

'It all happened so fast, it's a bit of a blur. I must have pulled the trigger by mistake. There was a horrendous bang, and then a door flew open and I saw Tony on the floor. I stepped towards him, then everyone arrived and there was a lot of unnecessary shouting.'

She finished with a small hiccup of emotion and an involuntary shudder.

'There, there,' soothed Daniel, taking one hand off the steering wheel and giving her leg a consoling pat. 'You're quite safe now. Look around, isn't the view magnificent? Just imagine all the fun we can have – going for walks, having picnics, watching the sunset over the sea.'

It struck Dee that he was going to keep her very busy over the rest of her holiday.

'And when the winter comes, we can be like the swallows and fly south. We can sit February out on a tropical beach.'

'Sounds very, er, romantic. Very Lavinia Loveday,' was what Dee said while her mind raced. *February? My flight is booked for the end of next week! I'm not at all sure Cat would like it here. Of course, she'd love the mild climate but then there's all the rain to consider. Could I leave my garden? I've only just got the delphiniums to take. And there are Zara and Amelia to think of.*

She sneaked a shy look at Daniel. *On the other hand, he is extremely good-looking, it would make a wonderful change waking up to him bringing me coffee instead of Cat demanding breakfast. And Zara might well remarry, then she wouldn't want me under her feet. Amelia is bound to move away when she's no longer a student. Is it a bad sign that I'm being seduced by the notion of romantic cocktails in exotic locations with a dashing hero, when I haven't totally ruled him out as an illegal gambling chief slash drug smuggler slash murderer? Oh, dear! I'm getting a headache.*

She wound down her window.

When they arrived at Tove Bay, Dee took a deep breath and

just stared. 'This is even more spectacular than I remembered.'

They stood for quite a while simply enjoying the sounds of the sea and the look of the quaint fishermen's huts nestled against the rugged grey cliffs. Lobster pots were stacked neatly alongside fishing nets. The bay was sheltered by a curve of ever-diminishing hills that dipped into the sea that sparkled with the sun.

'Yes! I could live here!' declared Dee.

Daniel swept her up into his arms and kissed her.

She allowed herself to be carried away by his strength and passion. It was a long time since she had felt like this.

It was only when he released her, and with joy suffusing his face he declared, 'Let's go and celebrate. I've booked us a table at the café,' that Dee began to regret what she'd said.

Oh, dear! I really should have kept that thought in my head rather than saying it out loud. I need to clarify things. But when? Why do books on etiquette focus on the obvious, like 'Always write a thank-you note', rather than useful things like, 'How to tell your childhood sweetheart that you might have spoken a bit hastily? Is it better to raise it over the starter or wait until the pudding?'

Daniel, totally unaware of Dee's inner turmoil, was leading her up the hill to the café, all the while keeping up a happy monologue of his plans for Dee to change his home to suit herself. He was laying particular emphasis on the kitchen, so perhaps her dream of him bringing her a morning coffee was just that – a dream. It appeared from his comments that in his vision of a life together, she would find true happiness in making him endless meals.

The moment they walked into the delightful café, with its rustic chic décor, Dee was aware of the stares. A silence fell – one woman actually pointed. Dee felt a familiar prickle of unease. She had a sense of déjà vu from when she'd been embroiled in the clown murders and her village turned against her.

Even Daniel noticed the hostility mixed with curiosity; he broke off talking about how much she would love cooking culinary masterpieces with an Aga to say, 'Oh, dear! The newspaper must have got a picture of you.'

They were shown to their table with its stunning view of the coastline and Daniel took out his phone. After a few minutes of scrolling, he said, 'Oh!'

'Let me see!' said Dee reaching across the table.

'Probably better not to look.'

She snatched the phone. 'How bad can it be?' she said with a hollow laugh.

It was bad – extremely bad.

After a moment or two, Dee regained her power of speech. 'Do you think it was the flash that gave me that crazed look in the eyes?'

'Could be, but then it didn't help that you tripped going down the steps of the villa – from these photos, it does appear that it took three burly police officers to carry you off, rather than them just breaking your fall.'

'I think the headline is a little harsh: "*Crazed clown killer allowed to run amok on the island.*" And who is this Gladys Elms who claims she could tell I was evil from the moment she spotted me grabbing some man outside the villa before the show began? The man was Nicholas and I just wanted to tell him something – he certainly didn't have to tear himself from me in order to save his own life.'

Daniel's forehead was creased with concern. He spoke hopefully but there was a shade of doubt in his voice as he suggested, 'Why don't we forget about this and enjoy our lunch?'

Dee had lost her appetite but nodded.

Halfway through their soup, Daniel broke the silence by saying, 'You haven't told me if you like my gift.'

Dee swallowed, tried to smile sincerely and said, 'I wanted to wait to open it until we were together. I have it here.'

She fished it out of her bag. There it was – a neat black jewellery box. It looked small and innocent. She stared at it with a mixture of fear, dread and giddy anticipation.

Daniel's eyes were sparkling, his voice was rapturous. 'Perfect – it's only right that I should put it on for you.'

Dee swallowed and found she was unable to move. The seconds ticked by, the soup cooled and still, she was paralysed.

Eventually, Daniel muttered, 'Let me open it for you.'

He did and she stared at the beautiful piece of jewellery. She blinked in surprise.

'Do you like it? I designed it myself.' For the first time, Daniel sounded unsure of himself.

'It's a ...' Words failed her.

'It's a necklace,' helped Daniel. 'A pendant with a seagull on it. Here, let me put it around your neck.'

As he carefully stood behind her and fiddled with the clasp, Dee's mind ran riot. *Am I relieved or disappointed that it's not an engagement ring?*

Then, as he blushed and looked modest while she gushed about how kind he was and how beautifully he had designed it, a second thought struck her.

Where does he get all his money from – Manx gold? Commissioning a highly-skilled goldsmith smacks not only of high romance but of conspicuous wealth! Daniel is certainly a man of mystery and not in a good way. Oh my! When did I become so cynical? Why can't my life have a fairy-tale ending? Why does it have to be full of murders?

Fortunately for Dee's overworked mental capacity, Zara texted just then.

'Oh good!' she said. 'They are back at the B&B. Let's go.'

Chapter 13

As Dee and Daniel drove home, she touched her new and unfamiliar love token. *A pendant is more romantically ambiguous than a ring. But a seagull personally designed and commissioned by one's loved one? Now, that is quite a statement! Why do I feel uneasy? Manx gold? Commissioning a goldsmith? Where does Daniel get his money from?* Her stomach tightened. *Surely not from being an artist and part-time teacher? And is it just a coincidence that he is always where the drama is, be it murder or illegal gambling?*

Daniel hummed some unidentifiable song. *Jazz? Debussy? Something contemporary? Would his tuneless humming prove to be the death knell of a life of joy together? Would I always be frustrated by trying to work out whether it was Puccini or Kanye West he was attempting to replicate? Or would I get used to it, like people who live by a motorway often don't notice the constant buzz of traffic?*

Dee gave up trying to decipher the tune Daniel was failing to mimic and instead, she thought of all that had happened in the short time she'd been on the island.

There seems to be a lot of romance around – I wonder if it's something to do with the invigorating ions in the sea air? I've reconnected with Daniel after all these years, which is either the most wonderful and romantic thing that has ever happened to me or is highly dubious as I can hardly live happily ever after on what may be illicit earnings. Zara seems to be getting on very well with Nicholas when she isn't being distracted by the charming Sean. Amelia and Josh are definitely – definitely what? If Benedict hadn't appeared I think Amelia and Josh would probably be going out by now. But Benedict did appear.

She spent a few moments visualising her granddaughter with each prospective beau. She could see Benedict and Amelia forming a little Goth family, painting their children's toenails black and giving them skulls to play with. *Such a shame, as I rather like smock dresses and sailor suits. I always think the Princess of Wales dresses her children so beautifully.* She sighed. *But then I mustn't be judgemental. It would be convenient if I married Daniel, but I am rather torn. Benedict seems troubled and Josh is a fine upstanding young man. Who knows, if they were together, Amelia might ditch the Goth look for the traditional Korean hanbok – she'd love all the flowing silk and she is very good with chopsticks.*

Dee's musings only extended to her immediate family, while elsewhere on the island people were far more troubled in their thoughts.

Sean was having a cigar and his favourite Jameson whiskey while he perused the Sporting Times but he was too worried about what had already happened and what was about to happen to enjoy either.

At Police Headquarters, Hadrian Macintosh was sitting at his desk trying to write his report without using swear words.

The skinhead was sulking in an alley, wishing he'd chosen a different career and had become a solicitor like his mother had wanted.

Jill and her bodybuilder boyfriend were having a row. 'Why do I have to do everything?' hissed Jill, and her boyfriend scowled.

At the hospital, things were no better. Tony was still unconscious and as John sat by his cousin's bedside his mind went over on all the arguments they'd had. His hatred for his cousin had fuelled his life; they were inextricably intertwined. What did he think of him? No, that was the wrong question – what feeling did he evoke? Was it hatred? Loathing? Or was it possibly stability, like the hills nestling protectively around his home?

They had shared a lifetime together. When his father had died – carried off by the same vicious influenza that had had John prostrate in bed – Tony had been there. When John had staggered down the stairs and out into the cruel blizzard that had wrapped around the valley, he hadn't found the hungry stock and distressed milkers he'd expected. Instead, all the beasts were content, even the sheepdogs and yard cats. And there was Tony just finishing off the morning chores. Neither of them had said anything, they had just exchanged a silent nod as he'd passed by.

Mind you, he'd done the same when Tony's wife had died at such a tragically young age.

John wasn't sure if his kindness to Tony in his hour of need hadn't bound the cords of their relationship more tightly for John than when Tony had been generous to him. Did doing an act of kindness for a neighbour acknowledge a certain responsibility towards them? An obligation of care, even?

He reached for Tony's hand and clasped it, a tear trickled down John's rounded cheek and in a raspy voice he said, 'Don't you dare go and die on me, you old bastard! I want to beat you in the Fur and Feather competition.'

In the waiting room, Christian was ashen, too shocked to process his thoughts. Juliet, on the other hand, had a mind full of plots and plans.

I need to do it now, however dangerous it is! Now more than ever we have to get a load of cash and get off this island. I won't tell Christian; he'll only try and stop me.

In fact, the only person who was happy and serene was Betty Hobbs. In a cloud of rose scent, she was beaming at Joe while Reggie stood awkwardly to one side. 'Look what I've knitted for you!' She held up a bright garment. 'I knew you'd love it! I can see it's quite taken your breath away!'

Joe ran a bony hand through his strawberry blond hair and stammered, 'It's very striking.'

'That's the contrasting stitching – I always think scarlet looks good on yellow. It will be the perfect sweater for you to wear at school when the weather gets cooler.'

'Is that why you put *Best Teacher* on the front?'

Betty nodded enthusiastically. 'And all the mathematical symbols. After all, you are a maths teacher. I especially like the way the division sign came out.'

Reggie's usually blank stare morphed into a smirk.

Dee was relieved when they arrived back at the B&B. She found Amelia, Zara, Josh and Nicholas all waiting for her while they had afternoon tea.

Joyfully, she threw open her arms and greeted them, but her family and friends did not mirror her excitement at being reunited. They were decidedly downcast.

'I'm afraid you've been mentioned in the press,' explained Nicholas.

Dee gave a weak smile. 'Oh, I saw that! But it's only the local news. I can put up with a few pointing fingers. After all, it's only for a few days and then we'll be back home and no one there will have even heard of sheep shears.'

Zara sadly pushed a couple of national tabloids towards her mother. 'I'm afraid it's a bit more serious than that!'

Under the banner '*Killer Granny?*' there was a photo of Dee in the charity mud run in aid of nature conservation.

'Oh! It's not a very flattering picture, is it? I was exhausted – climbing up that rope obstacle while covered in wet mud was testing, to say the least. I can see how I look a touch ... wild!'

'This one doesn't help,' said Amelia pointing at a rival paper's front page.

Dee tried to sound nonchalant. 'Honestly, where do they pick up these headlines? "*Is This The Most Evil Granny in Britain?*"'

'Well, you have to admit Granny, you do look pretty evil in that picture,' said Amelia, strain and worry etched all over her young face.

'I was meant to – I was playing the villain in last year's

village pantomime. I did a frightfully good job and had the audience booing and hissing like mad. Everyone said that I was very convincing,' replied Dee defensively.

Josh sighed. 'Slightly too convincing. There are calls for the police to take you back into custody and I think the phrase they're using is *for the protection of the Blom people.*'

'Oh!' said Dee deflated.

Amelia tried to inject a bit of hope into the conversation. 'Perhaps Tony will come out of his coma and clear things up.'

'I'll go and ring the hospital,' said Daniel taking out his phone and rising to go and make the call outside.

When he was safely out of earshot, Dee said, 'Good, I'm glad he's gone. There's something I need to tell you and I don't know how much Daniel is involved. On the night of the dance contest, I saw—'

Nicholas wasn't listening to Dee; he was wrapped up in his own train of thought. Without having heard a word she said, he rudely cut across her, saying, 'I could try speaking to Hadrian Macintosh again.'

Dee had had more than enough of men in general and Nicholas, in particular, brushing her off. She was thoroughly nettled. 'Nicholas, will you please shut up and listen to me!'

A shocked Nicholas finally gave Dee his full attention.

Patiently, as if addressing a slightly annoying child, Dee explained, 'I've been wanting to tell you about Hadrian. On the night of the competition, I saw him with that unpleasant man with the broken nose and the shaved head – you know Zara, the man who bumped into me outside the B&B.'

Zara nodded enthusiastically. 'And I saw him near where Patrick was killed and then he got involved in that punch-up at the bar.'

Nicholas was confused, 'So? Hadrian was probably reprimanding him.'

'No!' declared Dee emphatically. 'It wasn't that sort of a meeting. They were hiding down an alleyway – I would have missed them if I hadn't had to pause to adjust my heels. They were head-to-head, whispering. It was a cosy tête-à-tête, not an official police reprimand and I should know, the number of times I've been hauled off by the police.'

'I knew it!' exploded Zara. 'Mr Macintosh is crooked! A bent copper in league with a murderer! That skinhead is a scoundrel if ever I saw one. No wonder he was so keen to pin the blame on Mother!'

'Keep your voice down!' whispered Nicholas, his brow creased. 'This is going to take careful handling.'

'There's more,' said Dee in suitably hushed tones.

'Yes?' asked Zara and Nicholas simultaneously as they both leaned across the scones towards her.

'It's about that skinhead – I can't be sure but I think it was him who pushed the gun into my hand.'

Zara leaned back in her chair and gave Nicholas an *I told you so!* glance.

Nicholas pressed his lips tight and pulled his brows together. Gently he shook his head as he softly said, 'I have to admit, Hadrian Macintosh's meeting with this man is suspicious.' He glanced at Josh. 'We must find out his name and who he is. Dee seeing them together explains why Hadrian shut me down when I asked him questions about the chap – I thought it was just because I had rubbed Hadrian up the wrong way.'

Josh nodded, his slim dark eyes assessing his superior officer. His voice was quiet and steady when he commented, 'The question is, if we can't go to the local police, how do we find out about him?'

Nicholas gazed up at the ceiling for inspiration. 'And how does them being in some sort of relationship link into Patrick O'Connor being found stabbed with some sheep shears on Chough Drive?'

Zara drummed her pristinely-polished nails on the table. 'We need to find the answers as soon as possible! My mother can't go around being hauled in and out of prison and being pointed at by every passing stranger!'

Dee made a frail attempt at a smile. Amelia thrust out her hand to clasp her granny's hand and held it tightly.

Nicholas spoke again. 'Our best bet for swiftly clearing Dee of all hint of wrongdoing is if Tony comes round and is able to explain things. If he can provide a clear testimony that links Patrick O'Connor to the illegal gambling ring, that would put Dee out of the picture. She has only just arrived on the island and she could hardly have been running a complex criminal organisation capable of staging illegal gambling events here from the safety of her Cotswold cottage. So—'

Nicholas was interrupted by Daniel rushing in with his phone still in his hand. Dee rather liked the way excitement animated his chiselled features. Even though he was simply hurrying into the room, his face reminded her of a Greek god.

I do wish I didn't have my doubts over where he's getting his money from. If only he wasn't so evasive when I ask him questions. Manx born and bred; he could so easily be involved in all sorts of things. And he was 'on the scene' so to speak when I found the body.

Daniel, unaware of his love's thoughts, happily declared, 'Tony has regained consciousness!'

Chapter 14

As they drove the short distance to the hospital, there was the ominous sound of thunder.

'A storm's coming!' stated Daniel, sounding rather more Blom and at one with nature than was his norm.

The sun was still shining and the sky was largely blue but there was that edge in the atmosphere that set Dee's nerves on edge. She wasn't sure if it was the electricity in the air or her hope that Tony was going to clear everything up and she could relax without fear of wrongful imprisonment.

There was another rumble of distant thunder, which brought to mind her large Persian feline friend. She said, 'Cat hates it when a storm is coming – she prowls around the house and growls rather than purrs.'

'The crops and the gardens could do with the rain,' continued Daniel, still at one with the weather and oblivious to Cat's suffering.

'I hope she's alright. She doesn't like it when I leave her in the cattery.'

Dee liked to pretend that Cat missed her, but in her heart, she knew it was more that Cat felt outraged that her appointed slave dared to desert her duties.

They pulled into the car park as the sky suddenly darkened. Zara and Nicholas had followed in a separate car. Fortunately, there was another parking space nearby for them.

'It's just as well Josh and Amelia stayed behind, as I doubt they'd have let us all into Tony's room,' commented Daniel as he locked his car with a clunk.

There was a swift drop in temperature and the first fat drops of rain heralded the approaching storm. Daniel, gently holding

Dee by the elbow, called to Zara and Nicholas, 'Follow me!'

He speedily shepherded them into the spacious hospital lobby. With the whoosh of the electric door, they were thrust into a brightly-lit lobby filled with a mass of people, some in PJs but most shivering in their summer clothes. There was the smell of coffee and the clink of china from a café to one side and close by was a crowded shop with magazines, gifts and *Get Well Soon* cards.

In a prominent position was a desk with *WELCOME* emblazoned on the front. Behind it in a haze of rose perfume and pink floral was Betty Hobbs. 'Welcome!' she bellowed across the hall.

As her high-pitched call echoed around the glass and metal surroundings, people turned and stared. Inevitably some people recognised Dee and the pointing fingers began.

'Come on, Mother,' said Zara, protectively putting an arm around her. Much to Zara's chagrin, she realised that they needed to approach Betty in her role as official "welcomer" to ask which ward or room Tony had been put in.

Next to the desk, pale-skinned and slim, was Joe. He was clutching a bunch of pink flowers that clashed with the red in his hair. Betty was looking at him with the unmasked admiration of a pet pooch.

Dee regarded the tableau. *Personally, I can't see the appeal. He is rather too thin and spindly for my liking. Still, he is obviously very kind – just look at those flowers, they must be for Tony. And the way he looks after Reggie is admirable. Even so, I can't help thinking that Betty's teenage crush on his dad colours her view of Joe.*

Reggie, as ever, stood – or rather slouched – by Joe's side.

Dee regarded him with compassion. *Some water steeped overnight with parsley would do wonders for all those spots of his; the only problem is how to tell him. He gives the impression that he would be more comfortable having a bare-knuckle fight than chatting about herbal remedies with a granny.*

Joe smiled as they approached. 'Betty has just been telling me the good news about Tony being out of his coma.'

Reggie regarded Zara and Dee with no hint of recognition but then, as Dee noted, there was rarely any sign in Reggie's face that he had registered anything.

To Daniel, Betty said, 'You must be relieved your cousin has taken a turn for the better. Of course, it's rather embarrassing if it turns out he's a criminal. I understand he has something to do with those infamous sheep shears and that he has a bit of a troubled past.'

She didn't notice Daniel's annoyance as she immediately turned to Nicholas and in one of her stage whispers asked, 'Do you think it's wise letting *her* anywhere near Tony? She might try and silence him before he can *spill the beans*. I'm sure my Ron wouldn't like it.'

All this was accompanied by vigorous head nodding in Dee's direction. Dee attempted to look demure, a bit like the Queen Mother visiting the blitz-devastated East End.

I will simply rise above Betty Hobbs and her opinions. In a little while Tony will clear all this nasty business up and my good name will be restored.

She let Betty's voice wash over her; a bit like the scent of roses with its undercurrent of roll-your-own.

'Well, I suppose if she's with you, Nicholas, it will be all right. Sort of like being in police custody – just keep a close eye on her.'

In her normal voice, she addressed Joe. 'Be a love and show them the way. You can tell Nicholas all about that lovely sweater I've just given you. Nicholas loves my knitting. I'll keep Reggie with me.'

She gave Reggie a rather patronising smile. 'You'll like that, won't you?'

Reggie looked nonplussed and she returned to Nicholas and her standard stage whisper. 'So good for him – a bit like doing community service but without the orange vest.'

'They don't wear orange vests any more,' stated Nicholas.

Betty took no notice; she was already working on Reggie. In a brisk, enthusiastic tone she said, 'Now young man, the trick is to give the visitors a big welcoming smile as they come through the door. I like to think of it as capturing their little fragile hearts in a net of warmth and love. So, let's see your smile. Umm – well, I suppose for a first attempt it's quite good, but do you think we could try something a little less ... menacing?'

Joe said, 'Shall we?' Clutching his flowers, he led the small party away.

The visitors were already out of the lobby when Reggie turned to Betty and so they all missed a rather touching exchange between the two of them.

Betty was arranging her biros and pink Post-it notes when she became aware of Reggie's watery eyes upon her. She glanced over at him and managed not to wince at his spots.

He blinked at her, his mouth slightly slack.

'Yes?' she asked.

He blinked again and she thought that Joe really was a total saint to spend so much time in this youth's company.

A young couple – pink with blushing pride – approached the desk to ask where they should go for their first baby scan. Betty smiled benevolently at them and showed them on the desk plan the easiest route. As they left, she looked up again and was taken aback to see that Reggie was still staring at her, slack-jawed.

'Yes?' she queried again with a hint of exasperation in her voice.

He blinked, swallowed, then flushed and said, 'I wish you were my gran.'

Betty drew in her breath with horror. Evidently, the idea of this unprepossessing child as a relative did not fill her with unmitigated joy, but then her features softened and she smiled at Reggie.

He smiled back at her, a warm smile that reached into his eyes and he blushed an even deeper red.

Joe guided Zara, Dee, Nicholas and Daniel along miles of corridors. 'It's wonderful news. I was so worried about Tony, and Christian, of course.'

'Are they close friends of yours?' asked Nicholas.

He was walking by Joe's side while the others walked behind.

'Not really. I missed teaching Christian by a few years but with Tony being hurt at an event I was helping to organise, I do feel slightly responsible.'

Dee, overheard this comment and had to stop herself from saying, 'Why? Was it you who coshed him over the head?'

At the end of an anonymous corridor was the door to a private room. A neat policeman stood outside.

Joe declared, 'Here we are. They have given him a private room for security and as luck would have it, that police officer stationed outside is a good friend of mine. We've both served on several Rotary committees. I'm sure he'll let us all in if I have a word.'

The officer did indeed let them in. They crowded into the room to find Tony, John and Christian. Tony was pale, with a lot of monitors attached, but he was awake. Rain was pounding against the large plate glass window that made up the far wall.

Christian looked to be in a worse state than his father. He seemed to have lost a lot of weight in a couple of days and was positively gaunt. Dee couldn't help noticing that John definitely hadn't shed any pounds due to stress – if anything he'd gained. *Comfort eating?*

'Come on, lad,' said John gently, putting a hand on the young man's shoulder. 'Let's give these people a bit more room and get you some fresh air. Although with this storm we won't actually go outside.' He ushered Christian out of the room.

Daniel took the vacated space by Tony's side. Dee wasn't sure if Daniel automatically assumed the role of group commander out of natural leadership or by right of being related to Tony.

'Hello, how are you feeling?' Daniel asked.

Tony gave a weak smile through cracked lips, 'I've felt better,' he whispered hoarsely.

'Are you up to telling us what happened?' asked Daniel, squeezing his hand.

Tony nodded, shut his eyes for a moment as if gathering

strength, and then began. When he spoke his voice was so weak that it was difficult to hear what he was saying above the rattle of the wind on the window.

'It was when Zara was doing her bit on the dance floor that I got an urgent call of nature. I went to find the bog. It must have been all the excitement – who'd have thought Juliet and Christian could—'

'Yes! Yes! But what happened when you got up?' Daniel was keen to clear Dee's name and had no time for fond fatherly reminiscences.

'Well, I wanted to check something out.'

'What?' urged Daniel.

Tony glanced nervously past Daniel at Police Chief Nicholas, and his voice faltered. 'I'd seen one or two blokes from Gamblers Anonymous coming and going. I wanted to make sure they weren't getting into any bother. I'm a mentor.'

Daniel raised his eyebrows. 'What, at Gamblers Anonymous? I didn't know that.'

Tony closed his eyes again and lay back against his pillow. 'Well, we take confidentiality very seriously and don't tend to go around talking about our business. Do me a favour, give me some squash, will you?'

Daniel took the plastic beaker by the bed-stand and held it to Tony's lips.

He took a sip and continued. 'Anyway, with all those passageways, I got a bit lost.' He swallowed. 'I opened the wrong door and—'

A clap of thunder reverberated around the room. Tony shut his eyes again.

'And?' prompted Daniel.

'The moment I opened the door I knew I'd stumbled on something I shouldn't have. There was a blur of people jostling and scrambling to escape, and then the lights went out.'

'You must have seen something before the lights went out.' Daniel's normally calm demeanour was cracking.

'Don't press the man while he's so poorly,' whispered Joe.

Dee diagnosed that the part of Joe's nature that Betty so admired, his empathic side, was coming out. His pale eyes were full of concern as he looked at Tony, so frail in his stark hospital bed.

But Tony carried on with his story. 'All I saw were some betting slips and I think I picked up a cashbox. I was just wondering what to do. I didn't want to go to the police as it wouldn't help any of the people fighting their addiction, but I couldn't just leave it.'

'So?' Daniel was leaning forward in his plastic chair.

Tony squeezed his eyes shut. 'I felt a blow to the back of my head and the next thing I knew that John Pringle was by my bedside rabbiting on about his cockerel beating mine in the Fur and Feather. Ridiculous.'

At the mention of John Pringle and cockerels, his voice shook with anger rather than fragility.

Zara and Dee swapped glances.

'This doesn't help us clear your name,' sighed Zara, deflated. Her eyebrows pulled together and her lips were tight.

Tony opened his eyes and slowly looked around the room, from Daniel and Dee to Jo, Zara and Nicholas. He licked his cracked lips and swallowed before whispering, 'Oh, there's one more thing, I probably ought to tell you – I've been keeping it to myself to maintain privacy. Daft really but I guess keeping things quiet, like – confidential – becomes a habit.'

'Yes?' urged Daniel, leaning forward.

'The thing is, I knew Patrick O'Connor.'

The room took a collective breath and exchanged surprised glances. It reminded Dee of when she was part of the Greek chorus in a rather ambitious production of a classical tragedy by the local Am Dram society.

'How?' asked Daniel.

'Actually, I have a confession to make.'

'About Patrick?' asked Zara, pushing Daniel out of his prime bedside spot.

Tony nodded.

With a flick of her hair and the snap of her tote bag, Zara

had her phone out. She held it close to Tony's mouth and pressed record.

'Go ahead, Tony Pringle, of The Isle of Blom.'

'I was his sponsor at Gamblers Anonymous. He was doing really well. He was totally focused on his training.'

Confused, Zara blurted out, 'Training?'

'He was going to do the Parish Walk – and you know that's quite a test of stamina. Touching all those parish churches.'

Zara was even more confused. Putting down her phone, she demanded clarification. 'What?'

In an offhand manner, Joe explained, 'It's an annual island race. As a test of endurance and speed, the participants walk all over the island, from one church to the next.'

'So that was why he was walking along Marine Drive,' said Daniel.

Tony nodded again.

'Hang on!' interjected Zara. 'So you're not confessing to murdering Patrick O'Connor?'

If it was possible, Tony went a shade paler and looked around the room with wide, frightened eyes.

'What? No! Of course not!'

'But what about the sheep shears? How did they get from your front room to Patrick's chest?' Zara's voice rose to a nearly hysterical pitch.

'Search me?' shrugged Tony before, exhausted, he collapsed back into his pillow.

Lightening flashed, illuminating the room and Zara's stricken face. Dee counted, 'One', before thunder shook the hospital's foundations.

Chapter 15

'You'd better get some rest,' said Daniel firmly. He gave his companions a significant look, then glanced at Tony and added, 'We'll leave you in peace.'

Tony lay still. His eyes were closed and only the regular beep of a monitor reassured them that he was still alive.

Dee, Daniel, Nicholas, Zara and Joe filed out, quietly murmuring their goodbyes and good wishes to an unresponsive Tony.

Once outside and in the corridor, Joe commented, 'It's good that Tony is recovering. Now I really must go and either rescue Betty from Reggie or save Reggie from Betty, I'm not sure which.' He smiled but no one else felt like grinning just then. With a nod of his head, he turned and walked briskly down the corridor, humming happily.

Daniel patted Dee's arm. 'I'll just find Christian and have a word with him, then I'll run you back to your B&B.'

Dee, Zara and Nicholas silently watched as he strode away.

Nicholas regarded Zara with her drooped shoulders and Dee who looked as if she was trying not to cry.

'Shall we go to the coffee shop we saw in the lobby? We can talk through the implications of what Tony told us?' he asked.

'Not the coffee shop – I don't feel strong enough to face Betty's exuberance right now,' implored Zara.

'I noticed a waiting room just a bit along this corridor; let's go in there,' suggested Dee.

But when they pushed open the door marked *Waiting Room*, they found it was occupied not only with a couple of green pot plants but with an agitated Juliet.

Her normally luxuriant long blonde locks fell limply around her face. She was pale and looked as if she'd been crying. At the sound of their arrival, she glanced up. Wide-eyed and startled, she leapt to her feet, then – registering who it was – she glowered.

Undeterred by the girl's hostility Dee stepped towards her with her arms outstretched. 'Juliet, you poor child, are you alright?'

'Fine! I'm fine!' muttered Juliet as she pushed past them and out into the corridor. Above the sound of the rain, her footsteps resonated, echoing away down the passageway.

'Oh dear!' mused Dee. 'This must all be very stressful.'

Zara sat down on one of the foam armchairs and crossed her legs. 'I didn't have her pegged as the emotional type. Less sensitive, more hard-nosed and ruthless.'

Dee glanced at her daughter. 'That's rather harsh!'

Zara shrugged while Dee and Nicholas both sat down.

With a sigh, Nicholas commented, 'I'm afraid that Tony regaining consciousness wasn't as helpful as I'd hoped. We're not that much further on.'

Dee sat forward in her chair and in a tone ringing with forced brightness said, 'I'm so glad that Tony isn't involved. Christian has already been through such a lot and Daniel would have been so upset if Tony had actually confessed to the murder.'

Zara slumped back and spoke languidly. 'So what we now know is that Patrick O'Connor was no longer actively involved in gambling. He had swapped his obsession with gambling for a far healthier passion of long-distance walking.'

Dee commented, 'I can't help feeling sorry for the chap. He was turning his life around and then someone sticks some sheep shears into him and it's all over.'

Nicholas cleared his throat and said, 'He might still have had links with the wrong people. We can't just focus on the gambling aspect; there could be other forces at play.'

Zara sat up straighter. 'You mean like that beefy boyfriend of Jill's? We saw him go from nought to sixty, aggression-wise, at the bar.'

Nicholas nodded. 'And we can't rule out there being some other link with organised crime. Betty Hobbs was explaining to me that there has been a recent increase in illegal drugs coming into the island and that's why Ron is in Liverpool conferring with colleagues.'

The direction of the conversation had re-energised Dee. 'Drugs! That skinhead must be involved!'

'That's a bit of a sweeping statement,' chided Nicholas, 'but I do wish my friend Ron was back on the island. He's an excellent chief of police and I'm sure he would swiftly sort everything out.'

Zara glanced at him in irritation. 'Why don't you just ring him or send him a quick email?'

Nicholas glanced at her and was torn between being annoyed at her tone or full of admiration for the flash of brilliance in those jade-green eyes. Evenly he replied, 'None of this is the sort of thing one can put in an email or talk about over the phone.'

Dee eagerly enquired, 'So are we thinking that Patrick O'Connor's death is simply an act of passion by Jill's boyfriend or are we looking at it being drugs-related?'

Not to be left out, Zara put in, 'Or is it linked to illegal gambling?'

Nicholas looked from Dee to Zara and then slowly articulated, 'If we discount the jealous lover for a moment, I don't think we should be looking at it as an either-or question. The real issue is who is behind it all? Who is pulling the strings? Who is making a packet out of illegal drugs and gambling on the island?'

Dee was perched on the edge of her seat and with gusto, she gushed, 'Oooh! What fun! A master criminal! A Professor James Moriarty! I haven't come across one of those before!'

Nicholas's phone went off and he glanced at the screen. 'It's my mother – I'd better take this.'

He rose to go into the corridor.

'Send Myrtle my love,' called Zara as he exited the room.

An uneasy feeling swept over Dee as she thought about illicit profits and Daniel's wealth. Fortunately, she was able to deflect as Zara's expression clouded. 'You suddenly look worried, dear. What are you thinking of?'

Zara glanced at her mother. 'Oh nothing really, I was just wondering where Sean is.'

Outside the hospital, shivering in the cold and drenched by the rain, Juliet was walking around the car park, trying to get her thoughts in order.

I have to act now! There isn't any time left! I must get some cash so Christian and I get off the island and start a life together. A few thousand quid is chicken feed to them.

With hands trembling from cold and fear she took out her phone, dialled a number and said clearly, 'Don't speak, just listen. I know it was you. I have proof you murdered Patrick O'Connor and that you are behind the illegal drugs and gambling. Unless you meet me tonight at nine at the top of the Sloc I'm going to the police. Bring a bag with £5000 in cash.'

In the lobby at the Welcome Desk, Betty was preaching to Reggie, 'Put your mobile down immediately! We've only got another five minutes on our shift – the least you can do is—'

Her tirade was interrupted by her own phone ringing and she broke off what she was saying to answer it. She didn't notice Joe walking up with his phone clamped to his ear, his face like thunder.

Upstairs, Daniel walked into the waiting room, his phone in his hand. 'I've just had a call – I need to go.'

Chapter 16

The murderer was not happy about Juliet's call.

Who does she think she is? Too big for her boots by half! Still, I'll take care of her tonight and her pretty face won't save her. Stupid really – she doesn't know what she's got herself into or who she is messing with.

And with that thought they left for their appointment at the Sloc.

Tears were streaming down Juliet's face, burning her cheeks and making it difficult for her to see. Rain drummed against the windscreen. The wipers swished frantically but they were of little avail against the onslaught of water. Other cars had slowed right down, their headlights on to try and mitigate the danger. Juliet felt sick, but these days she was always nauseous. She knew she was driving too fast, she knew what she was doing was reckless but she pressed her foot down hard on the accelerator. She overtook a slow-moving Mini and nearly collided with an oncoming lorry. There was a spray of water, a screech of brakes and the wail of an angry horn but still she pressed on, heading south.

I have to do this! It's not just Christian and me anymore. I have to make sure our baby has a chance.

At the thought of Christian, she had a moment of doubt. *Perhaps I should have told him about the baby. I wanted to but there hasn't been the right moment. If we'd won the dance competition and got the prize money, I would have let him know. We could have made plans.* She gulped back a sob. *We would have been so happy. But everything is ruined now. We didn't win, Tony got hurt and Christian is a total wreck.*

She wiped her running nose with the back of her hand and

overtook another car. *If only our dads weren't so stupid, if only they didn't hate each other so much, we could get married here and bring our baby up playing on the beach and riding the steam train. But they would never accept us or the baby. They would make our lives hell. No! It has to be like this!*

Clenching her teeth together so that her jaw ached and clutching the steering wheel so hard that her knuckles showed white, Juliet drove on.

Back at the hospital, Nicholas joined Dee, Zara and Daniel and noticed they were all looking sombre.

He asked, 'Mother wants to know if you can all join her and Dad for a late supper.'

He might have issued the invitation to all of them, but his eyes were on Zara. The drama of the evening appeared to have energised her rather than exhausted her and her skin glowed. She was standing very straight.

Nicholas regarded Zara, thinking of their rehearsal times together. *You can tell she's a dancer by the way she holds herself – by her poise.*

Daniel was shaking his head. He was quite a few inches taller than Nicholas so Nicholas had to look up to see his expression.

'I'm afraid I'll have to decline. I, er, I need to go south.' He paused for long enough for Nicholas to wonder if he was trying to think up an excuse. 'Benedict called. With Tony, Christian and John here, he volunteered to check the livestock on Tony's farm. Anyway, one of Tony's heifers is having problems calving. He's phoned the vet but the vet has been called out to an injured horse and doesn't know when he'll be there, so I need to go and help the lad.'

Zara glanced at the window, where a torrent of rain was running down the glass. Glossing over the unhappy cow she turned to Nicholas and smiled. 'Supper sounds lovely.'

Dee tucked her arm in Daniel's. 'I'll come with you.'

'No! Don't!' said Daniel hastily and then at Dee's hurt look he softened it to, 'It's a filthy night and I've no idea how long it will take.'

To Nicholas, they looked like an unusual couple, with Daniel tall and well-built and Dee so petite but there was no mistaking the mutual affection in both their eyes as they looked at each other.

'Alright then,' conceded Daniel, 'but we'll need to get you some warmer clothes and a waterproof or you'll die of cold.'

Down south of the island, Juliet swung into Tony and Christian Pringle's farmyard. She checked her watch: eight-thirty, she still had plenty of time. It would only take fifteen minutes by the field tracks to get to the Sloc. Her body was wracked with adrenaline. She could feel it coursing through her body both terrifying and exhilarating.

I wonder if the baby can feel what I'm feeling? Isn't stress cortisol one of those hormones which are bad for babies? I'm a terrible mother – I don't know anything. I think I'm meant to take things easy and rest, not charge around the countryside in the pouring rain.

She put a protective hand on her flat belly and said, 'I'm doing this for you.'

In her agitation, she couldn't get her seatbelt undone. She fumbled with trembling hands, swore and finally succeeded. Slamming the door shut, she ran towards the old Land Rover. A couple of the sheepdogs scampered up to her, barking through the rain. Recognising Juliet, they began wagging their tails but she ignored them.

Hearing the door slam, Benedict gave the cow a comforting pat on her wet black-and-white fur. 'Don't worry girl, soon be sorted. That'll be the vet.'

But it wasn't the vet. At the sound of the ancient Land Rover's engine turning over and grinding to life, Benedict scrambled to stand up. Straw scrunched beneath his feet in the dim shed, lit only by a naked bulb and he looked out on a muted world obscured by a veil of rain. Through the downpour and the rising mist, he could just make out a figure struggling with the gate that led through the fields to the Sloc. Just in front of it was the Land Rover, its driver's door was open and the engine was chugging.

Benedict blinked, stared and recognised Juliet, 'What the—?' he muttered, but a groan from the labouring cow drew him back into the shed.

Juliet's heart pounded as she took off in the Land Rover. She tried to glance at her watch again, although she knew it could only be a minute since she last looked. The rain made it too dark to see. She swore and the loss of concentration caused her to swerve. She almost drove off the track but managed to right herself just in time.

She put both hands firmly on the steering wheel and focused on staying on the track while the Land Rover bucketed and rattled over the rough surface.

'I must admit, I'm rather excited. I've never seen a calf being born,' confessed Dee, as with window wipers swiping, they sloshed through a puddle and into the Pringle farmyard.

Daniel pressed his lips together and he looked at her steadily as he turned the engine off. 'Don't get your hopes up. It may be grim. From what Benedict said we may be looking at a dead calf and if we're unlucky we might lose the heifer as well. There is livestock and dead stock. Just don't expect it to be a like a scene from James Herriot.'

But Daniel was wrong. As Dee squelched across the yard in oversized wellies and waterproofs, the scene that met her eyes was straight out of the original James Herriot film. There was a ramshackle shed, poorly lit but just visible against the sheets of rain. Ensconced within, a young man was valiantly aiding the stricken beast.

Of course, in the film everyone is in tweed, thought Dee, *but then there weren't a lot of Goths hanging around rural, pre-war Yorkshire. Benedict looks very dashing in his winged white-collar shirt and drainpipe black trousers but I'm afraid his tailcoat will never be the same again, not with all that muck on it. Shame.* She had a vague recollection that Benedict was meant to be taking Amelia to a nightclub that night. *That explains his pointed patent leather shoes.*

Daniel was soon scrubbed up. He gently put his hand inside the cow and winced as there was a contraction before saying, 'You're right, Benedict, one of its legs is caught back. I'll see if I can get it in the right position.'

Dee watched, mesmerised by Daniel's gentle strength. His patient endeavour was rewarded as he removed his arm from inside the cow and two perfect little hooves appeared. The cow groaned, and with a whoosh out came the calf along with blood and mucus. The calf lay lifeless on the yellow straw. Dee swallowed and fought back burning tears. Daniel cleared its mouth and Benedict set to rubbing its pathetically limp body with straw. After a minute Dee detected a flicker of movement around the calf's eyes. She blinked and refocused. *Is the calf alive or is it just the motion of Benedict's massaging?* Another few seconds and the calf tried to lift its head.

'He's alive!' squealed Dee.

'He's a she,' smiled Daniel, as he manoeuvred the calf around to its mother's head. The mother, exhausted now, started to lick her baby. The pair nuzzled against each other and Dee thought she had never seen anything so beautiful.

While Daniel cleaned himself up, she regarded him speculatively.

Feeling her eyes upon him, he grinned and asked, 'What's with the look?'

'Oh, nothing much. I was just wondering why Lavinia Loveday has never set one of her romance series in a farm setting – perhaps I'll write to her and suggest it.'

Chapter 17

They barely had time to relish this triumphant miracle of life before there was the sound of screeching brakes in the yard.

'That'll be the vet. Sounds like he's driving like a bat out of hell,' commented Benedict.

Once again, Benedict was wrong. It wasn't the vet; this time it was Christian.

He ran through the rain and muddy puddles oblivious to the damage done to his white trainers. His blond hair was slick with rain and the look in his blue eyes was wild.

'Is Juliet here?' he screamed desperately while sending darting looks around the shed as if she might be hiding behind a pile of straw or even under a cowpat.

The atmosphere in the outbuilding instantly changed from euphoria to concern.

Dee and Daniel both shook their heads.

Christian spluttered, 'I called her – she was crying and saying something about needing to be at the Sloc by nine and that she was going to take care of everything. Then she cut me off and I haven't been able to get back through to her.' Benedict stopped wiping his hands and said, 'She's not here now. She blasted in a bit ago and without saying a word, took the old Land Rover and headed off up the field track as if she was driving in the Monte Carlo rally.'

'We've got to stop her!' In his distress, Christian's voice came out as a screech.

Daniel put a calming hand on the young man's arm and said, 'I don't understand.'

Annoyed, Christian roughly shrugged the arm away. 'She's got this thing about us getting enough money to leave the island.

She reckons she knows who is behind all the organised crime on the island and that murder.'

'I still don't understand,' said Daniel. Even in the gloom of the shed, Dee could see that his eyebrows were raised.

Savage-eyed, Christian blurted out, 'I'm afraid she's going to the Sloc to meet the person who is behind the drugs and gambling and to get cash from them via blackmail.'

Shocked, Daniel said, 'That would be suicidal! The chances are whoever it is doesn't mind killing. They might well be behind Patrick's death.'

'But how does she know who's running the organised crime on the island?' asked Dee.

Benedict spoke up. 'She's always had a lot of unsavoury friends – I think she likes the thrill of it.'

Dee was about to say, 'We must ring the police' but then she thought of Hadrian Macintosh, temporary head of the Blom constabulary and of what she witnessed in the alleyway. *There is definitely something dodgy about him and that skinhead. Perhaps calling the police isn't such a good idea.*

'I'll stay here with the calf. If the three of you hurry, you may be in time to save her,' said Benedict.

'Come on!' declared Daniel, leading the way to his immaculate Range Rover with its plush, valeted interior. He glanced at it and hesitated.

'We'd be better off in mine!' shouted Christian over the noise of the storm.

'OK,' agreed Daniel, adding, 'but I think it would be safer if I drove.'

He took the keys.

Dee was relieved, she didn't fancy being driven, in a howling gale, over rough terrain by a young man driven half-wild by terror over the safety of his lover.

They all piled into the beaten-up red pickup. As they pulled through the gate, the two sheepdogs jumped into the back, screwing up their eyes against the rain.

'Do you want to take them back?' asked Daniel.

'No time. Just drive!' shouted Christian.

Dee was buffeted and bounced across rocks and through roaring streams. She presumed Daniel was negotiating all the twists and turns by Braille as the driving rain made it impossible to see out of the windscreen. Occasionally they came to a gate and Christian leapt out to open it. They were climbing higher and grassland gave way to heather.

Eventually, they swung onto a road with a steep rugged hill beyond.

'We're here!' exclaimed Daniel, scrambling out of the pickup truck and scanning the horizon for Juliet.

'The Land Rover is there – you can't take vehicles further than this, so she must be on foot. But where is she?' yelled Christian.

'That white van by the Land Rover – it was at Chough Drive when I found the body,' stammered Dee, but Christian wasn't listening.

'*Juliet!*' he bellowed but his voice was carried away by the storm.

A crack of lightning illuminated the sky.

'There she is!' called Dee, pointing to where Juliet was silhouetted against the skyline. She was standing on a rocky outcrop.

Christian started to run up the steep incline.

'Careful! She's right at the cliff edge,' called Daniel.

'And she's not alone!' screeched Dee as she spotted a menacing figure joining Juliet, but her words were drowned out by a clap of thunder.

Dee and Daniel followed Christian up the narrow track.

'What are these fluorescent orange markers?' panted Dee, pointing at an arrow indicating the uphill path.

'There is a fell race here this weekend. They are to show the runners the way,' Daniel replied.

The pathway was unstable and running with water. Dee slipped on the loose stones. Daniel caught her arm to steady her. She prided herself on being fit, but the combination of oversized wellies and a near-vertical incline made for hard going.

A scream carried over the sound of the storm. Dee looked up.

'It's Christian, he's fallen,' said Daniel and they both increased their pace.

Scrabbling up the rocks, at times on all fours, they soon reached Christian. He was on the ground cradling his ankle.

'I'll stay with him, you go on,' prompted Dee.

Daniel nodded and carried on.

'Do you think you can stand with my help?' asked Dee. She was aware from her first aid training that he should not be moved until the paramedics arrived and were able to secure his ankle but she knew, with total certainty, that if she didn't assist the boy, he would crawl on his belly through the stony cascade that constituted the path. It would be a misguided attempt to help Juliet but Christian was young and in love.

She had just got him on his feet, his arm leaning heavily on her shoulders and her arms giving him what support she could, when she was startled by someone breathing heavily beside her. A familiar voice asked, 'What on earth is going on?'

To her amazement, she realised it was Joe, in a running kit.

'Joe, what are you doing here?'

'Training for the weekend.'

'In *this* weather?' queried Dee.

He ignored her question and repeated, 'What on earth is going on?'

Relief overtook her surprise. 'Quick, Juliet is in danger! Up there! Daniel has gone to help, but please hurry.'

Without asking any more questions he began a steady jog uphill. Dee craned her neck to see what was going on and despite the rain and the burden of Christian's heavy arm, she could just make out that he was swiftly gaining on Daniel. She found herself thinking, *Betty is right, Joe is wonderful. I'm sure he can help.*

'Steady does it!' said Dee out loud, more for her benefit than Christian's. Inch by inch they crept up the hill.

With the best will in the world, Dee was only able to take a few steps before she had to stop and catch her breath.

What am I doing here on this heather-clad hillside in a

thunderstorm? This is not what I was hoping for when I booked a relaxed Manx fortnight.

She glanced up at the rocky outcrop.

'I can see Juliet,' she said then wished she hadn't as Juliet was cowering and an ominous figure was looming over her.

Christian had seen it too and screamed, 'Hurry! They're right on the cliff edge there – it's a sheer drop down to the sea!'

Dee struggled on with all of the strength inside her. She ignored the burning in her legs and the sensation that her lungs were about to explode. Upward they toiled and when they next paused, they were still not close enough to hear but they could see from Juliet's tilted head and open mouth that she was screaming. She was struggling against the grip of the man. Her slight body looked so slight and helpless against his powerful form.

Dee had an overwhelming sensation of helplessness. She could feel the thrum of her own pulse – her blood pressure must be through the roof. Her mouth was dry, her stomach tight. Her mind raced.

Who is he? Did he ruthlessly stab Patrick and leave him to bleed to death? Who could be cunning enough to ruin people's lives with drugs and gambling? Who is unscrupulous enough to wrestle a young girl to her death?

He had a bandana tied over his nose and mouth but even with his face half obscured she had a growing realisation.

I know him! But it can't be!

Tall, hefty and muscular …

'*Reggie!*' Dee screamed.

'For God's sake don't stop. We *must* get up there,' urged Christian.

'Daniel is nearly there,' she said hoping to comfort Christian and not adding that she didn't fancy his chances against Reggie, especially after a fast climb.

They stumbled on keeping their eyes on the action above them. It was like watching a horror film in slow motion.

Reggie spotted Daniel and swung Juliet in front of him as a shield. He had her throat clamped in a stranglehold by his beefy arm, and was slowly squeezing the life out of her.

Daniel held his hands open and outstretched, in an obvious gesture of calm. What he was saying was lost in the wind.

Dee's mind was in a whirl. *Somehow, I don't think reasoning with Reggie is going to work.*

'My God, Reggie is backing towards the edge, one gust of wind and they'll be over the cliff!' howled Christian trying to break away from Dee. He took half a step and crumpled in pain.

Dee caught him. She clutched him tightly as if she could only hold him tightly enough she could protect him from the tragedy that was unfolding.

Mesmerised with horror they watched helplessly.

Daniel was standing stock still.

Juliet has stopped struggling. Is it because of fear or has Reggie's stranglehold of her rendered her unconscious?

'No! God, no!' wailed Christian to the angry heavens.

Dee didn't want to watch but she couldn't drag her eyes away. Her jaw ached from clenching her teeth together. All of her senses were heightened; she could smell the wet peaty earth mixed with heather and their own sweat. Wind and rain reverberated in her ears and she thought she could feel the hammering of Christian's heart as well as her own.

A blast of air caught Reggie's windcheater; as it billowed out behind him it looked like a sail. He stumbled and Dee gasped.

This is it! I'm about to witness the death of two people.

Then when all seemed lost, Joe dashed forward. He grabbed Juliet and in so doing he dislodged Reggie's mask and pushed him over the edge. Dee saw the boy's eyes, wide and terrified, gape at Joe in disbelief before, with flailing arms he plummeted over the edge.

Speechless Christian and Dee stared.

As they focused, Daniel, Juliet and Joe were joined by a man and a woman. The pair were dressed for running, like Joe.

Who can that be?

'Thank heavens Juliet is safe,' sobbed Christian, tears mixing with rain on his cheeks.

Out loud Dee wondered, 'But who are those two?'

'I think I know them,' said Christian. 'The woman is Jill; she's Sean's secretary and the beefy bloke is her boyfriend.'

Dee narrowed her eyes. *I know they're kitted out for running but can all these sporty types really be training at this time of night and this weather? There is definitely something fishy going on!*

It was then that the shock set in and the next hour was quite hazy for Dee. She registered that the storm was passing over, leaving the hillside pungent and steaming.

Somehow the muscly chap took Christian off her and he seemed to find his weight no problem.

Joe and Daniel were more or less carrying the semi-lifeless Juliet between them.

Joe was in a bad way; he kept muttering useless words of remorse and regret such as, 'Poor boy! I should have done more. I blame myself. If only I'd grabbed his arm.'

Jill obviously had a lot of medical experience as she was doing a lot of checking pulses and barking out orders.

In her fog of emotions Dee pondered, *Odd that she's being so commanding; I thought Zara said she went to pieces in the bar. Perhaps it's something to do with the bracing sea and moorland air?*

When they reached the car park at the bottom, the red pickup and Land Rover were still there. The white van had gone but it had been replaced by Betty Hobbs. She leapt out of her diminutive car resplendent in a pink rain hat, coat and coordinated flowered ankle wellies and was brandishing a flask.

'How fortunate I came with a hot drink for Joe – so important he keeps hydrated while training! I could see there's been some sort of an incident so I've rung for the police and ambulance.' Betty looked hopefully from Daniel and Dee to Joe. She was clearly expecting to be praised; instead, she was greeted by a weary shocked silence.

She gaped at Joe. Now he had put the burden and responsibility of Juliet down he had crumpled in on himself. His normally slim, muscular body resembled an abandoned rag doll. His wet red hair was plastered to his scalp. His white skin was splattered with mud and his sodden running kit hung limply on his slight form.

'Don't sit on the wet ground, you'll catch your death,' she shrieked.

Still in command, Jill snapped at her burly companion, 'Let's get these two into that red pickup.'

When Juliet and Christian were sheltered in the vehicle, Dee was touched by the tenderness with which Christian was cuddling his girlfriend.

Betty looked at Daniel. Ignoring his weary limp body and exhausted face she demanded, 'Put Joe in my car and leave the door open. What's wrong with him?'

'He's had a terrible experience,' murmured Daniel as he manoeuvred Joe into the passenger seat.

'What's happened? Someone tell me what's going on,' shrieked Betty.

With an icy hand, Joe grabbed Betty's arm. His pale, translucent face had a maniacal glint. 'I killed him!' he hissed.

Betty opened her eyes wide, silently shaking her head. She tried to pull away from Joe but his bony fingers bit through her mac and into her flesh. 'What? I, er, I don't understand.'

Daniel calmly extricated Betty and perched himself on the running board by Joe, his long legs crumpled uncomfortably on the gravel. Soothingly, he patted Joe's shoulder and murmured, 'It's alright, it wasn't your fault.'

Dee led Betty a few steps away. She was trying to come up with the words to explain what had happened but was interrupted by the wail of sirens. Snaking up the hill, towards them was a cavalcade of vehicles. An ambulance was sandwiched between two police cars and they all had their blue lights flashing.

Dee blinked. 'Is that Hadrian Macintosh? What's he doing here? I imagined someone as high up as him stayed behind a desk.'

Betty could not resist jutting her chin out and puffing out her chest. 'Well, an officer as excellent as Hadrian would keep his finger on the pulse. Did I mention my Ron appointed him?'

As the cavalcade of vehicles screeched to a stop, Hadrian Macintosh leapt out of the lead car.

He glanced at the assembled group, his dark eyes alert and his immaculate moustache impeccably in place. He eyed Dee with what she felt was quite an unnecessary dislike.

Forcibly, he demanded, 'What has been going on here?'

'It was Reggie!' wailed Joe.

'What?' queried Hadrian.

'Reggie attacked Juliet at the top of the Sloc.' Joe's voice faltered. 'Right on the cliff edge.'

Betty's shrill voice cut across the valley. 'What? Why? Where is Reggie?'

Hadrian attempted to silence Betty with a stern, 'I'll ask the questions here!' but his police training was no match for Betty's lifetime of being bossy.

Joe slumped in the car, his eyes dull. He stammered out, 'I've no idea why he attacked her or what he was doing here.'

While Hadrian, standing tall and with his shoulders thrown back, tried to take command, Betty, with all the feminine softness of Attila the Hun on a bad day, said, 'She must have done something to him. I mean, I know Reggie is a bit rough around the edges but he has a heart of gold. He wouldn't just attack her.'

Daniel looked directly at Betty, making eye contact as he spoke. 'I'm sorry, Betty, but I think he was responsible for the crime wave on the island and Juliet tried to blackmail him.'

Hadrian took a sharp intake of breath and began to say, 'I really must insist—'

Betty interrupted him. 'Don't be ridiculous.'

She scanned the group. Jill and her bodybuilder boyfriend were hovering around Christian and Juliet, Joe was in her car and Dee and Daniel were standing by her.

'But where *is* Reggie?' she asked.

Joe's face contorted with pain, 'I— he …'

Daniel was straight back beside him, putting a hand on his shoulder and explaining, 'There's been an accident. I'm afraid he's gone.'

Betty stared from Daniel to Dee. 'Gone? Where?'

Dee tried to explain, 'Reggie had Juliet on the cliff edge and, well, he slipped.'

Reality slowly dawned on Betty. Her perky commanding demeanour morphed into shock then slowly she began to cry. To begin with, it was just a solitary tear trickling down her plump cheek but soon it was a torrent. She sobbed uncontrollably and extended her arms out to Dee, as the nearest available mother figure. Dee held her and tried to ignore the cloying smell of roses and roll-your-own tobacco.

'I can't believe it!' whimpered Betty. Her voice came out muffled as she had her face pressed against Dee's shoulder. 'I was only with him a couple of hours ago. He was really getting the hang of his welcoming smile.'

Jill was handing over her care of Juliet to a brisk paramedic.

'What's your name?' he asked in loud, distinct tones.

'She's Juliet,' said Christian with an arm still around her.

The medic called her name and she roused slightly.

'How could I be so stupid?' she wailed. 'I could have killed us both. I could see the cliffs – that drop into the water! We could both be dead!'

The final statement she screamed. Her arms were flailing and from where Dee stood it looked like Juliet was hysterical and fighting to get away from Christian and out of the car.

Christian was becoming just as alarmed as his girlfriend. 'We're alright! We're safe now!'

Juliet shook her head frantically and shouted, 'You don't understand! You'd hate me if you knew the truth.'

'I could *never* hate you!'

'You would if you knew what I'd done!'

The paramedic was hyper-calm, 'Juliet! Look at me!'

Juliet continued to shout. What she was saying became incoherent as she battled to run.

The paramedic turned to his female colleague who was attempting to examine Christian's ankle. 'We need to sedate her.'

'*You can't!*' Juliet's words rang out.

The medic was impressively unperturbed. 'It's for your own safety, Miss.'

'I'm pregnant.'

The statement hung in the air. The only person who seemed not to be shocked by the news was the paramedic. 'In that case, Juliet, you need to calm down and breathe. Look at me!' She turned her head towards him. 'And breathe in with me, and out – again breathe in, hold it and out. Good. Feeling better?'

Juliet nodded. Christian was looking dazed, but eventually, he managed a quaky, 'What did you say?'

'We're having a baby,' she said and a soft smile crossed her lips as she patted her belly. Then a frown creased her forehead and she added, 'And I put her in danger.'

Christian was still staring at Juliet, slowly he asked, 'Was that why you thought I would hate you if I knew? Because our baby might have died?'

Juliet nodded and Christian threw his arms around her. 'I love you! Both of you!'

Dee felt a lump in her throat and she noticed Daniel swallow and brush away a tear.

Betty Hobbs had stopped crying when she'd realised something interesting was going on with Juliet. Leaving Dee with a smear of pink lipstick on her coat, Betty pulled away to get a better look at Juliet, the paramedic and Christian.

She gave an 'Umph' of satisfaction before saying, 'Well that explains her running off the dance floor at the competition.' She giggled, 'I'd like to be a fly on the wall when they tell their fathers.'

Chapter 18

It wasn't until mid-morning the next day that the police had finished processing them. Dee blinked as she came out of the police station and into the bright sunshine. She wanted nothing more than a hot bath, clean clothes and a long nap. She knew she must look terrible – no sleep, crumpled clothes and she dreaded to think what her hair must look like. For once she didn't even crave her morning Taekwondo drill – she didn't think that any amount of mindful breathing with movement could restore her mind and body to tranquillity.

Daniel stood next to her. When he looked at her it was clear he thought she was the most beautiful woman he had ever seen, which was gratifying but did make Dee wonder how good his eyesight was.

'So that's that then!' he declared happily, giving her a great bear hug that lifted her feet off the ground.

'What do you mean?' laughed Dee. She was still suspended in the air and she had to crane her head back to look into his blue eyes.

They look like the ocean when the sun is sparkling down on it, she thought as he spun her around.

A young couple with a pushchair waited patiently as he twirled her a few times, totally blocking the pavement. When Daniel noticed them, he flushed with embarrassment and put Dee down.

'Oh! I'm so sorry,' he stammered sheepishly.

The mother laughed and said, 'That's quite alright,' as they wheeled the pushchair past.

'Well, you are off the hook. We can finally relax and enjoy having found each other again.'

'But there's still no direct evidence to prove that Reggie killed Patrick.'

Daniel's buoyant spirits were in no way dampened by Dee giving him a dose of reality. He tucked her arm in his and began walking towards the prom.

'No, but it's only a matter of time. Now they know that it was Reggie who was behind all the organised crime, they'll soon put all the pieces together. The main thing is that the police are happy that you had nothing to do with any of it.' He patted her hand and then looked serious. 'I can't help being annoyed at Juliet, though. If only she'd gone straight to the police with what she knew.'

Dee thought of Juliet: so young, so foolhardy and now about to be a mother. 'I hope they don't prosecute her for obstructing justice, or whatever the phrase is,' she said. 'The stress wouldn't be good for the baby.'

'I think that's very generous of you after all the bother she's caused you.'

'I can't help feeling sorry for Reggie,' continued Dee.

'What?' spluttered Daniel, pausing their walk to stare at her in disbelief.

'He was little more than a child.'

'A pretty dangerous one,' grunted Daniel as they continued to walk.

'What chance did he have, in and out of juvenile detention?'

Daniel's lips tightened and his voice was quiet but hard as he stated, 'He had a lot more opportunities than most young men – think of all the time and effort Betty Hobbs and Joe gave him. If you want to feel sorry for anyone, feel sorry for them; they are both shattered. An experience like that will probably haunt Joe for the rest of his life.' He gave Dee another hug and smiled down at her. 'Let's not talk about it anymore, let's focus on all the fun we are now free to enjoy.'

As they strolled back along the prom towards Dee's B&B, there was a wonderful, post-storm freshness in the air. The sun was shining again but it had lost its feverish heat and a few white clouds dotted the sky. There were several picturesque sails out to sea and on land lots of young families were enjoying a walk without the risk of sunburn.

While Daniel talked happily about proposed walks and outings Dee thought, *I can't leave things like this. Reggie might have had a role in the gambling, drugs and even the murder but he couldn't have been working alone. This isn't about my name being cleared; this is about all the lives already ruined or tainted by gambling, violence and drugs and about all those lives that will be affected if I don't get to the bottom of the organised crime on the island. I must take action! The only question is, where do I start?*

Chapter 19

All very satisfactory, thought the Blom malefactor as they sipped their coffee and read the local headlines: '*Crazed Criminal's Sensational Sloc Slaughter.*'

'Oh! Give it a rest, Gran! Reggie's gone and that's the end of things.' Amelia was leaning her chair back at a dangerous angle while sipping her late brunch coffee. She was looking rather dashing in a sort of floaty top whose romance was offset by several narrow black-studded belts – this was paired with faux leather shorts whose minuscule length was softened by several wafting diaphanous petals. The outfit had been a gift from Nicholas's mother, Myrtle. It seemed that Amelia's Goth sensibility had inspired Myrtle's costume-designing heart.

Rather sweet, mused Dee. *It's a bit like Julie Andrews in The Sound of Music; she thought Amelia ought to have some rompers or play clothes so she could enjoy all the healthy outdoor activities the island has to offer.* She said, 'A tight lace corset and a stiff tutu is all very well in its way, but it's not ideal for cliff-top hikes.'

She took a leisurely look at her granddaughter. *I can't help thinking that it's a shame Myrtle made it in purple but I suppose she's right, it is rather fitting with all the Manx heather that's out – and unlike Julie Andrews, she didn't have any old curtains to hand.*

She glanced from Amelia to Zara, who had gone for a more classic look, three-quarter-length white jeans and a navy polo T with a sporty little green scarf knotted at her throat.

She realised that Zara was giving her a stern look. 'Although Amelia could have phrased it with more respect, I do agree with her. The police are happy, so let's just forget about all this nastiness and enjoy the rest of the holiday.'

Dee had no intention of doing any such thing. 'But do you really think Reggie had the mental capacity to organise a gambling ring? Think of all the maths – I struggle to add up my household bills. And as for the drugs, that must be like running an import-export business and I just don't think Reggie was the entrepreneurial type. He didn't have any of Sean's sharp wit.'

Amelia shrugged. 'Perhaps what he lacked in intellect he made up for in animal cunning. Juliet was absolutely certain she had witnessed him selling drugs.' She glanced at her watch. 'And speaking of enjoying the rest of our holiday, I must run. Josh will be here in a minute; we're taking the electric railway – Josh says it's really ace, something about it being the first electric railway ever. I think I read that the Isle of Man insists that it had the first electric railway but no one here takes any notice of that. Anyway, it's going to take us to the base of Ullr Mountain and then we're going to climb it. On a day like today, we should be able to see Scotland, Ireland, Wales and England – actually, its eight kingdoms as you can see the Isle of Man too but they like to pretend it isn't there.'

Dee nodded. 'The fabled seven kingdoms: the Isle of Blom, Scotland, Ireland, England and Wales, the kingdoms of the sky and the sea.'

'What about Benedict?' asked Zara.

She shrugged again. 'He says it's not his thing, you know, all the fresh air and exercise.'

'And it is yours?'

Amelia nodded. 'Yes; until we came here, I'd forgotten how much I love it.' She paused and looked tentatively at her mother. 'It reminds me of all the fun we used to have with Dad.'

Zara didn't say anything but gave Amelia a half smile.

Amelia laughed, 'Who knows I might do a psychology paper on it, something along the lines of "*Early influences on hobby preferences*".'

Zara drew her eyebrows together. 'I thought you were focused on criminal psychology.'

'Well, if I throw Gran into the mix, I could combine the two. "*Hiking and murder, a psychological analysis.*"'

She pushed back her chair and stood up to leave.

Dee interrupted. 'But the case? There are still so many unanswered questions.'

'What like?' asked Amelia.

'Sean! He was all over the place – well, largely following your mother around – and then he just sort of vanished,' blurted out Dee.

'Oh, that! It turns out there was nothing mysterious about it. He rang me this morning; he's had food poisoning, something he ate,' explained Zara dismissively.

'And you believe that?' Dee sounded both outraged and disappointed in her daughter.

Zara shrugged. 'Why not?'

Dee was adamant. 'It's a bit convenient. And then there are all the other loose ends.'

Zara didn't try to hide her boredom with the topic. With a stifled yawn, she asked, 'Such as?'

Firmly Dee explained, 'The rough-looking man with the broken nose and shaved head who I saw being so cosy with the acting chief of police, Hadrian Macintosh. Then there are those sheep shears – how did they end up being a murder weapon? And what's more, I don't believe Jill and that bodybuilder boyfriend of hers were really on the Sloc for training like Joe. Seems a tad suspicious to be training in a storm, let alone to pick the one hill Juliet has picked for a bit of blackmail.'

Zara interjected, 'Betty says that Joe sticks to his training program with more precision than the Swiss railways; that's why she knew where to bring the flask to.'

Dee was only slightly deflated by this information. 'Well, that still doesn't explain the other two. And like I said before, I just don't think Reggie was up to all the organisation.'

Amelia glanced at her watch and then outside before saying, 'Juliet was very clear; she had personally seen Reggie selling drugs and she'd heard about his other activities.'

Zara poured herself another coffee and asked, 'Speaking of Juliet, how is the news of the baby going down?'

Dee smiled; she liked babies. 'According to Daniel, Christian is thrilled.'

'And the grandfathers-to-be?'

Dee laughed. 'They're fighting over whose barn the wedding should be celebrated in, where the couple should live, who the child will take after and even who will do the most babysitting.' She wrinkled her forehead and took a sip of tea before thoughtfully continuing, 'If we're talking about my suspicions, I'm still a bit concerned about Daniel; he's so evasive when I ask him where he gets his money from and he also seems too good to be true.'

Zara rolled her eyes. 'I'd hoped we'd moved on from your sleuthing but if you insist, how so?'

Dee pinched her lips together and stared at her teacup before blurting out, 'He's more like one of Lavinia Loveday's romantic heroes than a normal man.'

Both Amelia and Zara laughed at this, which made Dee blush.

Deciding that they had teased her enough, Zara said, 'Look, Mother, the main thing is you're off the hook.'

Dee looked pained. 'But it's about so much more than just me! We can't just leave things! Think of all the people who will still be in danger if Reggie wasn't the criminal mastermind?'

Zara gave Dee a glance laced with impatience. 'Sometimes I think you enjoy stirring things up. Can't you just let things lie?' She turned her attention to Amelia. 'Don't forget you're coming with me later to check that Joe and Betty Hobbs are alright after all that's happened.'

Dee had been gazing at the sea out of her window while toying with her tea but now she looked at Zara and Amelia. 'That's so kind of you both to do that. They really were in a terrible state. I would join you but I can't face it.'

Zara patted Dee's hand as it lay on the white tablecloth. 'You've had quite enough upset for one holiday. You should spend the rest of the day just relaxing.'

Amelia pulled a face. 'Visiting them is a bit over the top, isn't it? After all, we hardly know them.'

Zara was crisp in her reply. 'It's the right thing to do.'

'Fine!' agreed Amelia, picking up a final bit of toast. 'I suppose it could be interesting. I might take notes: "*The physical and mental effects of trauma*".' She glanced out of the window and waved. 'Josh is here. See you!'

Zara turned to her mother when Amelia left. 'Nicholas is picking me up and we're driving Myrtle and George to the far north of the island. George wants to see the Artic Terns. It should be fun; why don't you join us?'

'That's kind, dear, but no thanks.'

'If you stay here, you'll just brood.'

'Well, there's a lot to brood on. The police seem awfully keen just to sweep things under the carpet.'

'Oh, there'll be reports and investigations galore. There they are now!' Zara waved out the window. 'They're double parked – I must fly. Do come – I'll worry about you all alone.'

'No need, the nice lady at the desk, did a ring-round and found a good beautician who had a cancellation, so I'm booked in for the works: massage, nails, you name it, I'm having it.'

'Good,' said Zara.

Fortunately, she couldn't read her mother's thoughts. *Yes, you're quite right, dear, it is good. It will give me lots of time to think through the case.*

When Nicholas thought about it later, the outing had been … interesting.

The drive up north took longer than Nicholas thought it would – or perhaps it just felt never-ending – and it was way less romantic than he had hoped for.

Admittedly the countryside was magnificent. The view ranged from stunning heather-clad hills to gently rolling farmland. The occasional glimpses of the sea added drama to the scenery. The sun was shining and Zara was sitting beside him, as sophisticated as ever.

The problem was in the backseat. While George might be a

silent presence, Myrtle was anything but.

'No!' she'd said. 'I absolutely insist that Zara sits in the front seat next to you, Nicholas.'

I do wish she hadn't given me that wide-eyed look before glancing significantly at Zara, and the wink was quite unnecessary. Zara was very tactful pretending not to notice, but talk about embarrassing.

And why did Mother insist on sitting in the back when she gets car sick? If her aim was to create a sense of romance between Zara and me, why would she think that having her gulping and frantically winding down the back window would help the ambience? Still, thank goodness that when she did actually vomit, I had time to pull over – the sound effects were bad enough with her behind that boulder but it would have been an utter disaster if she'd lost her breakfast over the car.

He sighed. *At least Mother felt better having been sick. She recovered enough to start and maintain a monologue about the weather, the sheep, and George's athlete's foot. Personally, I would have preferred to spend the journey discussing literature with Zara while listening to classical music.*

Once they had reached their destination George had been delighted – well, Nicholas thought he detected a hint of a smile. The coastline was vast and the terns swooped and dived, elegant against the blue sky.

They deposited George and his binoculars, and he sat on a rug on a boulder while they walked along the pebble beach.

Nicholas had glanced across at Zara, the sea breeze was toying with her hair, and her trim figure moved with ease and grace. Perhaps it was the backdrop of the crashing foaming ocean but with the suddenness of a breaking wave, Nicholas was overtaken by the recollection of the passionate beach scene in *From Here to Eternity*. In his mind he was no longer the reserved policeman, Nicholas Corman, but the all-powerful Burt Lancaster. Gone was his buttoned-down shirt and carefully pressed chinos; now he was proud and magnificent, bare-chested and glistening with sea spray. In the blink of his eye, Zara was transformed into the demure Deborah Kerr; cool and in control on the outside but internally raging with volcanic desire. Nicholas could see it all so clearly, the unstoppable waves, Zara trembling and gazing with admiration at his aforementioned, magnificent torso. He could hear her breath quicken as he touched her sea-kissed flesh. Their eyes would meet, full of passion and understanding before they embraced, all inhibitions washed away by the surging sea foam.

'Haemorrhoids!' Nicholas blinked as his mother interrupted his fantasy, her voice carrying over the crashing waves.

'What?' he stammered.

'Haemorrhoids – that's what your father will get if he gets off his rug. You get haemorrhoids from sitting on cold stone and you don't want to mess with haemorrhoids!'

Josh, as he was unaccompanied by Myrtle, faired rather better on his outing with Amelia. The electric railway was a delightful Victorian carriage. Pristine in the sunshine it shone, red and gold as if it was newly minted rather than an antique. Josh gestured to the bit of the bench nearest to the open window for Amelia to sit. She gave him a ravishing smile as she settled down and he knew today was going to be wonderful.

With much clanking and rattling the train head off up the hill. The breeze blew Amelia's curls across her face and she laughed. They soon escaped the town and were treated to dramatic cliffs on their left and stunning seascapes on their right.

Amelia leant closer to Josh to be heard above the rattling of the locomotive and said, 'What a feat of engineering to carve this railway out of a cliff face.'

Josh, with his heart beating a little faster than was the norm due to Amelia's proximity, just nodded.

She settled back in her seat and he was able to breathe again. He gave her a sideways glance. *How come I go all weak at the knees when she's anywhere near me but she seems unaffected by being close to me?*

It was a new experience for Josh, having a girl act cool towards him; normally his sleek good looks guaranteed him more attention than he wanted. The electric train climbed steadily upwards.

They both gazed at the scenery until Josh spotted a wallaby out of Amelia's window. He leant across her to point. 'Look, a wallaby. I read about how a few escaped from the wildlife park a few years back and now there's a thriving colony living wild.'

He finished his sentence and realised that Amelia was sitting very still – she wasn't even breathing – and when he caught her eye she blushed and looked away, stammering, 'Oh yes, I see it now. Isn't it cute?'

A feeling of elation swelled in his gut. *So, she* isn't *totally unaware of me.*

They sat in silence for a few minutes, each consumed with new revelations about themselves in relation to the other.

Amelia's mobile phone rang out, an unmistakably dramatic ringtone of *Flight of the Valkyrie* – it suited her.

Josh felt a wave of irritation as he noticed that it was Benedict's ID that lit up her phone screen.

'I'll take this …' She glanced about her; the train was small and there wasn't much hope of privacy.

She looked behind them, at the back where the guard sat in his peaked cap with his red and green flags and decided that that would be as good a place as any to take the call. Presumably, she assumed that as it was behind Josh, he wouldn't be able to watch her.

She stood up and began squeezing herself through the small gap between Josh's knees and the bench in front. Josh made no effort to move. Had she been bold enough to look at him she would have seen he was scowling.

She was mid-manoeuvre when the train gave an unexpected lurch and she was thrown onto his knee. There was a shocked pause as they both registered their intimate proximity, her sitting on his lap with the relentless cries of the Valkyrie. The elderly couple on the bench in front of them turned and glared. Josh held his hands out, keen to demonstrate to both Amelia and his fellow passengers that he was far too much of a gentleman to take advantage of the situation.

Muttering apologies, Amelia flipped her phone to silent and scurried to the back of the carriage.

Josh might not be able to quite hear what was being said but there was a large mirror positioned at the front of the carriage so that the guard could clearly see what was going on throughout the train.

With growing satisfaction, he observed Amelia's body language as she spoke to Benedict. Whatever was being said, Amelia was not happy. Josh found he was smiling and when she returned to her seat, he was most obliging in making room for her. He even reached into his knapsack and took out a small bag.

'Toffee?' he offered, proffering the open bag in front of her pert little nose.

Chapter 20

Relaxed and refreshed, Dee strolled out of the beauty salon and into the late evening sunshine.

I could definitely learn to love living somewhere that has the sea on its doorstep.

She paused to enjoy the rolling waves and the calling gulls. Her muscles felt delightfully unknotted by the massage. The salon had perfected every element of its service for maximum tranquillity: the warmed bench with its thick cosy towels, the smooth, oiled hot stones that glided over her body and the skill of the masseuse. Her mind had been lulled into rest by the soft lighting, the aromatic candles and the soothing soundtrack of rhythmic waves overlaid by gentle music. She couldn't resist sneaking a peak at her burnished nails. Normally she contented herself with an at-home manicure to keep them neat and clean but being on holiday she had splashed out on having them polished with a neutral beige colour.

I feel so glamorous! I'm sure this is just the tone Joanna Lumley would go for, although perhaps she's a vivid red sort of a girl. Still, they look very attractive! And the best bit is there's no gardening while I am on holiday, so they aren't going to get chipped in five seconds.

She took her time walking back to the B&B, relishing in the light salty breeze, the ever-rolling sea, the boats and the people. It was quite late by the time she got back and she was surprised that there was no sign of either Amelia or Zara. She glanced at her watch.

They should have been back hours ago. Where can they be?

She called Nicholas.

'Zara?' he said. 'No, she's not with me. Isn't she at the B&B?

We had a lovely time but I dropped her back some time ago. Josh is with me; I'll just ask him.'

There was the sound of muffled voices then Nicholas came back on the phone. 'He says he left Amelia at the B&B. If it's any help, she said something about not going out for a drink as she and Zara were going to check on Betty and Joe after their ordeal.'

Dee thanked him and rung off. She had an uneasy feeling. She tried Betty and Joe's phones, but there was no reply on either.

Can they have both decided to have an early night?

She looked out of the window and the sight of the ever-present sea calmed her, then she regarded her own bed with its inviting fluffed-up pillow. She yawned. Everything about the room was relaxing. The décor of cream and blue whispered carefree seaside holidays. The prints on the wall were all happy beach scenes. And best of all was that luxurious bed.

A little nap – just forty winks.

She lay down on the bed and pulled the cosy bedcover over her. *The Americans are so right to call these cosy covers 'comforters' because that's just what they are.*

Whenever she travelled she always took a small lavender bag to tuck under her pillow. Now she inhaled the soporific fragrance and thought of the lavender fields of Provence.

Dee was asleep in an instant. Soon she was in the midst of a delightful dream where she was having tea with the late Queen. The Queen was offering her a cucumber sandwich and they were swapping notes on how to get rid of greenfly on roses.

It was then, in her half-slumber, that Dee heard a distinct noise from Zara's room. There was an interconnecting door, so sounds carried. After the crash of what could be a lamp or a vase smashing on the floor, the swear word that followed was unmistakably male.

Dee sat up and swallowed.

Silently she moved to the interconnecting door. Her skin prickled and her mouth felt dry. With her ear pressed against the gap in the door, she listened.

Yes, someone is definitely there and from the way they are banging into things it's not a chambermaid.

Her mind raced to every mystery book she had ever read or drama she'd ever watched.

This is the bit where I confront the villain and save my admiring family.

She had a clear vision of the 'baddie', in a striped top and mask, being led away in handcuffs while Dee stood, the picture of modesty as Zara and Amelia heaped praises on her.

Her fantasy hit a possible stumbling block. *I just hope Zara hasn't locked this door from her side or I won't be able to get into the room to do any apprehending.*

As she quietly turned the handle a more uplifting thought struck her. *I'm so glad I went to the beautician today; somehow one feels so much more able to face life's challenges when one looks one's best. Of course, normally, the challenges are a stroppy neighbour or a flat tyre rather than a criminal mastermind who may be responsible for the disappearance of one's daughter and granddaughter.*

Cautiously she pushed against the door and was relieved to find it wasn't locked. It opened just a crack. Dee moved slowly and with intent – her Taekwondo instructor would have been proud of her.

It's so dim in Zara's room; she must have drawn the curtains.

Sliding inside the room and controlling her racing heart, she regarded the figure. Even with his back to her, she could tell it was a man.

He was not particularly tall but well built. Dee suppressed an urge to scream. *I can always do that later if needs be.*

Instead, she flicked the lights on. Startled the man span round. It was Sean.

Dee scrutinised him and had to admit he didn't look much like an arch-villain. He was nattily dressed in pressed trousers with a handkerchief artfully arranged in his blazer pocket, and instead of brandishing a gun he had an enormous bouquet of red roses in one hand and a lavish heart-shaped box of chocolates in the other.

But appearances can be deceptive and I'm not taking any chances.

In a quiet but fierce tone, a bit like a mother grizzly bear who spots someone threatening her cubs, she demanded to know, 'What have you done with Zara and Amelia?'

The element of surprise was working in Dee's favour. He stared at her.

'What?' he stammered. He had entered Zara's room expecting to find Zara, possibly clad in silk and lace, not an outraged Dee asking obscure questions.

'I said, what have you done with Zara and Amelia?'

'I don't know what you're talking about.'

'What are you doing here then?' insisted Dee, still fierce.

He looked a bit sheepish and held the roses and chocolates a shade closer. 'I came to make amends to Zara for the way I disappeared so suddenly.'

Dee looked at him shrewdly; hair combed, clothes immaculate and bearing gifts.

'It looks like you were hoping to make more than amends.' He squirmed and blushed – in an instant, he was less the mature womaniser and more the awkward teenager caught hanging around his crush's bedroom by her mother.

Dee continued, 'How did you get a key to the room?'

He gave a roguish half smile. 'The girl at the desk owed me a favour.'

Tartly Dee commented, 'Pretty big favour if she's prepared to risk getting the sack as a result.'

She took a step into the room, leaving the door ajar in case she needed to retreat. The more Sean smiled, the less she trusted him.

In her best school ma'am voice, she enquired, 'Where have you been?'

With practised quickness, he replied, 'Food poisoning.'

Dee felt uneasy, he was too self-assured for a bloke who clearly wasn't all he purported to be. She moved sideways, carefully putting an armchair between him and her. Dee registered a glint in his eye as he noted that her action was an indication of fear.

She went back on the attack. 'So bad you couldn't text?'

He glanced away. 'There was a bit more.'

'Yes?'

'I had a spot of bother.'

'Yes?'

He looked upwards for inspiration then in a gush of honesty he decided to confess.

'It's the gambling; the illegal ring.'

He saw Dee's jaw drop and registered her intake of breath in preparation for a B&B-rousing scream and hastily added, 'Nothing much – just the odd flutter. I've been, what's the phrase? *Cooperating with police enquiries.*'

Dee's concern grew. She let the phrase sink in; her mind instantly went to Hadrian Macintosh and his odd choice of associates. No, his explanation did not bring her comfort.

Sean continued, 'I rather liked all the cloak-and-dagger stuff, gave a frisson of excitement to life.'

'I suppose it makes a change from the middle-aged cliché of taking up golf,' conceded Dee. 'But when things started turning nasty and Patrick turned up dead, why didn't you come forward with what you knew about who was involved with the illegal gambling?'

He gave yet another of his roguish half-smiles. 'Well, that's just it, I really never knew much. I never attended a shady meeting or met anyone in person – it was all done over the phone with cash left at set places in plain brown envelopes.' He looked wistful. 'Shame what happened at the villa; I had a tidy sum on Zara winning.'

'So, you don't know where Zara and Amelia are?'

'Would I be standing here looking like a twerp if I did?'

He does have a point! Right, so I need to get rid of him and get on with the important mission of the moment: finding my family.

'Go!' she commanded, pointing to the door to the passage. At this, his shoulders drooped. She softened it by adding, 'I'll tell her you popped in.'

As he was nearly out the door she called, 'Leave the chocolates.'

The moment he was safely out of the room, she seized the beautiful box, ripped the red ribbon off, ran a finger over the glossy offerings, selected a swirly one and popped it into her mouth.

I need sugar after all that excitement!

She closed her eyes and allowed the sensual richness to wash over her.

Her respite only lasted for a moment, for when she opened her eyes the first thing she noticed was Zara's hire-car keys by the bedstand and it was then that the text came through.

Chapter 21

The text was from Zara and it was brief:

'HELP! The Chasms! 1'

Dee stared at the message. She reached in her pocket for her glasses and put them on. She read the message again but having it in focus didn't help.

Eh? was all that came to her befuddled mind. Her fingers felt like an uncooperative bunch of bananas as she pressed call-back. For the second it took to click into operation, Dee attempted to calm her irrational breathing and pumping heart.

Pick up! Please pick up!

But there was no reply.

What now? Think!

She looked at the text.

HELP! It was in capitals and with an exclamation point – so typical of Zara, she's always been a bit dramatic but then with a killer on the loose an exclamation mark is probably warranted. Still, it would have helped if she'd sketched in a few more details like, 'Help, I need rescuing from 'X' or you'll never guess who the baddie is, it's 'Y'. And where is Amelia? Is she with her? A 'Love Zara and Amelia xx' would have been helpful or if she was pressed for time just 'Luv Z & A xx' would do.'

She took a deep breath, then popped another chocolate into her mouth. It was a sickly-sweet strawberry and Dee revelled in the taste.

Fuel for the little grey cells, as Poirot would say. Now let's see what I have to work with. The Chasms?

She typed it into the search button on her phone.

'The Chasms are located in the southwest of the island; they are an impressive collection of fissures cut deep into the cliffs.'

There were several safety warnings about watching where you walk and loose rocks underfoot but, Dee noted, there was no caution alert to watch out for villainous characters who had abducted one's daughter and possibly one's granddaughter too.

She glanced at the end of the text.

1 - presumably one o'clock. No mention of 'am' or 'pm'. I take it that it's 'am' as creeping around in the dark is much more the style of villains than prancing around in broad daylight. What's more, even hardened criminals need to have a break at midday and something to eat.

She took the hire car keys and went back into her room to get the essentials. She pulled on her light coat and selected a muted lipstick which she expertly applied in the mirror.

I was right! It wasn't all over with Reggie's death! There is someone else behind all these evil goings on. But now is not the time to say, 'I told you so!' That can wait till I've rescued Zara and Amelia.

Who can it be? Who murdered Patrick? Who is behind the gambling and the drugs? There are so many suspects. Take Sean for instance; was he really waiting for Zara or was he looking for something? If so, what? And then there was that unpleasant man with the shaved head, broken nose and no manners at all, and finally, Jill and her boyfriend seem suspicious.

She sighed and regarded herself in the mirror: neat pixie bob with auburn high lights, in place, no need to comb it, lipstick perfect, eyelashes tinted so no risk of unsightly mascara smudges and just a hint of blush. She was more than happy that she looked presentable for facing her foe. Being groomed always gave Dee confidence. That coupled with having a black belt in Taekwondo but ...

I am a pensioner – a very fit and healthy one but nonetheless I am, as the French would say 'une femme d'un certain age', coupled with being barely being five feet tall, sparrow-weight, alone and in a strange place.

She thought for a moment.

What do I need? Another chocolate? No, what I need is a

team. But who?

She mentally ran through who she knew on the island. First up was Betty and Joe. An awful thought struck her.

Zara and Amelia were going to see both Betty and Joe and I couldn't reach them on their phones. Could whoever has got Zara and Amelia also have Betty and Joe?

They would both make excellent team members: Joe is swift of foot and brimming over with compassionate public spirit and Betty, whilst rather annoying, is very reliable and practical. But as I can't get hold of them and don't know if they have also been abducted, they are out.

Now who else?

Daniel? Well, he does have the physique for villain catching and he didn't seem to know Reggie but ... is it just a coincidence he is always around when there's trouble? Chough Drive, the villa, the Sloc?

Something Dee couldn't even admit to herself but that subconsciously played into her decision not to call Daniel was that he had a tendency to take over and when it came to rescuing her daughter and granddaughter Dee wasn't prepared to yield leadership. She continued thinking.

Of course, you could say I was at all those places too. Still, who else can I call upon?

Nicholas and Josh.

Her heart lit up as she thought of them; Nicholas so calm and capable, Josh strong and dependable. But almost as soon as they came to mind, she knew she wouldn't, couldn't contact them.

They would be honour-bound to go straight to the local police and that means Hadrian Macintosh, who has to be suspect number one.

She sighed again. A wave of helplessness washed over her.

I don't think I've ever felt so alone!

She took a deep breath to steady herself. She stood at the mirror, looked herself firmly in the eye and said out loud, 'Dee FitzMorris, pull yourself together! Your daughter and granddaughter need you!'

And with that, she picked up the car keys and strode purposefully out of the door heading to the Chasms and all that awaited her there.

Chapter 22

Previously in the evening, Zara and Amelia had returned to the B&B and were soon ready for their errand of mercy; they were going to bring comfort to Betty and Joe, whether they wanted it or not. They decided to walk from their B&B to Betty and Joe's neighbourhood. As they walked, they mulled over their respective days.

An hour or so earlier when Zara had returned from tern-watching, she was flushed and animated. Amelia suspected it wasn't from seeing birds.

Zara ran her hands through her saffron hair. 'It's beautiful up there. The terns are so graceful – I could have observed them for hours. And the weather couldn't have been better; sunny but not too hot.' This was what Zara said to Amelia, but all the while she was thinking of Nicholas.

Once, when she'd been totally absorbed in observing the terns swoop and dive with finesse against a blue sky, she had glanced across to find that he was looking at her with much the same admiration she had bestowed on the birds. Even the thought of that look made her glow.

Then there was the time that they had been walking side by side along the beach with smooth pebbles crunching beneath their feet, the waves rolling in, the breeze on their faces, and the back of his hand had brushed against the back of hers. So in sync were their steps that they continued for fifty yards in this public intimacy, the sensitive skin on the backs of their hands brushing, caressing with each stride.

Butterfly kisses, thought Zara.

From behind the safety of her sunglasses, she had surreptitiously glanced over at him but his well-defined profile gave no hint as to whether he was as alive to the frisson of their touch as she was. She could but wonder if he too felt a tingle down his spine and an electric charge ignite his skin.

All, the while, Myrtle chatted happily on, walking a pace or two in front of them. 'Good thing we found your father a nice place to sit. He'll be happy for the rest of the day with his binoculars and notebook. As long as he remembers to keep his sunhat on he'll be fine. I must say it's a joy to stretch my legs. With your father hurting his ankle, I haven't got in nearly as much walking as I'd hoped.'

Zara let her words be carried out to sea and simply revelled in the moment. Now she smiled, reliving the memory.

It was just like something out of a film, complete with a scenic red-and-white lighthouse. Of course, if it had been a film, we wouldn't have had his purple-clad mother giving us a constant, chirpy commentary. Nicholas would have swept me up into his arms at the foot of that romantic lighthouse and gazed passionately into my eyes before kissing me. His kiss would have been gentle at first and then with fervour.

She allowed herself a few moments to imagine what that kiss would have felt like and the sensation of him caressing her face with gentle fingers while they kissed.

'Are you sure it's the terns that are making you smile like that?' asked Amelia in a tone that reminded Zara of her own mother and Amelia's grandmother, Dee.

Hastily Zara deflected, 'How did you get on with Josh?'

Amelia shrugged, 'Oh, it was alright, you know.'

Zara did know more than her daughter guessed.

Amelia had untied her hair and was letting a cascade of fiery curls run down her back like a river of molten lava.

She wasn't ready yet to share just how much she'd enjoyed Josh's relaxed easy company. They'd chatted all day but Amelia couldn't recall exactly what they'd talked about. She did remember that they had laughed a lot, over what she was unsure. The electric railway had rattled its way uphill, giving them glimpses of the sea and then the steep climb up Snaefell had been rewarded by the panoramic views of heather-clad Manx hills, endless sea and sky, punctuated by distant blue hills at different points of the compass.

'And did Josh enjoy it?' asked Zara.

Amelia shrugged again. 'Guess so,' she said carelessly, while part of her hoped that he had loved every moment as much as she had.

'Are we nearly there?' Amelia asked and then unnecessarily added, 'This street is on a seriously steep hill.'

Zara paused in her walking and checked the app on her phone which was guiding them to their destination. Now they were almost there, she was having doubts as to whether this philanthropic trip was such a good idea. She would much rather be having a drink with Nicholas, perhaps a local gin over ice. Besides which, she suddenly had misgivings over how their solicitude would be taken. What if Betty just thought they were being nosy or if Joe wanted peace to meditate his trauma away?

'Yes, we are virtually there. Good thing they both live in the same square.' Zara spoke with more confidence than she felt. Between heavy breaths, she glanced over at her daughter. 'How come you haven't got your phone out? Normally you'd be checking I'm taking the right direction.'

'I decided to embrace the whole *at one with nature vibe*, so I'm going tech-free – no phone, at least for the odd hour or so.'

'You sound just like your Granny – she's forever sipping dandelion tea and talking about cleansing and having a tech detox.'

Amelia laughed. 'Granny doesn't do it mindfully.'

'What are you talking about? She's forever telling me she can't be contacted by text because she's on a tech detox.'

'That's just what she tells you when she's lost her phone and she doesn't want you to nag.'

They crested the hill.

'This is it.' Zara declared, looking around an impressive Victorian square with an iron-railed garden at its centre, flanked on all sides by classic townhouses. 'Let me just check what their respective numbers are and we'll take the nearest first.'

As it turned out, Joe's home was the closest. A few minutes

later they were outside a neat blue door with a brass knocker. The path was swept but, unlike the other small front gardens, there were no welcoming flowers. No happy pansies or bright red geraniums, just concrete.

Amelia sniffed. 'You don't need to be a bloodhound to follow the scent trail Betty Hobbs leaves behind, do you? She's obviously been here recently.'

'Shush, someone might hear.'

Zara knocked but Amelia hadn't finished.

'Well, like I've said before, I think it's odd the way that Betty uses roses to cover up her guilt that she smokes. I'd love to know what else she's covering up. What's more, it's just plain weird the way she trails around after Joe – he must be younger than her son.'

'Be quiet! We're meant to be bringing comfort not condemnation and I'm sure that if you are doing a psychological analysis of someone, you're not meant to use terms like *odd* and *weird*.'

Zara knocked again, a bit more loudly, but still no one came. 'What now?' she wondered.

'The door isn't totally shut. Look, there's a crack so he must be in,' commented Amelia, pointing at the fine black line of a gap between the door and its jam.

'So?' enquired Zara.

'Don't you think we ought to check he's alright? Gran said he was in a dreadful state – full of guilt and remorse for having inadvertently killed Reggie.'

'I still don't quite follow?' Zara crinkled her brow as she looked at her daughter.

'In that sort of a mindset he might easily decide to take his own life,' said Amelia earnestly.

'Surely not!' said Zara, aghast.

Amelia shrugged. 'It's not unheard of.' She thought for a moment before adding. 'And there's another possibility.'

'What?'

'Well, if Granny is right, and if Reggie was only a cat's paw in the hands of an arch-villain, then Joe, with all his public-spirited ardour to do the right thing, could easily have got up the villain's nose.'

'Darling, you're not making much sense.'

'Joe could be lying in there on his kitchen floor with a handy pair of sharpened sheep shears in his chest.'

Zara shuddered. 'You have such a lurid imagination. You take after your grandmother. But I get your point, we should go inside and check all is well.'

Tentatively she pushed the door open. It creaked.

'Hello?' she called. 'Joe? Are you there? It's Zara.'

Amelia showed none of her mother's reticence. Boldly she strode into the bare, white hallway. 'The lights are all on so he must have been here recently. Perhaps he just popped out to get a pint of milk and forgot to shut the door properly.'

Zara followed Amelia into the house and with her professional estate agent hat on, gazed around. 'Shame they ripped out the original features; these Victorian houses usually have wonderful plasterwork and tiles. Let's go into the sitting room – I wonder if they've kept the fireplace? Buyers do love an authentic fireplace.'

'Mother! Will you focus? We're meant to be checking Joe hasn't topped himself, not scoping the place for one of your estate agent deals.'

'Sorry, occupational hazard.'

Zara led the way into a side room and scanned it. 'Oh shame!'

'What? Is it Joe?' asked Amelia, pressing in from behind.

'No! It's just they have ripped out the fireplace! I must say he keeps it all very neat and tidy. A bit too clinically white and sterile for my taste but still not the typical bachelor pad.'

Amelia glanced around the sleek white lines, with not a photo or an ornament to bring warmth to the room. She shuddered. 'Bit repressed!'

'Oh! For goodness sake, darling, give your armchair analysis a bit of a rest. You're a second-year psychology student, not Sigmund Freud.'

'This is odd,' said Amelia looking at a piece of paper on the coffee table. It was the only sign of habitation in the room.

'What's odd?' asked Zara coming over to look.

Next to a surgically-opened envelope, on cheap writing paper was a note that read, 'The Chasms – 1 am.' The only other information on the note was the next day's date.

Zara peered over Amelia's shoulder at the note.

'Yes! I see what you mean – people just don't learn how to write proper letters these days. I blame the schools, them and all the texting people do. There's no sender's address, no *Dear Joe*, and where's the *Yours sincerely* or *faithfully*? There isn't even a *Love from*.'

'Not that!' said Amelia, with a touch of asperity in her voice. '*That*!' she said pointing at the gun lying on the table beside the note.

'Umm!' said Zara. 'Could it be one of those novelty lighters in the shape of a pistol? Or a starter's gun for school sports days? Joe probably coaches the track team – you know, giving the youth of today something to do other than drugs.'

'It looks pretty real to me,' said Amelia dryly.

'That's because it is real,' came a cold, quiet, voice from behind them.

The other thing that was very real was a frighteningly calm Joe. Those pale eyes of his were glacial.

Before either Zara or Amelia had time to gather their wits, he had stepped into the room and closed the door. He placed the pint of milk he had in his hand down on the table and picked up the gun.

Pointing it at them, in a steady voice he said, 'This is unfortunate.'

Zara's heart was walloping in her chest and her thoughts were running amok. *Unfortunate? It's a bit more than unfortunate! Why, oh why did I drag Amelia into my misguided attempt to be a Good Samaritan? If I can just manoeuvre myself between that gun and my only child, then at least I can act as a human shield.*

Amelia's emotional response was more robust. She dodged her mother's protective gesture. Her only thought was: *This may be my only chance to observe a homicidal maniac in action. Now, do I think he's a sociopath or a psychopath? I'm sure he's one or the other; he clearly doesn't have much sense of right or wrong. Nor does he share others' feelings, otherwise he wouldn't be waving that gun around while poor Mummy is quaking.*

'Like I said, this is unfortunate, but it's not the end of the world.' He gave them both a grim smile. 'At least it isn't the end for me. I always intended tonight's drug drop to be my last big hit, then I will have more than enough money to live out my days in sunny climes.'

Amelia was still in psychology mode. *OK! So perhaps he isn't either a sociopath or a psychopath. Perhaps he's just plain greedy. How disappointing.*

Calmly Joe continued, 'If either of you makes a sound, the other is dead. You'll have to come with me.'

'What? Why?' faltered Zara, who was still trying to put herself between the danger and Amelia.

With the gun fixed on them, he replied, 'A town is no place to get rid of one body, let alone two, but the Chasms are ideal, with all those deep fissures between the rocks with their fatal drop down to the sea. Live bodies are so much easier to move than dead ones.'

'Hence the expression, *deadweight*,' said Zara absently. She couldn't help thinking of how heavy Amelia had been as a sleeping child. She brushed away a tear.

Rallying slightly Zara hoped to delay him by asking, 'So you are a drug dealer?'

He stood up a little more erect. 'I prefer the term *Drug Lord.*'

Pompous git, thought both Zara and Amelia.

Imperiously he continued, 'And don't sell me short – let's not forget the gambling.'

In what Zara thought was an unwisely mocking tone her daughter added, 'And then there's also *murderer*. Patrick?'

Fortunately, Joe missed the irony and simply replied, 'That was the only thing I hadn't planned. Stupid really – all chance. We met on Marine Drive by accident, I was out running, training for a fell competition while he was preparing for the Parish Walk. The idiot dared to tell me he was going to the police to inform them what he knew about me and my criminal activities. He wanted to give me the chance to do the honourable thing and turn myself in.'

His voice rang with derision.

Zara used Joe's self-absorption in his narrative as an opportunity to look at Amelia. She had been intending to administer a glare that clearly stated, 'Will you kindly shut up before your sarcasm gets us both killed?' but she swiftly changed her mind. A glance at her daughter, along with the touch of her hand, revealed that her resourceful child was taking advantage of her mother shielding her from Joe to reach for the phone in Zara's hand.

To give Amelia more time she hastily asked, 'And the sheep sheers?'

He laughed. 'That's a funny thing! When we met, I asked him why he was walking with a pair of antique sheep shears in his hand. He said he'd spotted them on the ground near the Douglas bus stop and had recognised them as belonging to the Pringles so he'd picked them up. He was planning on dropping them back.'

'They must have fallen out of Benedict's bag when he was getting on the bus,' commented Zara.

'What?' snarled Joe, clearly annoyed by the irrelevant interruption in his preferred topic: himself.

'Oh, nothing! But how did they end up in Patrick?'

Her mother had always told Zara not to ask personal questions but she did feel that under the circumstances a bit of curiosity was excusable. Judging by how Joe's face lit up, she judged he was pleased to be asked.

I do believe he's proud of himself.

'So, after we had got the small talk about the shears out of the way, Patrick brought up the police,' he chortled. 'I was explaining to him the inadvisability of him going to report me and we struggled, then they ended up in him, rather than me.'

He gave a laugh of satisfaction; it was a mirthless, hollow sound. He glanced around the room, checking he had everything he needed.

'Now, the drone is in the car ready for the drop so I just need to get you ladies in the boot. And we can be off. Move!'

'Someone will see us!' declared Zara desperately.

'I doubt that, since the car is in the garage, far away from prying eyes. It's one of the reasons I bought this house. I do think privacy is so important.'

Zara nodded. 'Garage parking is always a good selling point. But back to that note; are you telling me that you run a drugs deal all via Royal Mail?'

He nodded. 'Good old Royal Mail – no digital trail, so it's far safer. I arrange where and when the boat is to bring in the drugs by letter then I simply pick them off the boat with my trusty drone. I like to think of it as the perfect blending of the old and the new for maximum efficiency. Now move!'

Zara felt they were safer in a populated street than alone with a crazed killer, not to mention wanting to give Amelia as much time as possible to utilise the phone, so as a delaying tactic she blurted out, 'And Reggie?'

He shrugged. 'He was useful for a while – keen to please.'

His callous response made Zara feel sick but she pressed on, 'But why? You have a position here – you're a respected pillar of this community.'

He laughed. It was a full, heartfelt laugh that reverberated around the room and Zara had to fight against her body and mind freezing with fear.

'Money, of course. Now move!'

Zara persisted, wanting to give Amelia as much time as possible with the phone. 'But what about all that stuff about your father being your inspiration? That it was thanks to him that you wanted to spend your life helping others?'

His deathly eyes narrowed and his thin lips twisted into a half-smile.

'That twerp? Yes, he was my inspiration, my driving force, but not in the way you think. He was a lowlife loser. It was only Betty Hobbs, with her deluded sense of reality, who thought he was some sort of a hero. Inadequate, weak and penniless, that was my old man and I vowed never to be anything like him.'

Amelia said, 'It must have been hard growing up with a father like that.'

He sneered. 'I hardly saw him but I had to live with the ridicule and poverty every day. Now be quiet both of you – oh, and while I think of it, turn out your pockets.'

They obliged: the phone, a comb and a packet of tissues were all dropped on the ground.

As they walked towards the garage, Zara finally fully understood the phrase *lambs to the slaughter*.

With the gun waving at them, they climbed into the boot of his car. He slammed it shut and they roared off.

In the cramped darkness, Amelia tapped Zara's hand and whispered, 'Don't worry, Mum! I've texted Granny!'

Chapter 23

Dee, like her daughter and granddaughter, was soon in a car, hurtling south towards the Chasms.

She was saying her affirmations in a firm voice that carried over the directions of the GPS. She had settled for repeating, 'I am calm and confident' as the nearest affirmation she could recall that fit the bill. Her usual one of, 'Today I will choose happiness' was singularly inappropriate and she didn't think she'd ever come across an affirmation that proudly declared, 'Today, I will defeat a master criminal'.

It wasn't exactly dusk but that strange half-light of the far north where you can see but it's as if you're in a dream. Following the sat nav's instructions, she turned left by some thatched cottages and wound up the steep hill. Reaching the top, she found that the road stopped abruptly at a gate and that she was not alone.

Two figures were bent over the open boot of their car. At the sound of Dee's arrival, they swung around to face her. Startled and seized by incredulity they gawped at her.

She was not surprised to see that it was Hadrian Macintosh and his rude skinhead buddy. She was a little taken aback to see that they were both putting on flak jackets with 'POLICE' emblazoned on the front but she reasoned, *If Hadrian Macintosh has such faulty moral fibre that he's become a bent copper, then he probably wouldn't think twice about misappropriating police property for his own use and that of his chums.*

The thought of her innocent and much-loved daughter and granddaughter spurred Dee into action. Filled with maternal rage, she leapt from the car and marched up to them; fury in her jade-green eyes and her hand on her hips.

Blinking in amazement and in hushed tones Hadrian hissed,

'What are you doing here?'

Dee ignored his question and demanded, 'What have you done with Zara and Amelia?'

'What?' he faltered.

As Hadrian was spluttering Dee scrutinised the scene. She had obviously interrupted them as they were kitting themselves out with both bulletproof vests and firearms. While they'd been fiddling with their flak jackets they had, in what Dee could only think was a rather careless manner, put their weapons down in the boot of the car. Dee was sure there must be police protocol about getting one's flak jacket neatly fastened before one unlocks one's firearm but now was not the time to enquire.

Instinctively, she seized both heavy black Glock pistols. She hoped they were loaded.

The unpleasant skinhead smirked and it was then she remembered watching one of those interesting documentaries on the Discovery Channel, or was it BBC 2? Anyway, it followed the armed police unit in Manchester – or was it Leeds?

She slipped one pistol into her belt and using her free hand she slid it over the top of the gun and pulled back the mechanism; it made a satisfying cocking sound.

Just like on the telly! she thought.

The look of total terror on both men's faces suggested she had done it right. Dee felt relieved and smiled.

'Now! Where are Zara and Amelia?'

'Ms FitzMorris, put the pistols on the ground and for goodness sake keep your voice down,' whispered Hadrian, perspiration visible on his forehead and his voice less self-assured than earlier.

Dee did think it was a little odd that he wanted to conduct their conversation in hushed conspiratorial tones, but she didn't dwell on the point.

'Put the gun down,' repeated Hadrian then added, 'please.'

'Not likely! As if I'd do anything a bent copper asked me. You ought to be ashamed of yourself. You are a disgrace to your profession and what about your poor mother?'

'My mother?' he mouthed, his eyes wide in bafflement.

'Yes! Betty Hobbs says she's a lovely lady – have you thought what the disgrace will do to her?'

She swung her attention and the pistol towards the skinhead. 'And you can stop sidling around – I wasn't born yesterday. What's more, I've watched a lot of police dramas and I'm hardly going to let you form a pincer manoeuvre so you can rush me from the side.' She clicked the safety catch off. 'That's right, move back to Hadrian's side.'

'You're making a big mistake, Ms FitzMorris.' Hadrian's moustache twitched as he wrestled with how much to tell her. 'We've had a tip-off that a big drug deal is going down tonight at the Chasms.' Seeing the dubious way Dee was eyeing the skinhead he continued, 'Bob, here, is an undercover officer.'

'Tip off? Undercover officer? You expect me to believe that? Now both of you climb into the boot of the car.'

'We better do it. She's just potty enough to shoot us,' hissed the man with the broken nose; his shaved head glistened with fear-induced sweat.

Hadrian nodded and they climbed into the boot.

'Mind your fingers!' warned Dee before clicking it shut.

While she rather liked pretending to be John Wayne with a gun in each hand, they were both heavy and cumbersome. With Hadrian and his buddy secure, she decided it was safe to put one gun down.

After a moment of consideration, she slid it out of sight behind the front wheel of the car.

After all, guns are dangerous and I'd hate a child to find it – someone might get hurt!

That done, she turned her attention back to Zara and Amelia.

Where could they be? Hadrian mentioned the Chasms. That footpath sign by the gate points to the Chasms. Thank goodness I'm wearing comfortable shoes. Hang in there, Zara and Amelia, I'm on my way!

She climbed over the style by the gate and began to scramble down the steep path to the Chasms. There were some make-shift steps on the worse bits. The trail wound between clumps of heather, bracken and gorse, their earthy scent blending with the sea air. A couple of shaggy hill sheep stared at her as she stumbled past. Their soft bleats mingled with the hoot of an owl and the ever-present sound of the sea.

In the dim light, she could just make out where the land abruptly ended and the black cold sea began. At the bottom of the hill that Dee was stumbling down, there was a flat area of grass. On this plateau, between land, cliff drop and sea, she could see a car and a small concrete building. From the guidebook, she knew that just in front of this hut was a small safety wall with a gate that led to the famous and perilous Chasms. The guidebook had warned that in the yards of ground that led to the dangerous cliff edge, there were flat slippery rocks with hazardous cracks that yawned open ready to plunge the unwary straight down into the unforgiving sea, far below.

She paused. *Am I imagining it? What is that buzzing sound? Can that be a drone?*

She hurried past the car, unaware that Zara and Amelia were locked inside the boot.

It was as she drew level with the hut, that she was grabbed. Without warning, she felt two enormous muscular arms encircle her and a gargantuan hand clamp over her mouth. In her surprise, she dropped the gun. Lifting her bodily off the ground, her assailant transported her through an open door and into the hut. Years of Taekwondo training had taught her not to waste her energy in mindless struggling. She needed to assess the situation and her enemy.

The hut was dark and to begin with she could see nothing but a slight shadowy figure. As her eyes grew accustomed to the lack of light, she recognised who it was.

It's Sean's secretary, Jill – and a very angry, irritated Jill to judge by her expression! So she's involved in this! In her mind Dee brushed over the fact that she wasn't quite clear what 'this' was; all she knew was that it was no good, and someone who was no good had her family.

'What in the name of all the saints is she doing here?' Jill whispered.

The bloke – whom, Dee, had guessed by association, must be Jill's burly boyfriend – still had Dee's feet floating a good few inches above the ground. She could feel, against her back he had something hard strapped to his chest. In the poor light, Dee could just make out that Jill was wearing a black bulletproof vest.

You don't think of villains taking safety precautions, mused Dee, *but then why not?*

In a deep soft under-breath the man replied, 'No idea why she's here but as she is, what do we do with her? Shall I hand her over to the backup team?'

My goodness! They have a backup team? Is the whole island overflowing with criminals?

Jill glanced at her luminous watch. 'No time. The drop will take place in a few minutes.' She ran an agitated hand through her hair, then took a step closer to Dee. With her face inches away, she hissed, 'If my colleague puts you down and removes his hand from your mouth, you mustn't make any sound – do you understand?'

Dee nodded.

When her feet were firmly on the ground and she was free to speak, she looked Jill fiercely in the eye, 'What have you done with Zara and Amelia?'

'Keep your voice down – and what are you talking about?' hissed Jill.

'Boss, we really don't have time for this!'

Jill nodded. 'We need to trust you to stay here. You'll be safe if you remain inside this building.'

She looked up at the bloke. 'Unlock the firearms case.'

Firearms? They are definitely not about to do a little fell running training! I'll be safe if I stay here? I don't think so!

Both Jill and the bulky bloke, turned their backs to Dee as they bent over a metal case. Silently Dee tiptoed outside. As she passed the open door, she noticed a large padlock dangling on the latch.

Better safe than sorry! she said to herself as she shut the door and clicked the padlock.

Ignoring the muffled whispers of, 'Ms FitzMorris, you're

making a terrible mistake! Let us out! We're undercover Garda officers working in conjunction with the Isle of Blom police.'

The chance of them being Irish Garda police officers is even less likely than them being at the Sloc for a bit of fell running! thought Dee as she headed with stealth through the narrow gate marked 'The Chasms – enter at your own risk'.

The terrain underfoot changed immediately the moment she was through the gate; springy turf gave way to grey stone marked out by black fissures of nothingness with the sound of the merciless sea below.

There was that buzzing noise again and Dee scanned the horizon for the source. The outline of a man caught her attention. She surveyed the figure standing near the cliff edge.

Surely not? It can't be! But who else has such an elongated lanky figure? It must be Joe!

Her first instinct was relief. *Thank goodness, a friendly face. He really is a knight errant always there to help whether at the villa or the Sloc!* Then reality hit. She swallowed. *Oh, dear! Joe must be the master criminal behind all these crimes! Betty will be disappointed!*

He was silhouetted against the skyline. A drone buzzed and Dee guessed he was operating it. She peered over the cliff edge and saw a small fishing boat bobbing in the sea below.

Goodness! Hadrian was right! There is a drug drop going on! And how clever to use a drone to get the stuff off the boat and onto the island! But more to the point, he must have Zara and Amelia. But where? I wish I had an ally – someone to help.

It was then that another thought struck her. *Could Hadrian have been telling the truth about both him and that ill-mannered man with a shaved head being here as police officers to foil the drug drop? And if they were telling the truth then Jill and her companion are also probably undercover.*

She swallowed again.

Perhaps I was a little hasty locking them all up. I'll just tiptoe back and release them – all of them. And they can deal with Joe and they can find Zara and Amelia. After all, it is their job.

She took a step backwards. Unfortunately, her foot slipped and she gave an involuntary little gasp. It wasn't much of a noise, but it was enough for Joe to hear.

He swung around.

As Dee caught the glint in his icy eyes, she knew she was in trouble.

In the time it took for him to land the drone and put down the controls, Dee had sprung to her feet.

What now? The man's a trained runner – if I flee, he will easily catch me and if he seizes me from behind, I'll be at a disadvantage. I haven't a hope of freeing Jill before he gets me. My only option is to face him.

'Well, well, if it isn't Dee FitzMorris!' His speech and strides were languid as he walked towards her. He had a gun in his hand. 'It looks like I've scored the hat-trick and I'm going to have the pleasure of getting rid of all three FitzMorris ladies in one night.'

He chuckled; the idea obviously appealed to him. Dee took a deep breath of calming salty air.

'Where are Zara and Amelia?' she asked, pleased that her voice didn't quiver.

'In the boot of my car; you must have passed them on your way here.'

Dee thought of the car by the hut. *I must have been within a foot of them and I went right past. If only I'd known, I could have freed them and avoided all this trouble with a gun-toting maths teacher. I never did like maths.*

'But don't worry, they won't be there for long.'

'They won't?'

'No! As soon as I've dealt with you, I'm going to roll the car, with them in it, over the edge of the cliff and into the sea. Now, Dee, if you'll oblige me by walking towards the cliff.'

At his casual reference to the demise of her loved ones at his hand, Dee felt her head jut up and her hands tighten into fists. Anger swiftly changed to determination. Her gaze became focused and she set her jaw.

She assessed his suggestion and quickly decided that doing

as he said would put her in a better position where she was had a slight slope. She reckoned that the flatter rock on either side of the nearest fissure would serve her better.

She took a few steps in the direction Joe wanted. The closer she walked towards the precipice the wider the crack in the rock grew. She risked a glance down – sheer rock sliced down to black nothingness. She could hear the sound of the waves several feet below. A cold sweat washed over her. She swallowed and took a deep breath.

Dee was on one side of the gaping hole and Joe was on the other. There were multiple cracks surrounding them and Dee registered that she needed to step with care. It would be all too easy to take a single tread into the void and, like Reggie, plummet to one's death.

When the fissure was about two feet wide, she stopped.

'Keep going!' commanded Joe.

Dee, with shoulders back and head erect, turned to face him. She took her stance, her arms by her side bowed. She did feel it was so important to show respect; respect for herself and her opponent. As she stood erect, she raised her fists in preparation and centred her frame.

'You have to be kidding me,' was all Joe managed to say before Dee executed a neat front flick kick.

With the ball of her foot, she knocked the gun out of his hand and resumed her initial stance before he had a chance to draw a breath. He staggered backwards from shock and narrowly missed a fissure behind him.

Dee was totally focused; there was nothing in her mind other than the calm intent to channel her energy in the best possible way.

It's not much different from a training block in the studio. Won't my lovely instructor be thrilled when I tell her?

Joe, on the other hand, was consumed with rage. He swore as he staggered to his feet, clenching his fists, his head held low and with a vein visibly pulsating on his porcelain temple.

'You bitch!' he spat as he lunged towards her.

With precision, Dee executed a half-turn over the chasm,

administering a side-kick to his chest in passing before she retook her composed stance. The blow had winded him and for a moment he just glowered at her, sweat trickling down his forehead and into his demonic eyes. Dee breathed steadily and preserved the peace in her mind and body.

He threw a punch at her. His long arm gave him the advantage of an impressive reach but Dee blocked it with her right arm then she spun and dealt him such a forceful blow to his back that he was sent sprawling to the ground with his front half hanging perilously over the fissure's edge. His eyes widened in terror and, snake-like, he squirmed backwards, away from the treacherous fracture.

Both of them spotted the gun at the same time. When Dee had kicked it out of his hands it had landed a foot or so away from where Joe now was, lying wedged against a lichen-covered boulder.

Dee leapt, intent on kicking it out of reach but Joe was quicker.

He grabbed it and with a twisted smile panted, 'Not so fast, Dee FitzMorris.'

So, this is it! thought Dee, feeling the dull empty ache of despair for the first time since she had faced him.

'Not so fast yourself, Joe Smith-Jones,' rang out a high-pitched, familiar voice. There was a waft of roses, a flash of pink and Betty Hobbs appeared, Glock pistol in hand and determination set on her pink lipsticked mouth.

Joe sneered. 'Like you've got the guts to shoot me!'

'Don't be so sure!' said Betty, squaring her high-heeled feet and raising the pistol with both hands. Her body position was worthy of a skilled New York cop.

A shot run out. Joe stared at her in disbelief and dropped his gun. He lifted his hands to his left ear where blood was spurting out. He staggered backwards into the abyss as the fissure swallowed him up.

There was a moment when the only sound was the waves beating against the rocks a long way below.

Betty dropped the gun and breathlessly looked at Dee. 'Are you alright?'

'Yes, but—'

'But what?'

Dee was looking at her right hand.

'Are you hurt?' Betty's voice rang with concern.

'No, but I've chipped a nail and I've only just had them done.'

'Typical!' said Betty sympathetically.

Chapter 24

It was a couple of days later that Hadrian invited everyone to a celebration barbecue. The venue was a delightful traditional fisherman's cottage right on the beach in Port Erin. The scene was picture-perfect, with the sea embraced by a bay protected by benign cliffs. The sea lapped lazily, seagulls circled and the group relaxed.

The food sizzling on the outdoor barbecue smelt heavenly. It turned out that Hadrian was a bit of a gourmet and he had ordered a perfect summer menu that was both fresh and sumptuous. They had started the evening clinking glasses with his home-brewed elderflower and berry champagne; pink and delicately scented, it was both highly drinkable and equally alcoholic.

The first course was a chilled seafood salad with squid, shrimp, mussels and a fish Dee couldn't identify, all in a light dressing of olive oil, lemon and parsley. The star of the show was the local lobster grilled and dressed with butter steeped with lemon thyme, chives, garlic and chilli served with a salad of courgette ribbons, lemon and mint with a sprinkling of borage flowers as blue as the sky and sea. As they picked at a sweet pudding of almond cake and fresh peaches, they watched the sun slowly descend in a crimson blaze into the westward ocean beyond.

They were an unlikely group of collaborators. There was Dee, who was sitting with Daniel, his arm over her shoulder. Zara and Amelia were looking as radiant as ever, despite their recent ordeal. Sean was absent – he claimed he had an important meeting but Zara suspected he didn't want to attend any event where he wasn't the centre of attention. Nicholas and Josh, although slightly nettled that no one had contacted them on that fateful evening, were joining in with good grace. Jill, whose real name was

Gillian, looked totally different now she had dropped the façade of the dippy blonde. Her hair was pulled back in an artfully messy bun and she had nailed the casual chic look with well-fitting jeans, good shoes and a silk blouse.

Another person whose looks had been transformed was 'the skinhead' or 'Please call me Bob' as he was telling everyone. Dee regarded him and thought, *He's actually quite nice to look at now he's not scowling all the time and he's wearing respectable clothes. And I'm pleased to say that in real life – I mean when he's not pretending to be a drug-crazed villain – he has excellent manners.*

Betty was taking centre stage as the heroine of the hour.

'Well, Hadrian, I'm so glad you think Juliet will be put on probation rather than prison. I can't help thinking that the whole prison thing wouldn't be good for the baby. And speaking of the baby, I'm having such fun knitting tiny sweaters with matching ones for the two Pringle grandfathers – I've done them in pink and blue stripes. Daniel, you're not to tell your cousins; I want it to be a lovely surprise for them.'

Daniel raised an eyebrow and diplomatically said, 'It will certainly be a surprise.'

Dee couldn't resist asking, 'But Betty, back to the other evening, if you really aren't an undercover police person, how on earth did you know that Joe was a villain and that he was headed to the Chasms?'

'Well, that night I couldn't relax. I was all fidgety – it must have been all the upset the night before with poor Reggie – so I decided to have a little walk around the square. I saw Zara and Amelia go into Joe's house and then Joe went in with his shopping. I fancied some company so I decided to join them. The door was open and I went straight in, I was about to call out when I heard Joe talking about being a drugs lord – which I thought was odd and so out of character – so naturally I hid in the kitchen. When I peaked out and saw him marching them to the garage at gunpoint, I obviously nipped home for my car and followed.'

'But why didn't you call the police?' asked Hadrian. His walrus moustache looked none the worse for being squashed into the boot of the car; if anything, he had waxed the ends with an extra flourish, perhaps in honour of the occasion.

Betty smiled apologetically at him. 'Yes, well, as you can imagine my Ron is a wee bit vexed at me over that. It was just that I had spent so long building Joe up in my mind to be a saint, that I thought I must be mistaken. I really believed there must be some simple explanation. I didn't want to look a fool in front of all of my Ron's colleagues.'

It was Zara's turn to ask a question. 'If Joe killed Patrick, why did Patrick's body smell of your signature rose scent?'

Betty laughed. 'Did it? You couldn't have thought I might have been a murderer.'

There was an uneasy silence but fortunately, Betty was too wrapped up in herself to notice.

'I'd popped in to see Joe just as he was leaving for his training run and I had a bit of a butter-fingers moment. I spilt my emergency handbag perfume all over him.'

Dee then enquired, 'If you really aren't yet another undercover police person, how come you are so good with a pistol?'

'Oh, shooting is a little hobby of mine but as you know my true passion is knitting.'

As the evening progressed, the group broke down into intimate small conversational groups and Daniel seized his chance.

He squeezed Dee a little closer to him and whispered in her ear, 'Dee, my love, won't you please reconsider? Do you have to leave tomorrow? We could have such a wonderful life together.'

Dee looked into those beautiful eyes of his – they were alive with love for her and she wondered if she was making a terrible mistake. She patted his hand. 'You will always be very special to me, but I can't leave Zara and Amelia – they need me.'

He looked so crestfallen and forlorn that she nearly changed her mind but then a thought struck her. 'Daniel, I need to ask you a question.'

He nodded.

'And this time I want a straight answer, none of your dissembling!'

He nodded again.

'I've been puzzled about where you get your money from. You definitely have a lot more than you could possibly earn as an artist and part-time teacher. I even suspected you might be behind all the drugs and gambling.'

His face showed how horrified he was. He spluttered, 'Dee, you couldn't have!'

Dee nodded. 'Well, you were always so cagey whenever I asked you anything about your income.'

He blushed. 'Actually, I do have a bit of a confession to make.'

Dee nodded encouragingly, Daniel took a breath. 'I am Lavinia Loveday, the author.'

After a moment of surprise, while she digested the information, Dee laughed. 'That explains a lot – the flowers, the romantic gestures … I should have guessed!'

'Does this change anything for you? Will you stay?' he implored.

Dee shook her head. 'I miss my little cottage and my garden. I don't know that I could ever leave my garden. And the village, Little Warthing, is wonderful, it's so beautiful – the quintessential English village. The people are kind and quite frankly, I can't wait to get back to the peace and quiet after all the upset here.'

Daniel sadly admitted, 'I do understand.'

As Dee wistfully thought of her home, it was probably just as well that she was unaware that just a few streets over from her pretty cottage someone was sitting at their kitchen table and writing a list, in pencil, on the back of an envelope.

It wasn't a shopping list, there was no: *pint of milk, two lettuces and an onion* on it. Instead, it was headed: PEOPLE I NEED TO KILL.

The title was double-underlined and there was just one name on the list:

Dee FitzMorris (and that pesky cat of hers).

Books in the FitzMorris Family Mystery Series

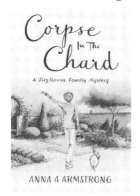

Corpse In The Chard
A FitzMorris Family Mystery
ANNA A ARMSTRONG

Murder On The Isle
A FitzMorris Family Mystery
ANNA A ARMSTRONG

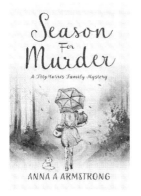

Season For Murder
A FitzMorris Family Mystery
ANNA A ARMSTRONG

Printed in Poland
by Amazon Fulfillment
Poland Sp. z o.o., Wrocław

32740508R00122